EMERGING ARAB VOICES

EMERGING ARAB VOICES

NADWA I

Edited by
Peter Clark

SAQI
in collaboration with
IPAF

ISBN: 978-0-86356-414-7

This edition published 2010 by Saqi Books

INTERNATIONAL PRIZE FOR ARABIC FICTION
www.arabicfiction.org

Emirates Foundation
www.emiratesfoundation.ae

SAQI
www.saqibooks.com
26 Westbourne Grove, London W2 5RH, UK
Verdun, Beirut, Lebanon
2398 Doswell Avenue, Saint Paul, Minnesota, 55108, USA

Contents

Introduction

The International Prize for Arabic Fiction (IPAF) was established in 2007. From the beginning it has had links with the family of Booker Prizes. The Man Booker Prize has, since 1968, offered an annual prize to a work of fiction by a writer from the United Kingdom, Ireland or the Commonwealth. It has been the inspiration for two other literary prizes – the Russian Booker Prize, founded in 1992, and the Caine Prize for African Writing, founded in 2000.

IPAF is modelled on the Man Booker Prize. It is managed by an international Board of Trustees (most of the membership of which is Arab) who determine the strategy, appoint the judges and are responsible for negotiating funding and supervising the budget. The Prize has been initially funded by the Emirates Foundation in Abu Dhabi, has an Administrator, based in Lebanon and is a non-profit-making company registered in London.

Publishers are invited to submit up to three works of fiction published in the previous year. An independent panel of judges is selected and over six months they announce a long list of sixteen and later a shortlist of six works. The end of the annual cycle is the award of a cheque to the six shortlisted writers and a bigger cheque to the winner. The third award was made in Abu Dhabi in March 2010.

The objective of the Prize is to reward writers, to ensure recognition for them and to encourage readership. It is also an *International* prize, so publishers outside the Arab world are alerted. The winning novel of the first cycle, *Sunset Oasis* by the Egyptian Bahaa Taher, has received critical acclaim all over the world. The author was invited to conferences and festivals from Indonesia to the United States.

The Caine Prize for African Writing has for ten years organised workshops for younger African writers and in 2009 IPAF planned a workshop for younger Arab writers. It was proposed to hold it in Abu Dhabi. When His Highness Sheikh Hamdan bin Zayed Al Nahyan heard of the idea, he immediately asked to be the sponsor and host. He generously arranged for the workshop – which we called in Arabic, nadwa – to be held at the hotel on Sir Bani Yas Island from 8 to 17 November 2009.

The judges of the first two IPAF cycles were invited to propose names of younger writers whose works of fiction were among the 120 or so books submitted for the prize in each of the years 2008 and 2009. The Trustees selected names from these proposals, bearing in mind the need for a gender and geographical balance. In the end the nadwa had eight participants – five men and three women. Two came from Egypt, a reflection of that country's proportion of works of fiction published annually. The others came from Lebanon, Saudi Arabia, Sudan, Tunisia, the United Arab Emirates and Yemen. Two other writers (an Iraqi and a Syrian) whom we had hoped to take part were at the last moment unable to do so. The age range was from 27 to 41.

Thus the participants were invited to take part. They were all published writers and had received some critical acclaim, either in their own country or beyond. Certainly all had attracted the attention of the judges who had suggested their names.

On the analogy of the workshops arranged by the Caine Prize, IPAF invited two more established writers to lead discussions and to provide more individual guidance and encouragement to the younger writers. The animators or mentors invited were the Lebanese Jabbour Douaihy and the Iraqi Inaam Kachachi. Both were experienced and respected novelists and each had been shortlisted for the International Prize for Arabic Fiction.

The nadwa met for nine days. Being on an island we were isolated from any distractions of a big city. Each morning the mentors had one-to-one sessions with individual writers. At seven o' clock each evening, writers and mentors met together for two hours and listened to readings from two of the participants. The writings were discussed. Comment was forthright. No quarter was given. No offence was taken.

Expectations were met, indeed exceeded. The mentors tell their own story. This volume is publishing the fruits of the nadwa, the stories or chapters that were written and discussed during the nadwa. It was an extraordinary experience for all involved, and IPAF hopes to make it an annual event.

Many were involved in contributing to the success. In addition to His Highness Sheikh Hamdan bin Zayed Al Nahyan I would like to thank Peter Cleaves, Stephen McCormick, Ahmed Arshi and Mohanna al-Muhairi of the Emirates Foundation; Zaki Nusseibeh and Peter Hellyer in Abu Dhabi; Nick Elam of the Caine Prize for African Writing; and the mentors and participators in the nadwa for making it such a positive occasion.

Peter Clark
Coordinator, Sir Bani Yas Nadwa, November 2009
Trustee, International Prize for Arabic Fiction

Preface

When our friend, the Sudanese novelist, Mansour el-Sowaim, disembarked from the small Cessna seaplane that landed or rather came to rest on the sea off the island of Sir Bani Yas, the trees planted in the salty terrain waved to celebrate the first man from Darfur to arrive on this isolated island in the Gulf. Mansour was not alone. We were a group of writers, men and women, from eight Arab countries. Two seaplanes brought us from Abu Dhabi to take part in a nadwa on creative writing. We spent ten days on this island ... ten days that may not have shaken the world, but did provide us all with new ideas and new friendships.

Is there any writer who has not dreamed of sitting on a deserted island surrounded by the sea and devoting themselves solely to writing? Sir Bani Yas was the ultimate in tranquillity before Kamel Riahi joined us. This untameable Tunisian volcano seemed as if he wanted to shatter the world to pieces and reconstruct it in accordance with his own narrative perspective. But Mansour and Kamel were just two of the group. There was Nadiah Alkokabany who came with diffidence and determination from the Yemen; Mansoura Ez-Eldin and Mohammed Salah al-Azab who brought with them the charm of Cairo and that city's finest narrative dress; Mohammed Hassan Alwan, the exceptionally amiable and sardonic Saudi; Lana Abdel Rahman from Lebanon, in love with writing; Nasser al-Dhaheri, the Emirati, confident in his style and his aesthetic choices. They were no ordinary tourists to the island that is one hour's flight from the mainland. They were explorers searching for new ideas that would equip them and clothe them with words from which they could fashion a text that would attract attention. That was no easy task.

They brought the first drafts of their writing that were fruits of varying tastes. Our task as animators of the nadwa, Inaam Kachachi from Iraq and Jabbour Douaihy from Lebanon, was to do what master cooks at a cookery school do, that is, to taste and get the amount of sugar right or to adjust the temperature while the dish was cooked. But from the first day we realised that we were encountering colleagues who were in control of their own experiments. We would be exchanging views, as equal to equal, and work together so as not to burn the dish. We had to give up the idea of a teacher/pupil relationship and work as a group of young writers and less young writers. And here we must acknowledge that the liveliest among us was the coordinator, the British writer, translator and Arabist, Peter Clark, a man of energy who tolerated sluggishness, or what may be called the caprices of genius, on the part of some of us.

Ten days. The two animators each morning met two or three of the writers who read the draft of a story or the chapter of a novel. There was discussion about style, language and characters, and suggestions for developing an idea. Meanwhile the others would be in their rooms, each of them working on their own texts, benefitting from the facilities of the comfortable and peaceful hotel complex. Seven o'clock each evening was the time for a plenary session around a conference table when we listened to what approximated to the completion of the novel chapters or short stories. It was a time for exchanging ideas freely, touching on practical issues of writing and looking for solutions to questions raised by the drafts in our hands.

Of course, this daily togetherness, with time divided between sleeping, writing, taking meals and even after-hours socialising in the open air coffee bars, gave rise to occasional temperamental spats. But one of the blessings of this nadwa was that it included personalities who succeeded in living together and blending together. Each of them accepted the comments of their colleagues with an open mind, and absorbed what they thought was appropriate. When it was otherwise, a quip was all that was needed to move on. Even the Tunisian volcano, Kamel, capable of puncturing the grandest of texts with his critical firepower, never managed to upset anyone. Indeed he provided the necessary salty ingredient to the nadwa.

Day after day, the qualities of the texts began to be clear and the first chapters of novels disclosed what made them work. Perhaps what we most enjoyed observing in this encounter was the individual style of each of the eight writers. Their texts emerged naturally from the soil in which each of them lived. They bore the stamp of their local personalities, a geography that was depicted and a unique fragrance and language that did not hesitate to borrow colloquial expressions when necessary in dialogue. And so Nadiah Alkokabany wrote a piece based in Sana'a where family events play a principal role. Mansour el-Sowaim described the characteristics of "the Frenchman", that man of Darfur who is almost mythic. Mansoura Ez-Eldin made the heroine of her story a woman of Cairo, and revealed the violence and sufferings of the oppressed, just as Nasser al-Dhaheri revealed the sufferings of a woman hungry for love. Kamel Riahi found his subject in one of "Bourguiba's children", those foundlings who were so described all their lives. Mohammed Hassan Alwan introduced us to the members of a Riadh family to show us their contradictions, telling us an intricate story of love.

Similarly the heroine of Lana Abdel Rahman was oppressed when she wrote about her ideas to a distant Frenchman whom she did not know and who did not know her. The central character of Mohammed Salah al-Azab's contribution was a loner who dies a number of legendary deaths and returns to life to enchant us with his story.

Had such visions from the Arab world, east and west, been encountered by the Arabs of Sir Bani Yas before? I imagine them content under their tents hidden from view, witnessing the emergence of novels by young people who are knocking authoritatively at the doors of Arab literature. Our thanks to them.

Inaam Kachachi and Jabbour Douaihy
Translated by Peter Clark

The Gorilla
The Last of the Leader's Children

The gorilla collapsed into orphanhood, uniquely and alone. Naked like a puppy abandoned in a street. His skull sprouted crows that swooped down, consuming identities and swallowing whole worlds.

Revolt

About one o' clock in the afternoon. The wind is busy rolling along some beer-can that has been drained of its contents in the deserted street. A massive silence links the arch of the Sea Gate with the enormous clock-tower where Muhammad V Street crosses Avenue Habib Bourguiba. The tranquillity of the deserted capital city is shattered by its well-known nutter: a suspicious man is circling the tower for the last time, before detaching him from people, warning them of the poison of the hands of passing time above. He then starts to throw stones, pieces of iron, houses, trees, crows and goats at imaginary enemies; things that are invisible to anyone else. He imagines that he is picking things up from the marble base of the clock of steel that is adorned like a whore in her last years of struggle. People are enjoying the blessed siesta of the great month of August. The temperature stands at fifty degrees, and the devil of midday clears its innermost parts from the stains of lust.

Suddenly the slumbering siesta is slaughtered by the sound of ambulances and police cars, and everyone rushes, with the traces of drowsiness and love-making on them, to the street of streets. Something is happening at the lofty clock tower. Cordons of police officers surround the place. Teams of emergency intervention forces hide behind cold helmets, and press back with sticks the onlookers at whom car horns honk from every direction. Human beings without number look up to the top of the stern clock. A small remote figure, apparently no bigger than a finger, is climbing the clock-tower with the speed of a cockroach. Everybody is amazed. He is about to announce the end of the world.

Necks strain to look at the bold climber who finally reaches the top of the clock, holding on to one of its hands. He takes a flask out of his back pocket. He has a drink and then empties what is left on his head. He removes his leather belt and secures himself with it to the iron surrounds of the clock, and turns to the crowds that have gathered below like ants. Nervous police surround the crowds. Auxiliary police run in all directions, talking into their radio sets. Gesturing nervously they ask the man up there to come down from up there; it is out of bounds. Meanwhile he mutters something the content of which is lost in the air. Only fragments of what he says fall like turds from a ram. There is a movement of his left hand and he waves right and left, indicating that he refuses to come down. The police carry on pushing back the people who are circling the tower like dung beetles. They try to ban any photography, to silence voices and to prevent mobile phone cameras being focussed on to the hands of the clock. Traffic comes to a standstill and the cars throb like the veins of a hundred metre sprinter.

What is happened is serious. No one has been bold enough to get near the clock since a soccer fan two years ago fell off it in a delirium of happiness after a famous team had won the Republican Cup. On that day, the water bubbling up from the fancy fountain beneath the clock turned into a pool of red blood.

From that evening the clock was subject to strict surveillance: it occupied a strategic site in the heart of the capital, regardless of what fools may sometimes say about it.

The crowds grow and the front rows are joined by lively tourists who pour in from the beaches and from hotels nearby. The auxiliary police assistants do not use their sticks so much, but they are worried by the growing numbers. They run about everywhere, barricading the pavements and extending the restricted area. Meanwhile the man clings to the end of the hand at the top of the clock like a gecko.

For years there was on the site of this clock a green statue of Bourguiba on a horse, with one of its forelegs raised to the faces of those who looked up. It was said that it raised its foot to the face of Ibn Khaldun whose nightmarish statue had been planted facing Bourguiba and at the latter's request. After he was swept away by order of the present rider, the statue was removed and there sprouted in its place a giant clock-tower with a cold cement pedestal. It was not long before it gave seed to smaller versions that were planted in each town and village, and statues of the Leader were cleared away from every part of the land.

The clock was changed for another that came from Switzerland or England or America – there were conflicting reports about the nationality of the new clock – and a bronze plinth was decorated in the style of Arab art. A statement without any evidence or proof about the clock of unknown parentage was installed in the heart of the city that was heedless of its sons. No trace of the Leader whose statue was moved to La Goulette, gazing at the bitter sea.

Spiderman remains above the restricted zone, supporting himself with the leather belt from which he hangs as he swings about, like a professional mountaineer. Below, the world, bewildered. The crowds grow after office workers leave their places of work. One whole hour passes by and the police are chewing their sticks, unable to persuade the man on the clock to come down. Among the crowd strange things are going on. Thieves and pickpockets are busy stealing mobile phones and necklaces from the women onlookers, and groping baffled bosoms or hidden bums.

Climbing to the top of the clock is a serious crime, an unforgivable act of rebellion and what is happening on this day is a problem affecting security. The police are facing a dilemma: how can they get on top of the situation and prevent the scandal that is unfolding in front of everybody – citizens and foreigners and the whole country at the height of the tourist season.

The officer almost bites the head off one helpless policeman, asking him for the thousandth time, "How have things reached this pass? Where were you? How did you let him get near the clock and climb up it?"

Elsewhere an auxiliary policeman pounces on a tourist and snatches the camera that he was pointing at the clock. The policeman rips out the battery and nervously hands back the camera, cautioning him against using it again. The barricaded area is a restricted security zone.

The crowds start to grumble about the behaviour of the auxiliary police as they clear a large space between the people and the location of the incident. Murmurs became louder when people see the man on the clock waving his hand and addressing the chief of the emergency intervention forces. They understand he is asking for water, as he is waving the empty water-bottle about. Another bottle comes. One policeman scales a stairway inside the clock-tower. He passes the man the bottle, suspended on a piece of string. The man grabs it and tells the policeman who wants to negotiate to get down.

We hear none of what is said. We are busy listening to the ravings of one young man who is shouting, "They're showing what's happening on the television and you can hear what the guy is saying. Look, I've had a text message giving the news with which channel it's on."

People take out their phones. The message has reached everybody at the same time. The auxiliary police get more excited and frenziedly start to look for something or other among us. Another group of policemen come and busy themselves searching buildings all around for the source of transmission and for the camera that is covering the incident.

Some people go home but crowds remain and others arrive until the pavements are packed and people pour out onto the roads.

The Funeral

I can still remember that day. The clear sky was like the bosom of an old widow, the thick skin of dead hide. The stars were eating themselves and the moon was hanging in the darkness. The trees by the road were like whores in a crowded brothel touting for custom.

The gorilla collapsed into orphanhood, uniquely and alone. Naked like a puppy abandoned in a street. His skull attracted crows that swooped down, consuming identities and swallowing whole worlds.

He tried to follow in his footsteps. His adversary was dazzling in the light. With a light touch, he played around like a skilled player passing the ball from one foot to another without it ever touching the ground. Like a magician he teased everybody just as he wanted. Sometimes, to the amazement of all, he balanced the ball on his head. Mouths were agape at the sight of this acrobat.

He did not adore Bourguiba in his time, but he had to do so. A target and a refuge, he was his opponent and his pretext for doing anything. Today he sleeps at peace in his earthly palace while the gorilla is torn to pieces by the din. He undertakes the impossible until he is at his side, guarding him from mischievous spirits, from worms and from memories.

An official uniform. There was no other way to him – only that blue uniform. To be a guard at the mausoleum. He had to be with him alone. Face to face. The gorilla created by the white god with two blue eyes.

Everything changed that day. Feelings were incoherent and the gorilla was full of contradictions. The body of the Leader advanced at the head, stretched out on a military vehicle, draped in a flag. The whole world followed, running. The Leader was like a god, as he processed towards his village that had been turned into a city. He was at the end of the procession, and had to put up with shoves and kicks. Faces and bodies around him pressed to look towards the corpse. Sometimes he was overwhelmed with curses and abuse. He got in the way of the movement of the final dash behind the corpse of the departing god. The gorilla saw himself shouting midst the running crowd, "I'm his child, the child of the great Bourguiba, come on to me, come and mourn with me!" He was drowned in tears of orphanhood and denial, mystifying them with riddles.

Alone he followed the corpse like some embarrassing truth. He was separated from him by savage lies. He was consumed by the fever of defeat and he remembered being in prison wearing a heavy German coat that protected him from the cold of a March cell. Suddenly he was possessed by an image of the Leader on the island of La Galite where he spent months of exile in the same coat.

Each of them was the same. Each of them had been in prison. Both have been eaten by the cold. The funeral procession continued like the Prophet's she-camel. Behind him the caravan proceeded as he had wanted, and behind the caravan a gorilla of his type who left him suddenly to his gloom.

He loved him only on that day. He took revenge on the mourners at the funeral, when the black car took the corpse. Faces scattered and the tears of the funeral ceremonies evaporated with the departure of the news camera. The gorilla was left all by himself to guard his black fur and the asphalt of the road.

He tried to utter his old cry, clapping his hands but was betrayed by his hands that fell to his chest like two cadavers. The self-image of the gorilla collapsed so he felt he was no bigger than a monkey forgotten among the rocks looking for a tree or a branch or some rope or a cobra to sting in order to end the pain. Haunted by gloom he sunk into his old depression. At another time it would have been necessary to take them on with courage. Another time they would have torn him to pieces and thrown him out and he would spend the rest of his life on the reserve bench.

Here he is then swinging around the top of the clock like an enraged tiger looking down for his prey among the crowds of ants beneath him. He disappeared two years ago and could not be found until he suddenly appeared on this clock during this murderous siesta time on 3 August, the birthday of the man with two blue eyes whom everyone soon forgot. If only he was the man hanging there on the clock, muttering incoherently for an hour and telling them about what happened to him that day.

Flight

On that day two years ago, the gorilla had not expected what happened to him to happen. Afflicted by hysteria, he opened fire on Bourguiba's mausoleum and then disappeared like a black cloud. He took flight and ran into the open country, far from the streets and alleyways, avoiding crowds. He ran away from the city and found his way to an abandoned railway line. The rust of its metal could no longer recall the last train that had passed by. Metal also dies, thought the gorilla as he was running between the lines to the unknown horizon.

His ears were now assailed by the screams of women, the shouts of men and the sound of anxiety among tourists in the square by the mausoleum at the moment that he had in his madness fired live bullets.

"You're all like him. Just like him."

He did not know how his finger pulled the trigger to fire the first shot and then not pausing after it. It was as if someone else was grabbing his arm and urging him to fire more shots.

His flight from the city of the Leader's grave was the beginning of his acquaintance with fear. He lay down on his stomach whenever he heard the sound of police cars or a plane or the boom of a hoopoe nesting in a lifeless carob tree.

He ran and with him ran adders and mice, lizards and scorpions. They all shared in the gorilla's flight.

A few hours later darkness took them all by surprise. It swooped down on them. The lizards, adders, snakes and rats turned tail as if the night was poison. The sweat on the gorilla's body dried up. The cold descended, accompanied by a devastating frost. The gorilla picked his way in the channel made up of discarded cement blocks by the railway line. They were what had been left over from a project for a sewage purification scheme. Like an aspirin in water, his weary eyelids dissolved into drowsiness. Not far from the railway line ambulances could be heard howling all night long. He expected they were transporting the wounded from the tomb to the hospitals of the capital.

Nightmares did not desert their ready prey. In his sleep the gorilla was chasing after impossible balls that were tearing at his rib like bullets spattering the channel of cement on the remote railway line.

He emerged from his nightmare to resume his flight to the unceasing symphony of the police sirens.

At dawn he arrived at a residential complex. He rushed towards a tobacconist's kiosk and asked for two packets of 20 March cigarettes. He bought a bundle of newspapers. The newsagent looked at him suspiciously.

"You're not from round here?" he asked.

"No, I'm from the south. I've come to see a relation."

"Now?"

"No, I'm off now. I'm waiting for a bus."

"There aren't any buses here. You have to take a taxi. Over there." The man pointed in the direction of some place higher up.

"Thank you."

The gorilla clutched the newspapers to his chest and headed off. As soon as he was some distance from the kiosk he changed direction and went off the road. He went to hide behind what was left of an abandoned house, and took out the newspapers. Alarm struck him as he found his picture on the front pages of all the papers. He turned to the second, third and fourth pages – his picture was in all the papers. They wrote about the foiling of a terrorist operation, committed by extremist groups in the capital and in Monastir. They said that the army had been called in to pursue the extremists, some of whom had escaped into the mountains and valleys and that the pursuit was ongoing. Beneath the headline were his picture, pictures of suspects, and an appeal for any information about them. Other pages published pictures of bodies described as extremists who had been eliminated by the authorities. They were wearing strange clothes, had long beards and thick hair. Their mouths were open. Their cold eyes were looking at the scene of the late crime before the bullets.

The gorilla ran off with a burden of fresh fear and distanced himself from the town, haunted by the vision of the suspicious looks of the newsagent.

He returned to the track in the desert. He was on his own this time without the creatures, running in the path of fear. Even his shadow vanished as if he had committed suicide or as if some false tranquillity was slipping away from him. By afternoon the track took him to the high fence of an unknown farm. He wandered around there waiting for nightfall. Suddenly he was surprised by the barrel of a machine-gun in his back and a voice ordering him to put his hands on his head. Thus did the gorilla turn from hunter to prey.

That was two years ago.

The voice pushed him into a position in which he was spread out on the ground. The voice was on top of him. He felt a pair of heavy knees crushing his back. His hands were tied behind his back. He was lifted up by his shoulders. He found himself facing a man in a mask wrapped in black carrying a machine-gun of a strange make. He was pushed forward into the farm through a gate that suddenly appeared.

There were dogs all over the farm. Ferocious dogs that did not stop barking aggressively. They seemed about to tear the world to shreds as soon as they were released from their leads. The barrel of the machine-gun was pushed into the gorilla's back again ordering him to walk forward. He stepped out towards the unknown in the dim light of an electric torch held by the man with the gun at his back. He was able to make out a faint track through a field of wheat.

The gorilla did not know where he was. The man with the gun ordered him to stand in front of a grass hut after some grim minutes of marching. He spoke in a foreign accent which the gorilla could not make out. Another masked man came out of the hut. He tied a black scarf over the gorilla's eyes and led him inside. He felt his feet going down some steps and his nose was assailed by the smell of freshly dug earth. The second masked man seemed to push him more violently and continued to push the barrel of the weapon into his back. The gorilla was helpless and did not know where on earth he was. He no longer thought of the number of victims that his mad machine-gun had left behind when he emptied it at the Leader's tomb. He had for some other reason become the object of pursuit.

This then is the gorilla today. Here he is on the clock. Precisely on the site of Bourguiba's statue. He throws away his shirt and bares his flesh. A fire engine turns up. It breaks through the crowds and an automatic ladder is extended to the top of the clock. Its steps are opened out until it reaches the gorilla who clings on to his leather belt. Through a loudhailer a policeman orders him to come down. They then listen to him. The gorilla gestures with his hands to right and left.

A Foundling

Do you still see him recalling that day on which he took on the epithet "gorilla"?

For more than thirty years the gorilla used to pause in front of the picture of Bourguiba smiling. It was there on the wall above the sandwich stall. He was smiling to him, waving at him with his white hand, the other hand holding a sprig of jasmine. The child gorilla below would chew at half a chunk of bread filled with *harisa* and sardine. His shirt was spattered with drops of oil as the man above smiled a smile that was like an open wound. Sparkling white. His hair was white. His smile was white. The palm of his hand was white. Even his suit was white. The oil with the smell of sardine trickled down the shirt of the little gorilla.

Terrible feelings simultaneously of pride and self-disgust then coursed through him like two raging bulls, as he examined his own identity, turning it round and round like a strange coin. On the one hand he is the child of the most important man in the country and this idea makes him look up to that the man in the picture looking down on palaces, gardens, enclosures, meat and fruit. On the other hand he is of no known family and that he is no son, not even of a rat or a donkey, and that he dropped, new-born, into a pile of straw and was smothered by oil and sardine, and shame. He melts into a white smile like the skull of a man who has never been heard of. He is simply one of the many children of Bourguiba.

When he was accused for the first time in his village of being one of the "children of Bourguiba" he gave a broad grin just like Bourguiba, as if he was confirming his parentage. But he did not smile after that when other words were hurled at him, such as pisser, bastard, foundling, whoreson. He then saw Bourguiba's teeth as if they were the fangs of some wild beast advancing towards him to crush his bones. That day he ran away from the playground to the cemetery where he stood and wept at his father's grave. He shouted and cursed until he lost his voice, as if he had dropped it down a deep well. Can you see him today as he remembers unzipping his pants and drenching the grave with hot piss? How much humiliation did he feel after that?

That evening he sat with his fair sister watching his "new" father giving his daily speech – "Directives of His Excellency the President" – on the black and white television screen. The screen made those two words – black and white – resemble each other. He realised that his sister was another adopted daughter. She was as white as milk whereas he was as black as charcoal. When he asked her, "Are we really Bourguiba's children?" his eyes filled with tears and she left and went to her room. She was older than he was and certainly knew of the matter or had heard about it. The family that had adopted them gave them no chance to make assumptions. He was the child of Bourguiba and after that he was the gorilla.

Here he is now throwing the water-bottle which he has filled with his own piss down on the crowd gibbering incomprehensively. The bottle was caught by some guy. He was standing under the clock looking up picking his nose as was his custom. News reached him from a girlfriend who was some way away on the other side, defending her groped backside in the crowds. He looked at the black guy up there and mumbled, "That's him. That's him. I remember him perfectly well." Memories from their childhood came back to him. The gorilla was playing football with him and his mates. They were making him goalie because no one else would be. He would go off each day to the playground and stand between two stones and kick away any balls they kicked at him. They shot ball after ball at him but he would save it time after time, returning it to the middle of the pitch with his hand. This guy remembered the strange look he had the day he stood in front of him, wanting to take the ball away. He noticed that his arms were strangely long, so long that his hands reached his knees. He said, "Gorilla. You're like a gorilla, Salih. Look at your hands." Kids around laughed and started to call Salih by this new name. Salih's cheeks quivered. He clenched his fists like a fierce boxer before he grabbed the ball and threw it onto another field. He left the field with the term "gorilla" stuck to him.

Urgent News

A globe on a screen with space as background and words in Arabic turning crazily to the rhythm of tense music announced the news programme.

A broadcaster with a prominent forehead wears a spotted black tie. He opens his eyes wide open. He allows a period of silence during which those viewers who have known this man's distinctive style hold their breaths. He then speaks in sombre tones,

"The main street of the Tunisian capital has been in a state of shock this afternoon following the scaling of the 7 November clock-tower by a swarthy young man. He reached a height of fifty metres. The young man has been clinging to the tower and all the efforts of the police and the police and the civil security forces have so far failed to bring him down.

"There are conflicting reports of the man's identity and objectives. Some reports from among the crowds that have been following the incident say that he is intent on suicide. The young man took some rope that had been handed to him to help him come down and twisted it round his neck, choosing to die rather than to descend.

"The Tunisian security forces have decided to ban the media on the spot from photographing the incident and will prosecute anyone who attempts to take photographs, by mobile phone or by any other visual recording device.

"We have heard that the young man has refusing to come down for two hours. Civil security officers have managed to get a small military parachute to him, intending that it assist him in coming down.

"We will give you more details in our next news bulletins."

The globe returned to the screen and revolved in some unknown sky before dissolving into a lather of Lux soap that a female hand toys with in some bath.

Translated by Peter Clark

Letters to Yann Andrea

Beirut, July 2006

Yann ...

Drops of water trickled on my bare shoulders, spreading out like fair freckles on a pale skin ... let it dry by itself.

You love these drops of water. In the cold weather their contact with the air stings me, but today the heat is stifling, and finding water for a bath at a time of war is a matter of fate: it might throw you into the camp of those migrating or you may be in the bosom of a home.

We are now in a house that has been closed up. Its owners only come here for a few days in the summer each year.

The words I write to you in darkness, these lines that I will email to you tomorrow, help me resist and to survive amidst this nonsense.

Perhaps Marguerite Duras found herself in writing. Perhaps this is the right thing. And so I write to you to discover the essence of my relationship with her, and with you.

I have been thinking for a long time ... why did Marguerite Duras love you and live with you until her last moments?

You stayed at her side, helped her pass away peacefully, and she continued to love you.

Moving to a safer place gave her no pleasure, even though there was water, electricity, a telephone and a television through which they could follow the news. When she left the house, she took only some clothes and her laptop, the novels of Marguerite Duras and the book about her by Yann Andrea. But when she reached the area of Sinayeh the mother looked scornfully at her daughter's cases and at her daughter who was preoccupied with putting her laptop in a suitable place. Zainab did not know this time whether to attribute this look to the long night they had spent to the sound of rockets or whether the scornful look was more or less fixed as far as she was concerned. The mother had almost lost her mind because of the war and had thought of moving up to the mountain where her sister went for the summer months. But there was no specific invitation from her sister and out of pride she would not impose herself and her children just because of the outbreak of war.

The mother felt ashamed at having to look for a place safer than her uncle's empty flat in Sinayeh. This showed up on her face whenever she spoke about having to leave Beirut altogether. Zainab looked out of the window and saw the displaced people setting up tents in Sinayeh Park. How could they live with war, with a shortage of water, food and cigarettes, and milk for the children? These people slept in tents on the ground and washed their kids in the open. Men and women had to resort to making their various arrangements such as washing in one part of the tent, sectioned off to conceal their naked bodies.

The mother looked all round the house, resentful and distressed about the comfortable life she had lost. Because of her marriage she had – from her point of view – moved to a lower social class. For the rest of her life she was to be a resident of Bir al-Abd in the southern suburbs instead of living in the centre of Beirut where she had been brought up and been educated. Living with the mother, for hours and days on end, was for Zainab most distressing, particularly as she had to sleep in the same room.

Her mother made her feel tense, especially when Zainab had to change in her presence. She tried to avoid this because the mother never missed an opportunity to criticise her daughter for her ungainly body – the thick hair that covered her legs and her upper thighs. Sometimes she was not slow to tell her that she had not inherited her own aristocratic beauty, but that her skin was swarthy and pimply, traits inherited from the peasant family of her father. Whenever she looked at her mother she felt cross; *her* skin was light brown and looked perfect. Her legs in generally were a deep wine colour, and her eyes matched the colour of her hair. Her nose was slender and small as if she was looking down on the world. Moreover she insisted on wearing elegant clothes inside the house even during the war. Her mother was also always irritated, gazing at the world sardonically and regretting her early widowhood and the years lost when she was busy bringing up children.

Her mother turned into a weak and submissive creature when giving in to her eldest son, Wisam. She gave him money on demand, and was happy because she felt he needed her. She would first resist at first but then hand over every time: opposition and then surrender. He continued to need her so long as she had any money. He would pay her attention and be nice to her in return. Wisam came, took money and then disappeared for a few days. He would return and settle down again in the house and so on. But now, because of the war, he had to settle with the family in the borrowed house. He would shift irritably from the living room to the bedroom. He would move from room to room, and refuse to allow his younger brother, Amir, to sleep in the same room. He had to have a room to himself, because he was the eldest brother. A room to himself, where he could hide his bottles of beer and whisky under the bed.

But he often irritated Zainab. She would find a box of matches containing a crushed cigarette and used matches. Sometimes her mother took the last cigarette from Zainab's packet, not realising she needed a cigarette. The mother knew that Zainab would be totally unable to confront her over this. Her mother used to smoke at night in secret and put the cigarette stub, ash and used matches into an empty matchbox. She would then forget to put it somewhere else, or would idly put off doing this to the morning. She never lit up in front of her children because she wanted to be the perfect mother. At home she used to smoke in her own room so it was impossible to notice these little details – but she would leave the empty matchbox in the living room, and there was no way to suspect anyone else.

Yann …

I am oppressed by a wearisome sameness. I look for her and for you. You know what I do not know, but you know nothing about me. I am confident that you will put an end to this oppressive sameness, that may be an illusion or a flight from reality.

Early this morning she looks at the ceiling of the room she sleeps in. Some of the plasterwork in the corner is flaking, dropping bits of dry white paint onto my bed. She hears Mother's voice, coming from the living room where she is chattering away about the war on the phone with my uncle in the Gulf who has lent us his house to live in during the war.

Yann …

The sound of the voices of the displaced children comes up from Sinayeh Park, as they sing about resistance and draw machine-guns and symbols of victory on the walls. Through the window I see a woman broadcaster from one of the satellite channels who has come to ask the children and their families about the war. Displacement has thus becomes a news item that the world must know about at close quarters; it helps to end it. Another woman was here yesterday from another channel. Sandra and I saw her when we were in the park. We asked their mothers what we could do to help. One of them shyly asked for some contraceptive pills and another asked for some cigarettes for her husband. A third asked for a cooking vessel and a saucepan for boiling water and heating milk.

I would not have noticed these little details but for the war.

Why do I keep writing to you when nobody remembers you any more? I go through your papers, I browse through your diary and I ask about her, that enchanting old lady with some elixir of life who has been able to capture your heart to this very day.

I will go on writing to you about her and about myself until I can be quite sure that I obtain release.

In her room at her home on the top floor Marguerite is alone. Only at home is she alone. She has a terrible sense of loss and writes about it. In the garden there are creatures who share her seclusion: birds, insects, cats, and a small mouse that scuttles by as quick as a flash. But here in this room which contains a table, a bed, and a blue cupboard – here the curtain is slightly drawn to admit a shaft of light, a fine long thread that is not enough to compromise her seclusion and the gloom. It occurs to her that she has been here alone for ten years writing her novels and crafting painful stories about her early sufferings. One would suppose that they would have been forgotten after such a long time.

Yesterday she had a row with him, slamming the door in his face and telling him to get lost. He just sat on the edge of the main entrance, waiting until the moment of her sudden attack of loneliness and alienation has passed. She was drunk when she asked him to go far away. She would be thinking of what this young man wanted from her. The centre of Paris was a carnival of pleasure, which this fool had abandoned to knock at the door of this old woman. She did not imagine that her existence as a writer gave any excuse for this young man to break into her isolation and to stay at her side

She looked through the curtains down at the garden. The bird was perched on the branch of a small tree. It will fly off as soon as it senses some distant movement. She would hate to be the cause of the bird flying off. Although she has been a long time in this house by this garden, the birds still fly off as soon as they are aware she is nearby. She passes her hand through her hair and thinks about going downstairs to make some coffee. In that corner she wrote *Le Ravissement de Lol V Stein*. Here she took off Lol to some unknown place and she never returned. She returned only to talk to her. Since *Le Ravissement de Lol V Stein* she realised that she was completely alone with her writing, along with images of her heroes that slipped away from her or were lost. She was always alone but the seclusion with her first books was different from what it is now. It was isolation in every place. Here Lol Valerie appears to her and here also the name of Yann Andrea first came into her life. Why did she Lol disappear and Yann stay?

And why has Yann Andrea now come to intrude into her seclusion?

For a long time she had been accustomed to take no heed of time. Time was like a shower of rain. We think it's heavy but it doesn't last long.

Marguerite realised deep down that her greatest trial was with the passing of time. And so it did not involve her. She ignored it utterly and arranged her life without regard to hours or days. She disregarded this foolish division into days and years, and consequently could never remember what day it was. She used to say, "Why can't today be Tuesday instead of Saturday? Why can't this year be last year or next year? Why must I submit to divisions of time invented by other people who have turned it into a law for the whole world?" She would not kowtow to this law. She would live her own life.

In her seclusion she has learnt the meaning of silence. She gets nearer to tranquillity. She sees the face of God, transparent like the mantle of a cloud, pure and innocent, uniquely joyous. As a result of this she feared intimacy all the more. She turned away from it as she flirted with deep silence. She knew that isolation provided her with the happiness of bringing forward her fleeting heroes. She had to be silent for a long time in order to allow them space to come to her, to disclose their stories for her to write.

While Zainab was writing on her laptop and following the war on the television, a whiff of hashish emerged from Wisam's room. She was able to identify the smell quite clearly, as did their mother. When Wisam had to stay at the house for some days he did not worry about having a joint in his room. He was sure the mother would not dare to be cross. She would turn a blind eye because he would threaten to leave the house for good.

The mother stood in her blue satin night-dress and claimed she was going to bed – escaping from the situation. She gave Zainab a shopping list – food and vegetables, that she would have to buy the next day. Zainab noticed that her mother's fingernails were painted pink. She also noticed a few freckles on the back of her hand that had appeared as years went by. She took the shopping list from her as her mother told her not to delay shopping in the morning.

It seemed that the war was important because it put away thoughts of suicide. Death was free and amply available; no longer an incident. For example, if she were to throw herself now out of the window of the second floor of this flat in the building overlooking Sinayeh Park full of displaced people, it would be nothing but an unusual news item, but it would not be an important event.

She thought her death would be gratuitous but it was not just this that banished the idea of suicide from her mind. Indeed it was death coming before reaching the idea of the release that she was seeking.

Her death at a time of peace, when her life was raging with emptiness and loneliness, might lead her to release. But now, war offered her the feeling that she deserved to live. She now understood the feelings of the fighter and the importance of his role in wartime, why he felt a sense of defeat after it was over. Indeed even in victory his role was over. He would have to return to life like any ordinary person. Then he would have to start struggling. If a sudden fight broke out between the two sides, he would be delighted because he would be able to turn it into a big war which would bring him back to a life from which he had been marginalised in times of peace.

Yann ...

Early in the morning.

I love to walk slowly in front of the vegetable cart. I love to look at his face that is optimistic in spite of the war. He sprinkles cold water on the mint and parsley and the wild thyme. He calls about his wares saying where they have come from. He announces that the things in his cart will shortly be split up and be distributed to many houses. This morning wake-up call from the street becomes a memorable event that spreads to every home.

Although I have been doing household chores for years, I usually forget about the tomato seeds in the fridge until they have gone off. I even feel a pricking of the conscience because I have been preoccupied with solving the eternal struggles that have started up inside me every morning.

"Why didn't they knock at the walls of the tank?"

You didn't hear this remark. Nor did you read it, did you? I took it from a story of Ghassan Kanafani that Mazin gave me. I will tell you about Mazin one day and about him and me.

And me? When will I knock at the walls of the tank?

What were you doing when Marguerite was watering the flowers in her garden? And why did you share in her depression so much?

When I am feeling gloomy I pass my left hand through the wintry locks of your hair and let my fingers rub vanilla cream in the wrinkles of your forehead.

Evening passers-by in the street are burdened by their stories of the day. They will not believe that dawn has brought a new love, as pure as water from a spring.

Then the breath of a sweet kiss remains suspended in air. It does not float in the upper air, nor does it fall on a fine body.

I will ignore this reality. I cannot believe that you have strayed from me. You have loved repose more than you have loved me. But this is what has happened.

Marguerite was sitting in the cafe and the table facing the door on to Rue Saint Michel. Marguerite contemplated the girl who was walking outside holding onto a coat and talking animatedly to a man who was walking beside her. She chided him, quarrelled with him. Yann was engrossed in talking about the text of a new play. She suddenly said to him,

"All this will be just a memory one day, just memories to be forgotten."

Yann seemed surprised at what she said.

"What will become memories?" he asked ruefully.

Both her hands went through her hair that was mostly grey.

"Everything, everything," she said. "It will all be memories, this meeting here, me, you, today, this moment, the plays you're telling me about, that girl arguing with the man she loves. All this will be simply memories that perhaps nobody will know about."

Marguerite lowered her head, and looked at the table for some seconds. Tapping her hand on Yann's hand that was lying on the table, she said,

"Finish what you were saying about your play, I'm listening."

Yann looked at her, into her face, at the fine lines around her eyes, at the two age lines round her pale cheeks. He felt how vulnerable she was, and how much he loved her. This woman he saw now was not very different from the frightened girl in her novel, *L'Amant*.

When Zainab writes she discovers the extent of her self-contained circle of isolation, where there is nobody but herself. She discovers this alienation in her compulsive writing. Writing takes her nowhere else but it does put her in touch with the self-contained circle in which he is isolated. In this passion for two circles being in touch with each other, examples of isolation that give rise to writing whenever she comes close to him and feels that her circle of cold iron is in touch with another circle that conceals him.

Perhaps mankind is isolated in circles of differing sizes. They are therefore looking for love. Perhaps they are living without realising their true isolation. They suppose that all their intense everyday activities are a barrier against isolation.

She discovered all this at an early time, after her first story with Hamid. She knew that humane feelings were genuine at some time and later on they change, in some way or other, in some form or other. There is no doubt that something happened, interrupting continuity so the eternal revolving movement of the greater circle would go on. And death. Birthdays. War. All this dismay and pain. All was nothing but a means by which the greater circle was given the continuity that would absorb all smaller circles within its orbit.

This war had changed her. Just as it had changed the only Easter party that she had ever been to. At that Easter party she became aware of her isolation. In the war she realised that she was freer and stronger. War tested our ability to suffer loss. War first tested us about things and then about people. The war had taught her to cling to humanity and to dreams. Then she learnt how to practise the game of resignation, dropping everything she had spent in the vanity of acquisition; it was a rehearsal for death, a rehearsal for the feeling of loss, then a rehearsal for death.

Yann ...

Do you know how it is bait for death? Did Marguerite tell you about it?

War broke out while I was preparing a present for you, a DVD of the film, *The End of the Affair*, the film of the story I told you about three times. But you were captivated by the voice of Edith Piaf as she sang about Paris, your first passion.

My loss of weight was not what made me think I lacked stability on the earth. It was rather my constant feeling that I was invisible.... . Sometimes someone would bump up against me in the street, then leave me and pass by without saying, "I beg your pardon" or "Sorry". This happened more than once. It was not his fault. It confirmed my feeling that I was invisible. But now I could die, my blood could be spattered on the ground, I could become a statistic among the casualties. Can I be sure then that I am visible, that I am alive, that I have a body I knew not how to love?

Shadows give us a deeper insight. So I realise that in your heart you know what I mean, just as Marguerite knew in her heart why you insisted on remaining with her.

Now at this time when I am in a dream, my writing offers

me a certainty about survival. I read through the novels of your beloved and seek your slender shadow between the lines. Then I read your book about her and I wonder whether this is indeed love.

Marguerite wished she was a beggar with nothing to do but look for enough to live on for the day. Or a gipsy who did not have to remember places and faces and names. What distressed her most was her failing memory, burdened with details from which she was only able to free herself after periods of seclusion and silence. For years when she used to invite her Paris friends to an evening meal at her house, she supposed that she would be eluding the heavy burden of loneliness. But when they came, the place was filled with noise. Friends spread out into the kitchen and the living-room, shifting from house to garden, and she found herself even more alone. She would sit in her beige-covered chair with its patterns of trees in brown and cream, lean back with a glass of whisky and ice in her hand – that had for years been her tipple.

Yann ... Yann Andrea, what a pair of radiant eyes that young man had, what a face of pale innocence. She repeated this expression to herself as she caught sight of him moving among the guests, smiling at her from afar as he put on a record of music she loved. He then turned to her and took her hand to dance with her. Three of her friends were discussing the policies of Mitterrand, while her journalist friend Irma who had had her fiftieth birthday a month ago was talking with great enthusiasm about the new policies of the Labour Party. Marguerite's eyes surveyed them all as Yann's hand encircled her waist. She felt how detached she was. Nothing aroused in her any wish to join in any conversation. She wanted to listen to silence. And also to dance in Yann's arms.

Together they made a strange tableau, a foolish mad picture

that defied all established ideas about the stages of love, age and time. In her relationship with Yann, as in her relationship with her body, all she expected was solace for the present, just for the present. Between herself and Yann there was only "the present", nothing more. Why did she want anything more? If the miracle of prolonging the present happened, she would reap great joy. But this would not happen because time was passing, because friends would move on, and with every day that passed she would become one day older. And Yann Andrea would bloom even more before he started to decline. He would also age as she did. His body would also commit various acts of betrayal. Time is the leveller and we advance in order to arrive, we bloom in order to fade, we grow old in order to die. We are embraced by this fear in spite of ourselves. There is no escape. If her body were to give her some comfort, pausing at some defined boundary of disappointment, she would be able to go on and to write more words. She would not be afflicted by old age, she would still have more to say, her writing would still be youthful and capable of moving actively amid this crowd. Writing is the only thing that stayed with her all the time ... all the time, and in all kinds of sorrows and joys.

She remembered something Daniel said to her: "One thing in your life is that you can view it from more than one angle, and always find reasons to be happy."

"And reasons to be sorrowful," she interrupted him.

"Happiness in your being alive," he went on. "Then happiness in continuing to live every day is something splendid."

That night, Marguerite stood a long time in front of the mirror. She looked at her breasts. They were firm and compact. She had been confident that they were the best part of her body. But it was no longer so. She was no longer herself. These calves with the veins standing out were strange to her. This callous skin was not her skin. When had these changes all happened? How had it happened without her knowing? Her physical decline had not happened suddenly. Her internal decay had started to come under a superficial exterior. When it became obvious it would be all over, repair work would be just cosmetic and would not prolong her essential being. She was no longer the young lass who used to run off secretly to meet her lover. She was no longer a woman bursting with a zest for life and love. There were things that had faded over time. As for Yann Andrea and his presence that shattered her seclusion, it caused her only confusion, throwing up questions about all manner of truths that she had ruined her life searching for.

The body's betrayal began swiftly. She felt out of control, for it was faster than expected. With the failure and betrayal of the body came the need for seclusion and silence. The compulsive need to write, to escape from a memory dripping with details and muddled up with the events of the day. She realised that there had to be a division between today and memory, and because of this she had imposed upon herself the habit of seclusion and had become used to it. Writing only came with long periods of silence. Then the images lurking inside her would move, looking for freedom, for a new life through the medium of her words. When this happened Marguerite became aware of the daily acts of betrayal that her body committed. Was there any greater betrayal than that committed by her hand when she wanted to write – the shaking of her joints, the failure of her fingers to grip the pen? You are weak, you are feeble. You have no word to tell your limbs what to do. In the course of time Margy – this is what Daniel used to call her – realised that she was coddling her body, negotiating with it, imploring it secretly not to reach a state from which there would be no return.

Translated by Peter Clark

MANSOUR EL-SOWAIM

The Ghosts of Fransawi
a chapter of a novel

Fransawi was not present for the events of this farfetched story,
nor was he entirely removed from them. The events took place
midst unseen influences at a toxic time. By the time the evidence
was obtained and the destinies known, Fransawi was hovering
with foggy wings over the isthmus between this life and the
next. From here, all journeys began, journeys to the isthmus,
earthly journeys, as well as journeys of no return, no sleep, no
rest, nothing. In this way, the story was plotted. You have to
remember that there was no Dafaq, no wild rice, no grey swans.
There were no old Arabian bustards, no Wadi al-Kassar wadi with
its turbulent waters. There were no drunken judges, no sergeant
or colonel, no dancing women, no soldiers hobbling on tired feet.
There was no past or no future, no you and no I. Look for loose
threads, my son, and mark them with post-its. But remember,
in his time Fransawi was part of this story. Don't forget, don't ...
don't let yourself to be distracted, son. Keep on going.

Guided by the call of the isthmus, the boy went away
overwhelmed by exhaustion and flashbacks of broken roads and
bouts of drunkenness. As he staggered past the thatched houses
of his childhood, he smelled the nasty smells once more. Then

the tears flowed through the cracks in his memory. Wishing he could forget, he remembered everything. His body kept on going blindly, propelled by instinct and pulled by the wind, until he was swallowed by the isthmus.

Where do we go from here, Fransawi? To what traps are you taking him as you stand there with your bleeding nose and shining eyes? You, Fransawi, burned seven lives. You wanted him to be the eighth because he deceived you and escaped early. Perhaps he made fun of you as you flew around the isthmus. Look at him. He is drawn to the triviality of words written by unqualified reporters. These charlatans fascinate him with their broken language and loosely woven ideas. But he has escaped since you hazily appeared in front of the computer monitors, between the blueprint pages and the copyediting on A3 paper. Now you have a real mission. You and the lad who does the proofreading will cover trivial sports news, editorials and scattered naïve reviews in the Arts section. Drawn by your idealistic style, he has always clung to you. Once upon a time, unseen winds whipped through the labyrinth of Wadi al-Kassar and battered your body. Do you remember, Fransawi, how the bullets once slid over your body shining like drops of water in the sunshine? You ran into the small bush where solders waited with their captain to ambush you with roasted gazelle and the cold Texas malt beer.

In his mind, Muhammad Latif exploited this magical scene and used it to rise above the never-ending tedium of court statements, company communications and the assignments of chief editors. He remembers the point in the story when Bashir organised exhilarating nights of debauchery.

Oh man, look! After all these years, Bashir has come back to dig up the past. He has come back because of your regular visits. He has come back because the troops disappeared in the labyrinth of a bigger cruel town. Oh Nyala. In this way, Bashir began to relive his madness. It was as if the waters of al-Kassar were flooding and Dishka machine-guns were firing again. Meanwhile, you, Fransawi, escaped into the bush.

So where is the proofreader? Muhammad Latif, the drunkard, the broken-hearted, is grateful for your seasonal appearances and your tireless hovering, Fransawi. He is back in the pool of his journalistic nausea. He points at you and asks you to lift him out of his isthmus.

Yes, it is Sergeant Bashir who joins Muhammad Latif the proofreader every Thursday. It is Bashir who plays the drunken companion crying with sloppy screams. Twenty-five years ago the same screams whistled in the quiet of dawn through an operating theatre in Nyala Civilian Hospital. Actually Bashir screamed only once. Then he calmed down and buried his head between his hands. His bosses had selected him from his company at the Southern Division of Police of the South Texas quarter. His mission was to accompany Awad Fransawi to the Nyala Civilian Hospital. Nobody asked him to stay with Fransawi's devastated body and broken bones. Bashir chose Fransawi's nurses. Then, wrapped in his uniform, he stood in Fransawi's room. With his severe face and red eyes, he was a formidable presence.

"His ribs are broken and his lungs have been punctured," said the doctor. Then he added, "He has a skull fracture and he may be bleeding internally."

Bashir did not hear the doctor. Instead he stared, fixated, at the tears flowing from Fransawi's eyes, moistening his light moustache and the white lines on his face, and trickling down his skinny neck.

"He may yet wake," said the doctor, patting Sergeant Bashir's shoulder stripes, "Everything depends on the will of Allah."

For the next three days, Bashir sat by Fransawi, with his broken body and cracked skull. For three days, Bashir did not close his eyes except when he took a nap. The flow of tears from Fransawi's closed eyes never stopped. Doctors came and went, mopping the tears with a cloth and ordering the nurses to give Fransawi tranquillisers instead of injections to keep him comfortable. For three days, Sergeant Bashir prayed for the first time to Allah. He asked Him to heal Fransawi's broken bones and to restore him safely so he could enjoy life and set traps again. On the fourth day, Sergeant Bashir fell asleep at dawn, overcome by three days of exhaustion. Slumped with his neck over the arm of the plastic chair, he slept soundly. When he woke up, he did not know how long he had been asleep. A soft hand was gently shaking him. He opened his eyes as if he was regaining consciousness. At first he thought it was a dream. Fransawi was smiling and taking his hands. When Bashir tried to stand, Fransawi whispered, "Sit, rest, Bisho."

Thinking Fransawi was recovering, Bashir clasped his hands, a smile lighting up his handsome face. He leaned over his friend's bed only to see Fransawi's face grimace with pain. Bashir dropped on his knees beside Fransawi's bed and embraced his hands.

Fransawi said, "I'm fading, Bashir." With an effort, Fransawi heaved himself up in bed so that he was face to face with Bashir. "I want to move, but I ..."

Fransawi fell back in bed with a groan, his almond eyes rolling in pain. Bashir squeezed his hands, trying not to look at the flowing tears. He said, "You'll be fine, Awad. Just relax"

With a slight smile, Fransawi said, "Don't be sad, Bashir. I'll visit you frequently." He tensed with pain and added, "I'll come and see the kids too." Fransawi's tears rippled again as he tried to raise his body, whispering, "Bashir, come here. I've got a present for you."

Bashir leaned close to Fransawi and touched with his hands the twisted face wet with tears. Awad Fransawi tied a small handmade leather amulet around Bashir's neck. Then he patted his face and whispered, "This will protect you over the coming years. Don't take it off."

In that darkest dawn Awad Fransawi's soul passed away, leaving Bashir weeping over his broken body. For the first time in three days, Sergeant Bashir again passed through the gate of Nyala Civilian Hospital. The cold air stroked his face as he approached the neem trees. He glanced at the crowds of homeless street boys, shamasha, leaning against the wall of the hospital and resting on the tree trunks. Bashir turned west and stared at the burning lights of the Central Police Station. From afar he could see the watchman standing in front of the gate. Two policemen strolled in and out of the station. He saw a Land Cruiser slowly crossing through the gate and heading south. The screams and shouts of the soldiers on the truck reached him in front of the hospital gate. He watched the sun rise and the flickering lights of old buses as patient tea sellers set out their wares under the neem trees near the hospital walls. Day workers, porters, small traders of the southern markets poured into the greater market. Columns of policemen in their uniforms drove north on the asphalted roads. Nurses leaving the hospital gathered in queues to wait for buses. Sergeant Bashir watched, his eyes misting over. He lit a cigarette and clenched his hand around the amulet round his neck, his amulet of protection for the years to come. This gift from his deceased friend would connect them forever. He whispered to himself, to the cold morning air, to the shamasha, tea sellers, traders, porters, nurses and running soldiers. He whispered to the faraway policemen, to the absent Lieutenant Yasser, to the Colonel, to Corporal Frini and to Afaf, "Fransawi died this morning."

Muhammad Latif was stuck. He switched the computer off, making sure to hide the file he was working on. Then he watched the monitor until it was dimmed. He remembers you, Fransawi, lying alone in a hospital bed. Sergeant Bashir finally left you alone to embrace your death. Muhammad Latif knew you would be washed in the room for foreigners at the Alcango cemetery. He knew you would be buried by a handful of hospital workers. Muhammad Latif knew all this. He also knew that your death would be classified and tucked away in a file that would be forgotten. Nobody would open this file for years. Nobody would know its contents except you, Fransawi. Right after you died, Muhammad Latif spent two wild drunken nights with Sergeant Bashir, a man of education, escaping from his police responsibilities. They spent the night shouting. They called you, Fransawi, and they apologised. Yes, Muhammad Latif apologised because he was alive and you were dead. Bashir apologised because your death landed him in Hell!

Muhammad Latif got up and walked from the Newspaper Building to the bus station. As he walked, he recalled random events. He remembered you, Fransawi, talking to Bashir about how the actions of the city officials would bring sadness and regrets to the Colonel and his cronies. Sparks would consume the Colonel and leave him in ashes. He attributed another thing to you, Fransawi, convinced he heard it from Bashir's boozy mouth. You predicted disaster, fires and death. You forecast utter devastation with no escape, bullets piercing bodies and heads being blown off.

Muhammad Latif kicked a small stone and lit a cigarette. Tonight he would not go to al-Samrab North to drink and rave with Bashir's outrageous friends. Instead, he would spend the night reading, or sleeping, or in the lap of the first woman he met in the street. As he moved slowly through the crowd at the bus station, he tried to free himself from your suffocating ghost, Fransawi. You appeared like a jinn and swallowed him up. As soon

as he was on the bus heading for al-Fitaihab, Muhammad Latif
rested his head against the window and let himself remember
you. He imagined he saw your silhouette on the surface of the
White Nile as the bus crossed the bridge. In Dafaq, on the border
with the Central African Republic, you cleverly guided the police
team from one water pool to another, from wadi to wadi, from
bush to bush. For fifteen days you wandered in the wild virgin
lands, hunting bustard, gazelle and wild hare. You swam in the
pools and wadi waters. You roasted bafra and corn and sucked
sorghum canes. You tested your rifle by firing at watermelon,
doum palms and papaya. You showed them your abilities hunting
and skinning a porcupine whose thorns stuck in your hands.
For fifteen days you misled the thieves and turbaned tribesmen.
You avoided the well-travelled roads. You guided them wisely,
Fransawi. All the while you chatted with Lieutenant Yasser in
his funny French.

At his mother's house in al-Fitaihab, Mohammed Latif lay
down on his bed feeling powerless and devastated. He unloaded the
burden of memories of you by dropping you off in Texas, in front
of al-Batallah's house. He pushed you through the zinc door with
its noisy creak. He heard you shouting "Bashsherhhheeeeerrrr."
Then he left you there and went to sleep.

Your elusive ghost is still coming to him in dreams and
nightmares. He sees you in his brief interrupted naps! He
imagines you hanging from the branches of a neem tree with
your feet tied. Someone wearing khaki approaches you and cries,
"Now ready." Then he pushes you with both hands and springs
back as you swing like a cradle upside down with your eyes closed.
He sees the khaki-covered bodies of many men standing nearby
with Kalashnikov rifles on their shoulders. The thundering sound
of bullets ricocheting off stone is deafening. They laugh and
shout as your slim body hangs helpless, swinging. You feel their

hands counting the holes in your torn clothes and then you black-out. The boy wakes up: damn Bashir.

Ever since he listened to the agitated delusions that poured from Bashir's mouth, Mohammad Latif spent his days tormented by thoughts of you. He swore to find every one of the men involved, even if he had to spend the rest of his life searching. In his hallucinations, Bashir reeled off the names: Corporal Frini, who studied engineering and is now a Police Captain Engineer, Judge Ismat, now a lawyer at Souk al-Arabi, Lieutenant Yasser who is now someone important in the Customs Police. The coffee trader Khalil now works as a guard for a relief organisation in Nyala, the only one who stayed on. And then there is Colonel Mudaththir al-Jack, oh Fransawi. Latif has written the names in the margins of his own hallucinations and nightmares, just like the corrections made by the editorial board. Muhammad Latif the proofreader, who scrutinises every letter, will tell your story, Fransawi, letter by letter. He will also rip stars off shoulders and mess up the papers of judges, advocates and other employees. Whose ghost are they chasing, Fransawi?

In the morning, before washing his face and greeting his mother, before he tied his shoes and put on his all-purpose shoulder bag, before he did anything, he bent over his papers to record his nightmares. He described the ocean of Bashir's hallucinations and added to them his own buried history. Muhammad Latif wrote the words to their story.

One boring evening, Sergeant Bashir used a hose to dampen the sand at the South Texas Police Station. He roamed the yard spraying the soft sand. The quiet of the evening lulled him into imagining the coming night. Everything was going as planned. At ten o'clock Ramla and her companions from the al-Thawra quarter would arrive. Fresh arrack could be found alongside the confiscated arrack in the station and a sufficient quantity was already reserved with al-Batallah, the arrack dealer. In addition, Khalil the coffee trader would send over three bottles of whisky. Abkar the agile maker of agashe will roast sheep. The guests will start arriving at nine. The Colonel will come late as usual. Everyone will enjoy the agashe, arrack and whisky. Most importantly, they will enjoy the surprise of Ramla and her companions showing up unexpectedly. The forthcoming meeting between Lieutenant Yasser and Judge Assam will be interesting, especially since Assam, the honourable judge, never gets drunk even were he to drink a barrel of old bitter.

Sergeant Bashir hauled the hose around the yard, thoughts of the coming evening piled up in his head. Suddenly he found himself approaching the main gate of the station. From his place under the flourishing lemon tree he could see six or seven pale and dusty villagers. They approached the station steadily and then stopped at the gate. An older man approached the lemon tree and shook hands with Sergeant Bashir.

Bashir said, "Hi, what's going on?"

The old villager replied, "Our cows were stolen and we came here to report the case."

Angrily Bashir tossed the water hose into the basin by the lemon tree. "Why didn't you go to the headquarters?"

The old man frowned. "We did," he said. "They sent us to this station."

Bashir turned away and pointed to the office where statements were taken. "Go over there. You'll find an officer there."

The old villager left, followed by his fellow tribesmen. Bashir stopped what he was doing to curse the villagers, their cows, their rubbish and all the thieves and tramps of the region. He tried to recapture his daydream about the coming night, but failed. What would happen if he was pushed into some new operation against armed robbers? He was bored with chasing robbers who had no fear of death. He wanted to enjoy life, to enjoy Ramla,

Afaf and the cold sand of the South Texas Quarter. His thoughts were interrupted by the approach of a lieutenant, followed by the filthy villagers. The robbery must interest him. What a pompous bum, Bashir whispered to himself. He straightened up to greet the young lieutenant.

The lieutenant straightened his hat and said, "Get ready. I'm off to headquarters to open a case." He opened the door of the Land Cruiser parked near the gate and added, "This could be a long mission."

The lieutenant winked at Bashir with a devilish smile. Bashir just stood there watching as the vehicle drove through the gate, loutish villagers hanging over the sides.

Bashir took a chair from inside the office where statements were made and plonked it in the mud under the lemon tree. He sat down, his feet propped against the tree's solid trunk. They may need personnel from our division, he thought. The force at headquarters is big enough, but it has been a long time since a force chased robbers. The idea pleased Bashir. The combined forces from HQ and Central Division were big enough and would not need reinforcements from the branch divisions. The lieutenant might be assigned to the mission, only the lieutenant, and perhaps the new squad leader sent recently from the capital. Bashir smiled as he saw himself excused from the errand while the lieutenant got stuck roaming around in the mud solving the puzzle.

Bashir stood up and headed into the welcome ambush of night ahead. He found Corporal Frini and a soldier, Salih, playing cards. Looking around, Bashir asked, "Everything alright?"

"Yes sir," said Frini, "There's plenty of ice, cola, snacks and beans ..."

Salih interrupted, "And grasshoppers, olives and stringy cheese ..."

Frini said, "We brought extra chairs and tables this time. I want everything to go smoothly. The people here tonight will be VIPs. The Colonel himself asked us to take care of them."

The three soldiers and their young officer had practically nothing to do during the day so they spent their time playing cards. As policemen, they dealt only with minor complaints such as the taking of domestic goats, bed sheets and old clothes. They also dealt with complaints about the occasional drunk or noisy quarrel at a wedding party. The Colonel's Thursday evenings were a welcome break in the soldiers' routine and the suffocating quiet of the South Texas Police Station. Those lavish Thursday evenings pandered to the whims of men of power. Bashir often thought the Captain who located the station on outskirts of the Texas Quarter intended it to be remote from the town.

Many of the Colonel's friends attended his unrestrained dissolute evenings. Among them were businessmen from the town, judges and lawyers, local politicians, bank employees, local traders and strangers. And of course women attended, including wives who prostituted themselves, the tea and fruits sellers of Souk al-Malaja, local singers, whores, pimps and lesbians. All kinds of freaks and oddities joined the Colonel. These parties were a release for the Colonel and his cronies, the most recent of the Colonel's psychopathic friends. The guests at the Thursday night parties witnessed the Colonel's explosions of frenzied anger and hysterical happiness. They also witnessed weeping, violent fighting, attempted murder and suicides.

The mad Colonel had carefully selected his men for the South Texas Police Station. He even selected a new officer, recently transferred from the capital. The Colonel saw in him what he needed, so he sent him to the South Texas Police Station to head the station and command the three soldiers.

As evening fell, Bashir forgot about the villagers from the south, their stolen cows and the lieutenant who accompanied them. The fever of the night overcame him as he considered his options. Perhaps he would cheat everybody in gambling, or he might win a voucher for the ration of sugar for a village from the municipal Administrative Officer. He could double the price of the confiscated arrack and sell it. He could squeeze Ramla when they were alone in the young lieutenant's office.

The Colonel's lack of discipline allowed a number of possibilities. Bashir lit a cigarette and took a plastic chair through the gate. He put the chair down outside at a corner of the station. From this vantage point, he could see an advance guard of Land Cruisers drive past the rows of thatched mud houses. He leaned forward in his chair as he watched three vehicles approach from the station. The vehicles were armed with Dishka machine-guns and filled with soldiers. A handsome young lieutenant smiled from the nearest Land Cruiser.

The lieutenant jumped out, holding a Kalashnikov rifle in his right hand and his cap in his left. "Be ready," he told Bashir. "We are leaving before sunset."

Bashir was suddenly angry at the bored young soldiers embracing their light gun machines and hanging their feet over the sides of the Land Cruisers. He did not see the villagers crammed in the vehicles at first. Then he faced the challenging glare of the same village elder he had seen earlier.

That Thursday, Bashir considered disobeying the lieutenant's orders. He even considered reporting him to the Colonel, the Administrative Officer and the head of the Smuggling Control Unit. He considered reporting him to the one doctor in town, to Judge Assam of the Special Courts and to the arrack dealer al-Batallah. He could report him as well to the princess of princesses of the prostitutes and to Kojin, the famous town pimp. Instead, he attached himself to the lieutenant's unit at the end of that afternoon.

As they drove away, Bashir sat beside the lieutenant in

the front seat of one of the Armed Robbery Control Land Cruisers. Bashir smoked a cigarette while a group of merry naked children ran alongside the vehicles. It was the beginning of the mission to restore the villagers' stolen cows. Those cows would never be restored.

Translated by Nassir Alsayeid Alnour

MANSOURA EZ-ELDIN

Déjà Vu

The scene flashed suddenly through Samiha's mind as she stopped her car in the old-style vegetable market. She had been driving extremely fast on the ring road from Heliopolis to the Ahram Gardens where she lived. As she hummed the words of one of "Little Najat"'s songs, she had lost her concentration and turned off at the Saft al-Laban exit instead of Maryoutiya. She had been surprised to find herself in a district that was completely strange to her — so strange, in fact, that she thought she must be in a city different from the one she had been born in.

A working-class district, with narrow, unmade-up streets, and a small vegetable market in the middle, making it impossible to drive a car through without colliding with the litter of tomatoes, aubergines and onions scattered all over the place. A district that was just like Karim's description of where he lived.

She started to feel uneasy, and slowed down. Suddenly, she felt she had been here before — it was as if she was not really in this place, so much as remembering that she had been there in the past. With everything going on around her, it was as if it was just a memory stored in her mind, a memory that had been captive for several years, then suddenly released to appear as a present moment.

It was not the first time she had experienced a state of déjà vu, but it was certainly the strangest. On previous occasions she had usually just felt that she had experienced the moment before, and forced herself to say certain words in conformity with what she remembered living through earlier. Then suddenly, everything would disappear from her memory, and the memory would become just a dimly lit spot in a vast desert of darkness.

Now, however, she felt that this place she was seeing for the first time had opened a door on a region of darkness inside her, on a life that she had possibly lived in the past. She saw herself apparently struggling to escape from the wreckage of a horrific accident. Then everything disappeared again, and she once more became a woman struggling to get her car out of this narrow, crowded area.

She emerged onto a street parallel to the market street but wider, then eventually found herself in the Maryoutiya area, from where she headed for the Ahram Gardens, and started to feel more relaxed.

As the scene emerged from nothing in her head, there also emerged the face of a young, wide-eyed woman with a deep look and a slightly protruding forehead, a woman exactly like her maid, Nura.

They had been driving together, in a place just like the market. Nura had been coughing violently, and Samiha was patting her shoulder, trying to keep her occupied by chattering to her without stopping.

The sound of Nura's coughing rang in her ear as if she were actually there. She could almost see her, with her body shaking slightly from the effect of the constant coughing. But the place they were moving through remained unclear. It was certainly like the vegetable market, with its crowds and clamour, but it seemed to be immersed in a thick fog.

Samiha tried to ignore the problem and just concentrate on the road ahead. But Nura's trembling body and her face with its wide eyes carried on dancing in front of her until she reached home.

She felt depressed, but did not understand why. She went into her bedroom, and lay down on the bed, her eyes fixed on the ceiling. Without any preliminaries, the events came back to her, as if in a dream. Nura was groaning beside her in a pained voice without her being able to see her, while she was crammed into the driver's seat, unable to distinguish anything around her, except the sound of groans mingled with an unsettling noise, a ringing that almost split her head open, and a continuous banging on the doors of the car. Amidst the clamour she could just make out the sentence "She's dead!" before everything faded away.

She fell asleep. When she woke up, she was still wearing her outdoor clothes. She was also suffering from a severe headache, as well as deep depression – the sort of depression that was usually followed by a night full of nightmares, even though she could not remember any of them afterwards. Her mind was weighed down with obscure fragments that induced an unfathomable sadness. The sentence "She's dead" started ringing in her head with no let up.

Nura seemed to be hiding from her in pitch darkness for some moments before reappearing. A cough, a shaking body, two wide eyes. Two women driving together in what seemed to be an old, traditional market, nothing more.

She grabbed the telephone on the bedside table beside her and called Karim.

She was sure that he would not be awake yet, so she did not give up when he did not reply the first time, but tried again, so persistently that it would be impossible for him to ignore it.

Her voice sounded tense, despite her best efforts: "Come here at once, come over to me!"

As usual, she ended the conversation before listening to his reply. She was afraid that he would go back to sleep and take no notice of her. She thought of calling him again, but she did not do so. She remembered the sentence of his that had assailed her ears in one of his rare bouts of anger: he was fed up with her repetitive calls, he had said; he only came over for fear of the whirlpools of complaint and lamentation that she would drown him in if he ignored her; he was no longer particularly afraid that she might be in real trouble.

She imagined him slowly getting out of bed after she had woken him, and imagined another woman, a younger woman, lying beside him. The thought disturbed her, and she invented an alternative scenario. She saw him throwing the cover vigorously from his body, as he got up quickly; then his foot slipped and he fell hard on his right elbow, cursing his bad luck. He recalled that he had not seen her for ten days, but he knew that his luck had not run out to that extent; it was enough that it was she who had called him, rather than him paying her a sudden visit, or pressing her to meet him.

This scenario also left her equally depressed. "How come that he had not contacted her for ten days?" she wondered.

At ten o'clock exactly she heard the door bell ring. She listened to Nura's voice greeting him excitedly and leading him to where she was sitting on the balcony looking out over the Pyramids.

Samiha sat sad and distracted. She had combed all her black hair up and was wearing a blue linen sleeveless dress. On the table in front of her was a bottle of wine and some plates of nibbles. She did not usually drink this early, but today she could not cope with her depressed mood without a drink.

She poured out a glass of wine for him as soon as she saw him. Without any words of greeting, she pointed to the chair facing her for him to sit down. For a while, she did not speak. She just looked absentmindedly towards the Pyramids nearby or gazed intently at the bougainvillea, jasmine and carnations in the garden, as she munched at the nibbles and sipped from her glass from time to time. He ignored her, eating his nuts and almonds. She recalled Mustafa, her previous lover, who had introduced her to Karim. She often compared them. She had liked Mustafa a lot, and had put up with his impetuosity and her constant doubts about his faithfulness to her. She often wondered whether he had introduced her to Karim because he was beginning to get fed up with her. Had he been so confident that she would like his friend, and could thus escape from her without her continual threats of suicide? Suddenly she regretted those threats, and wished she could erase them from her life as a whole, and not just from her memory. Had Karim told him that his relationship with her had started before he had left her? She didn't know why she had telephoned Karim right away the following day. Nor how they had ended up in bed.

She finally turned towards him. Her enticing smile had returned to her, as if she had pressed a button that had wiped away the sorrow and tension, and restored the smile of a PR person.

"Do you think I'm capable of murder?" she asked him. "Or at least of causing someone's death?"

"If you were capable of murder, you would have killed Mustafa," he replied without thinking.

She was extremely upset at the mere mention of Mustafa's name. They had an unspoken agreement not to mention his name. As with all the other bases of their relationship, it was she that had formulated this principle, without saying so explicitly.

She usually referred to her former lover as "him". She said that she was indebted to him for a lot. He had taught her how to enjoy Umm Kulthoum's songs, whereas before, she had spent the whole of her life listening only to foreign ones. She would speak at length about how he had made her appreciate oriental scents after having been unable to bear them. She could speak for hours about his little kindnesses to her, without any reference to the fact that he had taken a substantial part of her wealth. Like Karim, he was more than twenty years younger than her, and belonged to a poor family. He used to follow her everywhere like a shadow. When he was with her, he did not seem in the least like her lover; he was more like a personal assistant or a secretary, making himself agreeable to her friends of both sexes. That was just what Karim did now. He had almost turned into Mustafa's double, or heir. A less skilful, less attractive heir.

Her disgruntlement communicated itself to Karim, who greatly regretted mentioning Mustafa's name. Fortunately, however, she again started to ignore what he said, and went on speaking herself. "Karim, I imagined I had been the cause of Nura's death. Could I have harmed her in a previous life? Could she come back to take revenge on me?"

She noticed a confusion that he quickly suppressed, before asking her sarcastically,

"What life?"

She looked at him dubiously, as if she were thinking of putting him with Nura in a special compartment — the compartment of enemies in previous lives. But suddenly she wiped off her dubious look and started on a long monologue that had nothing to do with what she had been saying previously. She talked about climate change, about the populist morality that had taken hold of society, and the increase in poverty and fundamentalism. She spoke as if she was putting forward weighty views in a television programme, and from time to time looked around her discreetly, as if there were unseen onlookers following her carefully.

She spoke a lot, without noticing that Karim had not paid attention to a single word of it, because he was intent on following her pursed lips, and examining the details of her body that had begun to show signs of getting fat. The gaze of her eyes was cloaked in a thick layer of ambiguity, suggesting a challenge to the prints left on her skin by the harsh years. She looked at him, and recognized that look of his when he desired her. She wished he would make love to her now.

Even when making love, she never let go of the smile that was carefully drawn on her lips. She would close her eyes and seem to be in another world. When they had finished, her tensions would begin. Sometimes she would retreat into herself and weep, or else treat him with unjustifiable harshness before making her tearful excuses a few hours later, or sometimes the next day.

This apparent honesty in all her actions – especially when she was lying – was her most distinctive characteristic. It was not an act – or at least, it was the sort of act where the actor merges into the character he is playing so well that his original character disappears entirely. The surprising thing in her case, however, was that she was a different character each day. She would assume one character, then next day abandon it for another one. Sometimes she would switch characters with disturbing speed. In just one session, she could be an idealistic woman, a proponent of love, then a weak woman standing on the edge of a violent nervous breakdown, then a dangerous woman with a strong, power-mad personality – and so on, and so on. She would flit between these various alternative personalities, without ever abandoning her aristocratic nature or the gentle smile etched on her lips that gave her an added mystery.

Suddenly Nura appeared. She walked past the two of them at close hand, looked at her, and for a moment seemed confused. Nura left the balcony and Samiha quickly followed her, after excusing herself from Karim for a minute. She came back again, her enticing smile shining on her lips, but a deep sadness had begun to invade her looks.

She seemed distracted, wondering whether her angry mutterings with Nura had reached his ears. Until this moment, she had not wanted to tell him the real reason for her morning call to him, or her insistence that she should come over immediately. After she had decided to discuss everything with him calmly, she came back and hesitated.

Her voice was quieter than before, and from time to time she looked at the place where Nura had been standing just before.

Nura walked back in noisily, with a bunch of wild carnations in her hand. She had apparently just picked them from the garden. She gave him a searching look as she made her way to the flower vase that had been placed on a small table at the end of the balcony. She took the still open roses from the vase and placed the bunch of carnations in their place, then picked up the roses and left, vaguely humming the words of a song. Meanwhile, Samiha was completely silent, as a slight trembling came over her.

As soon as Nura left the balcony Samiha jumped to her feet, and Karim in turn stood up. "We won't be able to talk here, what do you say to a stroll together?" she asked quietly.

"It won't do any good," he replied quietly, taking his cue from her. "I'm broke and frustrated."

She disappeared for a few moments, then came back with some money, which she gave to him with a smile. Then she led him outside. As soon as they were together in the garden, standing among the bougainvillea shrubs and the wild carnations, she asked him for his address, with a promise of a pleasant surprise.

When he left, she went for a stroll alone in the garden. She went up to a wild rose bush and stretched out her hand to a red rose that was not yet open, only to be pricked by a sharp thorn. She retreated a little, tears welling in her eyes. She quickly wiped them away, and turned to go back inside the house. For a few moments she imagined that Nura was watching her through the window behind the curtain, but when she looked more closely she could not see anyone.

Some time after four in the afternoon, she told Nura that she was going to meet a woman friend of hers and that she would not be back till late. She left her car behind, and got into a taxi, telling the driver to take her to Karim's address. The man looked at her stylish clothes and aristocratic appearance, trying to work out why she should want to go there, but said nothing.

Suddenly, she remembered that Nura had put the wild roses in the flower vase, then come back an hour later to put the bunch of carnations there instead, for no apparent reason. She chased the thought out of her head, and tried to focus her mind on Karim. She had been disturbed by a particular surreptitious look she had noticed him giving her young maid. The taxi reached the Saft al-Laban district, with its narrow, dirty streets. She looked at the chaos stretched out around her, at the old houses almost falling on top of each other, and felt the distance that divided Karim from her. She was annoyed by that, and suspected that the same feeling must come over him when he walked beside her in the Jazeera Club or at cocktail parties in the houses of her friends.

The taxi stopped, and the driver pointed to a nearby building. She got out, to find herself in a market like the one where she had lost herself the previous day. She walked on, pretending to be calm, as everyone looked at her in astonishment. She realized that going into Karim's flat would certainly attract attention, so she abandoned the idea and stood in an out-of-the-way corner, staring at the place where he lived. She thought that if Nura had come here, wanting to creep into Karim's flat, she would have had an easier job. Nura would not have seemed so out of place as she did.

She turned round to go back to the taxi, which was still waiting for her. When she reached the villa, she did not ring the bell, but opened the door with her own key, for Nura usually went out when Samiha had told her that she would be late back herself.

She went in and heard Karim's voice coming from the balcony. She walked over, only to see him sitting deep in conversation with Nura. Surprised by her sudden appearance, Nura left quickly, while Karim informed her that he had come back to check she was all right, as she had seemed tense in the morning, but he had been unable to find her.

She sat listening to him talking at length without really hearing any of his words. She just pretended to pay him some attention as she followed him, while trying to retain her constant smile. She waited patiently until his visit ended, then went into her study. She shut the door, took out her photograph album, and started to look at old pictures: one taken while she was a child in her Ramses College school uniform; another wearing a swimming costume that revealed most of her yoga-tautened body at the age of twenty; a third in the sixties with her parents on a trip to England. She passed the rest of the photos by quickly, and when she reached the most recent photos, she closed the album. As she left the room, she avoided looking in the mirror by the door.

She did not ask Nura why she had been sitting with Karim, nor did she tell her off for letting him in while she was out. She just asked her to come with her quickly to the chalet on the north coast. She took only her handbag, which she had grabbed quickly as she dragged Nura along behind her.

She was driving extremely fast along the Cairo-Alexandria desert highway, humming again the words of Najat's song. She felt an elation that she had not experienced for years. Once again, she was a pretty girl revelling in her beauty and her elegant figure. Her voice became louder, increasing the speed of the car. The cold air seared her face but she did not notice. Nura asked her why she had set out so suddenly but she gave no reply. Suddenly, she lost control of the steering wheel and the car lost its balance; then she was no longer conscious of the world around her. She could only hear the sound of an injured groan, a ringing that almost split her head apart, and a noise that enveloped everything.

Translated by Paul Starkey

MOHAMMED HASSAN ALWAN

The Beaver

an extract from a forthcoming novel

Alone, my family is mute; but in the presence of other people, they are very talkative. We have created our own scandals under the cover of so deafening a silence that no one can tell what others are concocting in the next room. I wonder whether we really understand one another more than others understand us. This seems impossible because our circumstances have not changed since they were established by my grandfather and became fixed by my father after him. These circumstances have spread like some contagion through the family genes ever since.

Because we do not speak, we are forced to fake talk. This is one of our random attempts to understand and communicate with one another, in accordance with the suppositions we make about each other rather than what we really are.

On the basis of these suppositions, my elder sister, Hind, is not just a long-serving educational supervisor at the Girls' College, she is also the Hind who has monopolised most of the formal beaver genes. Her posterior gets bigger every year. Each time I see her, I get a feeling that it has grown much bigger than the last time I saw her. She blames cortisone, hormones and her big bones, and says no more. She is my only sister, which is why we are compelled to tell each other more about ourselves. This is what we do all the time, but we never believe it.

She is one year older than me, but as Francis Bacon says, "A man finds himself seven years older the day after his marriage." Because she has been married twice, and I have never been married, she acts as if she is fifteen years my senior.

Had Hind not been married a second time, she would have blamed me all the time for the divorce from her first husband, although that marriage had never been consummated. She was engaged when I was only seventeen. When I came home in the al-Nasiriya District, I found the red Cadillac of her husband-to-be in front of the door – the Cadillac they used to make in the eighties was long like a fishing boat and large like the broad shoulders of a wrestler.

I ran for the short club that I used to hide under my car seat for no reason whatsoever; and deciding to take a stand that would, as I thought, advance my passage from adolescence to manhood, I totally smashed the windshield of the car.

I remember my father spat contemptuously right in my face several times that evening. I shoved Hind hard in front of her would-be husband and faked a hysterical scream. I yelled at her to go upstairs. She did not go upstairs although I thought she did, because she walked past me toward the staircase while I was staring hard at her husband-to-be and he was looking at me disdainfully. She turned back suddenly, walked behind me and dealt me a blow of the fist on the upper part of my back, and then slapped me twice on the neck. The two of us came to blows in an uneven fight. Her husband-to-be looked on.

The red Cadillac was parked in front of the door of our house many nights. It had a new windshield. I could do nothing to push it away. Hind deliberately met him behind locked doors to spite me and to scorn my confused manliness. My father forced me to kiss her husband's head twice and to take a two-horned sheep to his house and to make my apologies. In spite of all this, the marriage was not consummated. And to this moment, I still do not know what the real details were.

It seems that the ugly fistfight Hind and I had in his presence had not helped to make her look beautiful, as he would have liked his wife to be. Nor had she shown the self-possession he expected. As far as he was concerned, she was the sister of a foolish young man who must never be the uncle of his future children. Something akin to destiny, or so it seemed to me, had stood between Hind and her husband-to-be, causing them to separate while she was still a virgin and half crazy. Had I been as foolish as they claimed I was, I would have played the game to perfection and smashed his head instead of the windshield of his car. But I was a young man who was only acting out the role of "being a man" that the children of the district were constantly playing and talking about, and which my confused unassertive soul had worn since the day I was born. I had finally found a use for my coward club that cost me a great deal of pride. Do we have anything but pride when we are seventeen?

Remembering these awkward details now that I am in my forties is like fighting dust with an old, second-hand pair of lungs. I just cannot understand the situation I had been in or what had spurred me to behave the way I did. Hence I find myself searching for justifications which I do not believe. The misery I am in now, a perplexed lover, makes me see life as nothing more than a project of destruction, although I am quite certain that it has not been a bad life. True, it has not been as good as I would have liked it to be, but it has given me enough to take up writing.

Sometimes, I think that my sister, Hind, was the most important woman in my life, even though she has been further from my soul all these days. I had shared with her a goblet of the most important part of life, and a loaf of salty memory which I could never have shared with anyone else. At times, I am surprised at how few things we share, but also at the strong and powerful influence of those few things. I do not think I would have chosen her as my sister if I had the choice, and I do not think she would have chosen me to be her brother either. But we were born in one womb; we were born successively to a father who was not wanted, and we grew up in a narrow bosom that had reluctantly sheltered our arid childhood.

I say this because I know for certain that you do not fake suffering when you are in your forties. Also because I know that Mother had never wanted to marry my father. Nor did he want her as a wife. A few years after I was born, Mother flew to join another man to whom she bore better children. I am sure Hind does not see it like this; she insists that it was Satin's wicked thoughts which she prayed would not occur between her and her husband, lest she might end up like our mother.

As a little girl, Hind had cold eyes, void of everything eyes have, except for the function of seeing. When I think about her life, I feel as though I am watching the documentary of the childhood of a potential shedder of blood. But fortunately life did not furnish her with enough rage. Heavenly providence has turned her into a serene and acceptable being, but she is still a stranger to everything. She likes nothing, prefers nothing, fancies nothing, and desires nothing. Or maybe she refuses to say. She knows that she has her own needs: she rushes when she can get what she wants; and when she cannot she recoils.

Hind was born on the edge of a dirty old rug; I came to this life one year later in a new hospital and in a bed as white as snow. This furnished Hind with more reasons to hate me whenever Mother mentioned this in family conversations which were very frequent in our household. The truth is that Hind's birth, which took place in a traditional gathering on the side of this old rug, was quite normal and happened all the time in many Riyadh families in those days. But my rich imagination had prompted me to make thousands of jokes about Hind's situation just to belittle her.

The cold night had aggravated Mother's labour pains. Hind would have suffocated several times but for the excellent experienced old Ethiopian midwife whom Mother had asked to look after her two months before the delivery. Without going into brazen details, Mother told us that she had to have one leg tied with her black veil to a metal bar in the window, and that Father's sister had to hold the short rope tied to Mother's other leg so as to keep her legs wide apart: for she could not keep them wide enough unaided. Mother said, "No pain I have endured in my life can equal the agony of that night!" So severe was the pain that she was unable to even faint. Then came Hind's scream; the midwife pulled her out fast, and Mother collapsed. Her thighs closed on the big wound. My aunt rushed out and vomited, after turning part of the rug over Mother's body to keep her warm and to shield her against the cold of the night.

Because Hind came as a tiny piece of pink flesh, Mother could not bear the sight of her; nor did she know how to carry or suckle her or look after her, and so Hind was suckled by two different women. One was from Yemen; she lived in the same district and agreed to suckle her free of charge. She only stipulated that she could not suckle Hind too long, because she had had twins of her own and did not have enough milk for a third intrusive baby. The second woman who gave suck was an African wet nurse whom the Ethiopian midwife had brought along as part of her many services. Thus through suckling, Hind ended up a sister of seven children both Yemeni and African, as well as my sister through lineage. Many a time I poked fun at her in a racist way, mocking what that old milk she sucked had done to her and what it had turned her into. Until quite recently I was calling her "slave" and "Zaidiya".

Am I writing this now because I want to chastise myself, albeit very late, for the insolence of the past? It is perplexing to harbour an obstinate guilt about a sister to whom you do not know how to apologise, whether she needs that apology or not, or whether it will make her a better woman.

Today if I utter an apology to Hind for my giving her offensive names, she will probably laugh at me, and that may rouse within her a vile beast that will suck out my repentant soul to the last drop.

The problem is that my calling her derisive names pierced her soul like poisonous arrows; but any acts in retaliation fell near me like a swarm of dead flies. It is just impossible for a girl to have a tongue that is bolder than that of a young man with an imagination as wild as mine, a young man who could be creative in inventing insults for his sister during his thorny childhood, but could also write elegant letters to his love when he was older. And when he was in his forties, he wished, albeit for a moment, to swap his conduct towards the two women so that each of them would get what she actually deserved.

I do not know if the breasts of the two foreign women who had suckled Hind were any different from Mother's peculiar breasts that suckled me. This did not last long because she separated from Father when I was still in her womb. She weaned me in my seventh month, and then walked away. A few months later she returned to spend a few years with Father, but the relationship was no better than before. They then separated for good, and she married another man. Thus the milk which Mother had poured in Hind's body was very slow flowing while that which she discharged in my body was fast. This is why Mother seems to us no more than a self-effaced familial being that carried the identity of motherhood. Some sort of paper affection kept us attached to her and made her our mother and us her children. If we had tugged a little on this paper affection in the way life usually plays havoc with people's feelings, we would have torn it to shreds, and this did frequently happen. Our situation was different from that of Hassan, our half-brother from her other husband, who loved Mother as much as she loved him. If it were not for Mother's merits which tended to develop into hasty good qualities as she grew older, we might have rejected her from our adolescent years, especially as she was living with another man while we were living with a father who had never had one kind word for his wife.

Mother did not live with us long enough to allow her motherhood to mature for us. She was the only beaver who renounced her family; her emptiness turned us into deadwood and filled us with lifeless sorrows. If Father had divorced her twice, it was only because she had failed to build the home he had always wanted. He believed she harboured ill intentions. I believed her to be an unruly, stubborn woman from the south. Hind believed that Mother had made a series of mistakes and always blamed her, Hind, whenever something bad happened. Hind had never mentioned these mistakes in front of Mother because of a new late friendship that developed between them; this new amity collided with my sister's veneration of Father, which Hind silently concealed to avoid having to wrack her brains inventing explanations. The sixteen years separating them made them good friends: they looked after each other when one of them was sick; they went shopping together; they lashed out at the same women with the sting of their tongues; and they slated all men, including me. The only man about whom Mother and Hind disagreed was Father. Whereas Mother had never had a nice word for him, and was constantly making fun of his illiteracy and ignorance, Hind held him in the highest regard and always spoke well of him.

Mother had always condemned me for my hollow pride, of which she had plenty and which she passed on to me. This did not help me lead a life of peace and tranquillity. When she left the house the first time, the only part of me that grieved for her absence was my hungry stomach and my mouth which sought a nipple that was not there. She came back home a few months later surrounded by messengers of peace from among the women of al-Nasiriya and their husbands who, according to Mother, filled Father's reception room. She insisted that her return home required the presence of all these middlemen.

It was not until I was twenty years old that I started to mend fences with Mother, not because she was getting old, but because she was the wife of that lovely man, Uncle Brahim, in whom I found qualities that my own father lacked. He was an intellectual, open-minded and easy-going – just the qualities with which Father's temperament could not cope. His had been hewn from rock and sand. As for Hind, she remained friends with Mother, and it seemed that she forgot all the bad things Mother had done to her, and she could find no one to remind her of her usurped rights.

Mother's genes prevailed in Hind's body, which made her forget that she was an abandoned child. They made up over a social condition. This did not make them seem odd, as a mother and her only daughter; but they did not share the same behaviour and qualities, except the fault of complaining about everything. The only difference between them was that Hind was an oppressed grumbler while Mother was a rebellious one.

I cannot say for sure that Mother hated Hind when she was a child, but it may be that the mother was unable to pour out her love on her daughter as she should have. This was perhaps because

Hind reminded her mother of an old picture of a wretched pregnancy, of a cold night, and of a husband who was displeased with the femaleness of his first-born child. Hind arrived at a season of hatred in a city that was very good at creating these seasons. Unfortunately, due to her stupid nature, Hind was unable to change anything of that. That was why she was what she was and always behaved in a random manner.

As for me, I grew up having only Hind in front of me. I watched her with great amazement as she sat in the midday sun without feeling the heat. She used to lick the walls because of an iron deficiency in her body; and at times she would swallow dirt and eat cold ash from the fireplace. She always had a runny nose, but that did not bother her. Her eyes would gaze into the void and took everything in. Her thighs displayed round, blue bruises from the pinches which Saida, the maid, had given her. Her arms had long red lines on them because of too much scratching in her sleep.

In those days, Riyadh was drinking petroleum, and getting fat very fast, and sprawling. Like many others, Father was panting for wealth. He did not have enough time to deal with the headache which Mother used to plant in his head every evening, and she did not accept a life marginal to him before the advent of the economic boom when he had nothing to do, let alone after the economic boom. Their divorce was more like a peace treaty than a family breakdown. Mother went to her maternal uncle's house but did not stay there long before Uncle Brahim asked for her hand in marriage. Then Father unrepentantly brought in the Ethiopian maid, Saadiya, to undertake all the household work that Mother used to do in the house.

We used to live in an ordinary house in al-Nasiriya District; it was the first house Hind and I lived in, and the second house in which Father had lived. Afterwards we moved to al-Murabba District then to the al-Fakhiriya District where my family lives today. Before I was born, my parents used to live in a mud house in the Dakhna District when they first arrived in Riyadh on an old rusty bus from Abha. The journey to Riyadh had taken four days and was full of dust, heat, fear and worry.

In Riyadh, I lived on the sides of the triangle of al-Nasiriya, al-Murabba and al-Fakhiriya before my capriciousness prompted me to destroy this geometrical shape and to travel to a faraway place called Oswego, south of Portland. Every time I looked at the map, I would ask myself about the potential geometrical shapes I might create in the coming years. Where might I move to? Who might I live with?

Studying maps took me to places that were too far away from what I wanted them to tell me. No map had ever before helped me to understand directions as much as it had contributed to my sense of loss and isolation. We look at maps to know where we are, or where we are heading. Because I was never able to answer the first question, the second one proved itself even more difficult.

The map of Riyadh, which looked like a huge scratch on the back of the desert, surrounded by pus and hate, had always spurred me to turn against the city. Every time I looked at this map, it raised in me issues of belonging, of love and also wretched memories. What survived were questions to which answers never brought me any peace of mind.

When Mother left the house the second time, everybody thought that she would return, but she did not. We did not grieve much at her departure. In fact it gave us a break from her constant nervous tension and her ruthless beating, as well as an opportunity for us to discover the new woman Father brought home whom he said was our new mother. We were very happy to receive. Because of her neutrality, it was safer for our souls and bodies to be with her than with our mother, who was always nagging us and beating us unexpectedly.

Mother travelled to Beirut with her new husband; we stayed in al-Nasiriya, trying hard to be the children of a woman whom we had never known. Hind quickly took to calling her "Mother" while I called her "Shikha", Matron, as Father called her. In spite of the fact that Hind was the first to have called the woman "Mum", I was the one who received her love, stories and was her favourite. I had no idea the reason for this, except that Shikha, who was then only nineteen years old, believed the road to my father's heart was through his only son, and that it would never be through his eldest daughter.

Regarding Father, our biggest beaver, who decided to work on a rampart in the face of Riyadh, even he did not escape unscathed from the whirlpool. It swallowed him up as it did tens of the migrants before him. He sold rugs in al-Zall marketplace, and he became a real estate agent of dubious reputation after the north of the city turned out to be a veritable treasure trove of land for the people. In the eighties Father got his share of the cake along with others, but when he fell, he fell alone.

Now Father is quiet, like an extinct volcano in which there lurk profound anxious intentions and from whose crater emerge angry gases that accumulate on the surface as a result of past eruptions. Father does not talk about the past, which only proves that there were dark episodes that should never be told in stories. The scanty details about his past come mainly from the tongues of others, such as Mother, my aunt and other relatives.

"He learnt to drive, and he became a driver," said the grey-haired man, whom destiny had brought from Abha to Riyadh to tell me what I did not know about Father.

This man had come to Riyadh to get medical treatment, and Father, whose custom was to welcome relatives, showed him great hospitality and invited him to stay in our house. I used to take him to hospital and bring him back home at different times, and show him into one of the guest rooms in our house.

Father would meet him only at meal times while I would spend most of the time with him. When he knew that I would never make a good assistant to a businessman, Father put me in charge of entertaining guests, entrusting me with trivial social responsibilities, daily household chores and any other task that would partly convince him that his bringing me to this world was not a wasted investment.

Thabit began to tell me much about Father, which made me feel that I had landed on an unexpected small treasure of information, especially as it came at a difficult time for me: my university research project was not completed when I finally left the university in 1993.

I was a sociology student at King Saud University. My professor suggested that I do research on the social impact of the families that had migrated to big cities. That was the only thing the professor and I had agreed on before we engaged in a series of disagreements and brawls that ended in my being dismissed from the university.

Although it was a short piece of research, I was overwhelmed by it, obsessed by it in a way that convinced nobody around. My dream grew bigger as my little research turned into first a book and then into a novel and finally into an encyclopedia. In this obsession, I detected a seed that could be fit for a project for the political opposition, then for a great theory in sociology, then for a major documentation concerning the whole of humanity, and which was likely to become a religion with its own followers in two hundred years' time. I dreamed of all this while I was in my early twenties. I was trying to build for myself a glory that would make Haifa grieve over the fact that she had left me for another man.

I have no idea where I left the box in which I keep my research; it must be in some place in the basement of my villa where my servants piled up all my belongings after I had moved into this new house. There was a bundle of pages full of revisions and observations, a collection of tapes full of insignificant voices, documents of old land transactions stolen from my father's safe, yellow newspaper cuttings which I had long been looking for in the archives of local newspapers, hand-drawn maps of our village near Abha which I had never visited, and a short video film which cannot be seen today because it is too old to be played any more. There are also records of my meetings with Uncle Thabit, as he walked down memory lane with Father in Riyadh.

My two years' work on imaginary research in the vast city of Riyadh was reminiscent of Marie Curie's discovery of radium whose radioactivity killed her, after she was exposed to it for many years. The difference between Marie Curie and myself was that I did not discover anything in the end, apart from what I had collected in terms of the ugly, the eccentric and the repulsive aspects of my city and the memories of my family; but in the end, I came out of it with no book, or university degree, or woman.

Undertaking university research was the worst decision I made in my life, not because of my failure to complete it, but rather because I had chosen it while I was going through a wistful mood, one that I had never experienced before. The crisis that had lasted for a quarter of my life was taking its toll on me while I was desperately in need of some achievement that would inject new blood into my confused life. I was living with my half siblings who did not treat me as their elder brother, and with parents who expected nothing more from me than the usual roles; at the same time I was dumped by the woman who loved me and whom I loved because she did not believe I could embark on a life that would give security for us both. All this was taking place in a suffocating void, in a boring city that had just shaken off the dust of the fallouts of the Gulf War, and had drifted into the coma of cement and sand.

The deluding holes left by that research in my heart are still gaping. Because I could not do anything to heal them, I left them open. It is simply a case of a failure that has not been turned into an interesting story from the past or into a curse that is now behind me – thank God! It still tastes bitter, with a tang which I still feel even when I try to free a small fish from the hook of my fishing line on the shore of the Willamette River.

Translated by Ali Azeriah

Temporary Death

a chapter of a forthcoming novel

1

The first time my grandfather died, all he owned was a rather flimsy wooden staff and a full-length djellaba. They hastily dug a shallow grave right beside where his corpse lay, so close to him that his face got covered in dust, obscuring his features. They shrouded his body in his djellaba, sewing him into it from the feet up, so that when they got to his head they found they had nothing left to cover it with and, perplexed by this, they ended up using his cotton food bag. They pushed him into the hole, and piled earth on to his body, and departed, not one of them lingering or looking back. But one small child returned to the graveside, in search of a frog he had heard croaking but had been unable to see. He found the djellaba and the cotton bag lying spread out on top of the grave, and the earth was as smooth and level as they had left it, and called the others back to the graveside. When they saw that the clothes had floated up to the surface of the earth all by themselves, without the body that had been inside them, they declared it a miracle. They built a domed tomb over the grave which became a shrine and was visited by the ill, the needy, the cursed and the barren, but it did not occur to anyone actually to dig up the earth and check that he was really inside it.

2

No one knew who my grandfather's father was, or his mother. They had found him lying on his back on the riverbank, reaching out his hand to scoop up and drink water, with a smile on his face. He was four years old, with the full beard and moustache of a man in his twenties. His memory of this moment never faded: they all gathered round him and carried him off to the village chief's house, and brought an elderly servant woman to him. They ordered her to feed him, but he refused to eat, and seemed to be perfectly satisfied with plenty of water. The servant woman tried to get him up on his feet and walking, but he could neither stand up nor talk, and just kept on smiling his broad and constant smile.

Most of the male villagers gathered together and sat in a circle around him, thinking that he could not understand what they were saying. Some of them said that the child was not human, some speculated that he was under a spell. Others protested that he was simply an illegitimate child abandoned by his mother at birth. The village sage said, "He will be the end of you all," so some of the men suggested that the child be killed – "so that people don't get led astray." But others objected, saying, "Don't kill him, just put him back on the riverbank where he was; he's got nothing to do with any of you." The priest said, "There is no mention of his condition in the holy books: he is therefore surely a demonic and ungodly creature." As for the doctor, he said, "His condition is unknown to science; perhaps this child marks the beginning of an evolutionary transformation which will turn out to have unholy consequences for the entire human race."

They talked on, staring long and hard at the boy as they stretched him out in front of them, and fiddled around with his body, seeing how it worked. They carried him back and forth, they tossed him up in the air, they fingered his eyes and nose, and one by one they all tugged at his beard and moustache to make sure they were real. One of them even opened the child's mouth and pressed on his teeth with great force to see how strong they were. But none of them managed to make him stop smiling.

He had already been through this same experience in several other villages, and he could still remember all the details of each of the occasions. He lay there contemplating the villagers who, to him, all looked exactly alike, as the discordant screech of their voices filled his ears. They did not arrive at any decision on that first day. Worn out by their discussions and arguments, they gave him to an old servant woman so he could stay the night with her. They then all went home, having agreed to meet the following morning to decide on the fate of this strange child.

She set off for home, managing to carry the heavy child at arm's length, gripping on to him with her hands rather than holding him close, so as to keep his body as far away as possible from hers. She covered the long distance from the village chief's house to her shack near the river in a state of fear and exhaustion, moving her feet with difficulty, sitting down every little while for a rest. She wanted him to stop smiling, or to cry as a child of his age should do, to reassure her; but he did not. So she squeezed him as hard as she could between her bony hands, as if to crush his whole body, and pinched his sides with her long thin fingers, but he gently and amiably pushed her hand away, stared into her eyes and smiled; so she stopped.

She considered leaving him in the middle of the road or drowning him in the river, and so be rid of him once and for all. She said to herself that if she lost him no one would care, and that they would believe whatever story she chose to make up about him. She could say that all of a sudden he had run off, or turned into a genie and jumped into the river, or hidden from her. But she was afraid of the way his eyes stared straight into hers, and she knew that she was simply incapable of killing a child who smiled the way he did.

She went into her hut and quickly lit the oil-lamp, laid him on her bed, and stayed standing beside him. She was hungry, but she was scared of getting distracted from him by preparing her food. She took off her shawl and put it over his face to cover his eyes, but he pushed it off. She tried to make him laugh by making faces at him, and throwing him up into the air a few times, and tickling his feet and his armpits. But he did not laugh: his smile just broadened a tiny little bit. She was too shy to change her clothes in front of him, so she sat down beside him, and eventually dozed off.

She awoke a little later to find that where she was sitting was soaking wet, and jumped up in alarm. Realising that he had wet the bed she smiled, despite her wet clothes, and began to undress him. As she did so, she exposed dense chest and pubic hair. When she saw that he had a mature adult penis she drew back in fear, but she did not raise her eyes from it, and she felt desire. She fetched a pot of water, and began to wash him. His penis grew erect in her hand. She prolonged the process of washing him, afraid to make eye contact; when she eventually looked up into his face, she found that he was smiling, eyes half closed.

She took off her clothes, climbed up on top of him, and soon felt him inside her. He was enjoying himself, and moved with the skill of someone well accustomed to lovemaking.

When she woke up next morning she was a little perturbed by their nakedness, so she fetched his clothes, which had dried off overnight, and got him dressed. She stood before him singing as she washed herself and combed her hair, while he contemplated her and smiled. She felt satisfied, and was surprised to find her body smoother than it had been the night before, and to see new black hairs had appeared among her snowy locks. She put on a clean djellaba, picked up the child and went outside to find almost the entire village gathered in front of her door, waiting to see this bearded child who neither ate nor laughed nor cried, but was content with water alone.

When they all crowded around her the child was scared of them, and she covered his face with her shawl so they could not stare at him, held him tightly to her and turned her back on them to protect him from their eyes. He felt reassured. The women of the group drew closer, looked hard at her face, and asked her how she had become so young. She hurried, with the crowd rushing along around her, to the village chief's house, where the male elders had gathered. When she went inside they demanded the child, and she asked what they were going to do with him. They scolded her for her question – she was a female servant, and certainly should not be speaking in the men's council. She clung to the child, refusing to leave him with them, and he gripped onto her clothes with his tiny little fingers, and pulled her towards him urgently so that she would not leave him. Then the men informed her that they had agreed to leave him on the riverbank of the next village, as they believed that was what the people of all the previous villages had done with him. He had been found, naked, on the riverbank in the first village, so they had dressed him and passed him onto the next one, as had a succession of communities, until he had turned up here. The old woman wept to hear this. Then, still clasping the child, she bolted out of the meeting, and fled towards her hut. The male council was not bothered by this in the slightest, saying only, "That old woman has taken a weight off our minds."

The rest of the villagers chased her all the way home, but they couldn't catch up with her until she had made it to the door, which she slammed in their faces. She put the child delicately on to the bed. Then she came back out to them, a knife in each hand, and threatened to kill anyone who came near her or the child.

The villagers were alarmed – they said the child was bewitched, and had driven the old woman mad.

3

At first the old woman didn't believe that he was a child, even though he had a childish face and he wet his bed. She was convinced he was an adult dwarf who was just unable to speak or to walk, and that she was the only one who had worked this out. She kept him hidden away in her bedroom, and shaved his beard and moustache regularly, which made him look as innocent as a baby. She taught him her name early on, and he would call her by it, even though he could not pronounce it properly. Gradually she taught him some more words, and got him accustomed to one or two types of food, and he took his first steps, holding on to her hand. By the end of their time together he had become quite proficient at talking, eating and walking.

She had sex with him several times a day; when he ejaculated inside her she never thought of him as a child, even for a moment. She often asked him what his name was, or questioned him about his life before he came to the village, but he did not seem to understand. The sexual maturity of his body bewildered her, and she also found it strange that he hardly ever slept. But she was glad of his wakefulness one night when a snake slithered in under the door of the shack as she slept, and he roused her just in time to escape being bitten.

She would sit in front of him, naked, observing with fascination the changes that had taken place in her body. She had grown a strong full set of teeth, and all her hair had regained its original black colour. She was tall once more, her wrinkles had disappeared, her skin had a youthful glow, her breasts had regained their pertness. She was able to walk long distances, to run and to carry all sorts of heavy loads – whereas previously she had struggled even to carry her pots and pans. The day she began bleeding from the vagina, however, she simply could not believe she was menstruating, and assumed it was a haemorrhage. But a month later it happened again: she was deeply shocked, and did not know what to do.

The other villagers grew scared of coming near her hut. They would stop a good distance away and wait for a sighting of the child when he came out to play. He had grown taller, but when she let his beard and moustache grow, as she did from time to time, he still looked as he had when they first found him. The women of the village were determined to discover the secret of the old woman's rejuvenation, so they sneaked up to her hut one night, peered in through the gaps in her door, and saw her having sex with the child.

No one employed her as a servant in their house anymore as, according to what the men said, she had gone mad, or had been bewitched; the women, for their part, feared the effect of her renewed beauty on their husbands. So, in order to feed herself and the child, she had started going to market once a week to beg, smartly warding off the stall holders' attempts to exploit her desperation and to seduce her. But on her last trip to market she let the haberdasher kiss her and came home with a piece of cloth, a needle and some thread, with which she made the child new clothes to replace the ones he had grown out of.

When her periods stopped she felt that she would grow old all over again, but two months later she was sure, from the size of her belly, that she was pregnant. News of the pregnancy spread like wildfire through the village. The women passed the news on to each other at first, and then began telling their husbands about it too, catching them at their most impressionable and pliant, whilst having sex. Even the children were whispering to each other about it in class, and so eventually the men called a meeting in the village chief's house and it was decided that the maid must be killed – but only after they knew who the father was.

They took her to the square in chains and all the villagers gathered around. At first she refused to name the father, but village law stipulated that any woman found to have committed adultery or to have become pregnant outside marriage should be tortured until she confessed. So they set light to her hair and her ears. Slipping in and out of consciousness, she eventually pointed her finger at the haberdasher. As they were dragged away together he shouted repeatedly that he had only kissed her. This made the accusation stick even more, and they were sentenced according to the law of fornication: stripped of their clothes, all their limbs were cut off, and they were strung up on two neighbouring palm trees, the amputation wounds having been smeared with milk and honey to encourage putrefaction. Insects and maggots soon covered them both, and carnivorous birds tore into their flesh.

The haberdasher died first, then the servant woman, who was by now in the prime of her youth. Her expression was as calm as if she were merely sleeping, and she showed no sign of being in any pain. The smile on her lips was exactly like that of the man who had spent a whole year in her home, whom she had loved passionately and had sex with many times until she had become

pregnant by him, without ever thinking for a minute that the
father of her unborn child was under five years old.

4

As soon as the servant and the haberdasher had been sentenced
to death the women of the village set off running towards her
hut, each hoping to get custody of the child. The old women were
at the back, but even they ran at a tremendous pace; the young
and the middle-aged women pushed and shoved each other with
their fists and shoulders, and when the crowd reached the locked
door of the hut, they fought – ripping each other's clothes and
tearing each other's hair until they were all half-naked, bleeding
from their mouths and noses, with scratches and cuts all over
their bodies. They did not stop until the village's eldest woman
had been killed – she had somehow extricated herself from the
middle of the battle, crawled over to the door of the hut and tried
to push it open, at which point twenty women hurled themselves
at her as one and trampled her beneath their feet, crushing her
bones and smashing her head.

The men arrived. When the village chief saw the women's naked
bodies he ordered the men to turn their faces away and the
women to try to cover themselves. He decreed that each woman
would be the child's guardian for a month, and their voices rose,
arguing over who would have the first turn and who would go
next. So he counted all the houses in the village, found that there
were 150, and told the women to draw lots to determine what
order they would go in. Out of the men's hearing, however, the
older women threatened if the rest of the group didn't let them
go first that they would reveal the real motive behind everyone's
enthusiasm for taking custody of the child. So the women asked
the village chief if the list of guardians could be drawn up in order

of age, starting with the eldest, then the next eldest, then the next, and so on. The eldest woman in the village came forward, presented herself, pushed open the door of the hut, and soon came back out leading the child by the hand. She clasped him close to herself, laughing, and hurried off home.

My grandfather did not realise that he had loved the old servant woman until he was having sex with the last woman in the village. He had always, with each of the women in turn, been searching for what he had felt with the servant, and each time he did not find it he would say to himself, "Maybe with the next one." By the time he had finished his stay in the last of the 150 households he was over seventeen years old, twice the size of an ordinary man, and his beard reached down to his knees. He decided to go back to the servant's hut, where they had buried her, but all he found were the tumble-down remains of a tomb. On this pile of rubble he built a little house, and dug a little channel to it from the river. People were astonished by this, but they did not say anything. As the men of the village knew about the child's relationship with their wives they said that he was blessed, and that it was this blessing that had brought such youthfulness back to the women in the houses where he had stayed. When they chanced upon him in the village they would kiss his hand. Once he had become independent, in his distant house, he did not allow any of the women to visit him. Water flowed along the channel right into his house, and he drank from it, but did not eat.

He made friends with the birds and the animals. He understood their language, and used to walk through the village with them in an awe-inspiring and solemn procession. At night he would take off his clothes and wash in the river, and the women would spy on him. When he caught sight of them he would throw them large fish. Eventually he decided to make the river his home, and spent several years in it, without ever getting out of the water, befriending the fish, the boatmen and the fishermen. In the end he decided it was time to get out of the river. He disappeared from the village altogether. The women stood in a vigil around his house, and by his usual place in the river, until they were absolutely sure he had disappeared.

There were those who said the river had taken him away again, just as it had delivered him on to the riverbank in the first place, on that day long ago; others said he was a merman. And some said he was just a normal human being, but that he had drowned in the river, and his corpse had drifted far downstream.

Several years later he came back to them, arriving, as he had left, by river – but this time he turned up on a big ship loaded with merchandise, perfumes, jewellery and livestock. He had shaved his beard off, and was dressed in clothes that were completely unfamiliar to the villagers. Etched on his chest was a tattoo clearly depicting the servant woman. The whole village drew close to the ship, and then caught sight of things they had never seen the like of ever before. He stood among them, saying that if any of them wanted any of these things they could have them, but that they would have to pay with everything that they owned: money, land and property. The men laughed at him and asked him who he thought would give all they owned for something they had never seen before. He gave no answer and waited. Over the course of the next day the women came along one by one, dragging their husbands behind them and forcing them to swap all their worldly goods for a set of silk sheets, or a glass *narghile*, or a pair of high-heeled shoes, or an hourglass. Once he had acquired the whole village and all it contained, and had driven out all the villagers, he began to spend his time constructing a high wall all around it. When it was finished he took to walking around naked inside the wall and drawing pictures on it of him and the servant woman, in all her different ages, having sex. He used to write her name beneath her image, and nothing under his own, and so eventually it dawned on him that he had did not have a name of his own. He would run his mind back over everyone he had met in the village and on his long travels: each of them had a name. He knew it was imperative for a person to have a name. He tried to find one for himself, but failed – he busied himself intensely with the task, but to no avail. Finally, having failed to work out his own name, he erased hers.

Most of the villagers had dispersed throughout the surrounding villages by this time, but some of them had settled just outside the wall, from where he used to hear their voices. They would peep in at him, watching as he spent his life demolishing all the houses of the village, dismantling them stone by stone, then throwing the stones in the river, until he had almost dammed it. White hairs began to creep one by one into his hair and his long beard. His body was becoming old and decrepit by the time he had finished his project. When he had demolished all but the farthest outlying houses of the village he dug a deep pit along its entire length, and no one could work out why. He dug it using his own invention, a hoe – a tool which no one had ever used before then and which was subsequently imitated all round the world. He would dig and dig, sculpting the edges of this huge hole with precision, then climb up a high date-palm tree to see his work from above. When he climbed up for the last time, he saw that the giant cavity had taken the form of a young woman's body, bearing a clear resemblance to the servant at the end of her life. He then knocked down the wall, dammed the river, diverting its flow so that it ran into the pit he had dug. It began to flow swiftly into her thighs, coursing through the rest of her body, and then went streaming out of her mouth to continue on its way. Many flowers sprang up all around her body, and the spot became a favourite trysting-place for lovers from all the villages in the area.

Having rerouted the river, he felt that he had completed his task. He put on his djellaba and, carrying his stick and his bag of food, he headed out of the village; but when he reached the woman's foot he fell down dead. By now the original villagers had all moved on to other places, so no one knew him; people were amazed by the length of his beard. They used his djellaba and his food bag as his shroud, buried him and stuck his wooden staff in the ground as a headstone, and that was that. That is, of course, until they came back and found his clothes on top of the grave, over which they built a shrine. Because they did not know his name, and he had died at the woman's feet, they named the shrine "Tomb of the Lady's Victim."

Translated by Alice Guthrie

My Own Sana'a

Subhiya

... tells how a special room called the mafraj on the top floor of old buildings in Sana'a make you nearer to Ilmaqa, the moon that is the object of your worship, and how there are alabaster windows in them, circular in form and with a faint light that comes in to give you the courage to spend the night there till dawn, gossiping about times past and times to come ...

The morning of the seventh of July 2009.

Lots of cars on Republican Palace Street and on roads leading to Sab'un Square. Soldiers bristling with arms were searching cars and frisking pedestrians very slowly. It did not bother them that they might be late for work or that students might miss their classes.

I was not the only one wondering why this was going on as I drove to work. One passer-by asked the soldier who was searching him the reason for these unexpected measures. The soldier replied with just the hint of irritation in his voice, "Security measures for the celebration of 7/7. Victory Day! There's going to be a parade of important people and their guests from here to Sab'un Square, where there'll be celebrations."

This guy did not seem to have taken much in. 7/7? Victory Day? But he moved on after he had been searched.

I then understood, 7/7. And the occasion, Victory Day. I rifled through my memory – as others did. Victory for whom?

Over whom? Another pedestrian passed by and repeated, as if he was reading my mind, the same words with biting sarcasm and inner anger. The soldier rebuked him and asked him to move on quietly or he would have to take certain measures!

The Secession War, that is what the press called the war of May 1994. They called its outcome on 7 July of that year a victory over those who were demanding a return to the partition after the passing of four years of unity.

The fact that there had been no celebrations of 7/7 for many years past was because they tried to make it just like any other day. There was much that was right about this. How could one family, when they had solved a problem that had caused them much tragedy, go back and have it driven into their hearts every year, forgetting what the memory of it brought back in terms of pain. Those children of one nation were damaged. The pain would not be over until the death of another grandchild of those who died on both sides.

One of the soldiers shouted at drivers, telling them to keep the cars to the right and to move on quickly. A huge parade passed by with an armada of black Mercedes cars reflecting in their tinted glass the despair of people, one third of whom were suffering from grinding poverty. The climax passed as the formidable procession went by, but this did not compensate for the fact that everyone the procession passed who was on their way to their places of work or study was late.

I continued on my way to the road that led to al-Sa'ila and entered the old city of Sana'a, winding my way through the narrow alleyways that allowed only one car to pass at a time. I parked my car as close as possible to a garden and walked the rest of the way to my place of walk. I was late but Salih had done what he had to do, opening the place up, cleaning it, welcoming visitors and making sales by the time I arrived.

A few minutes later Amm Muhammad came and asked me anxiously why I was late because I had not bought my daily potato sandwich from him. I reassured him, saying, "Today's 7/7, Amm Muhammad." He seemed surprised at the date. He left, striking one palm against the other once I had explained things to him, and went back to his cart from which he sold egg, potato and cheese sandwiches for the pupils at Nishwan school and to anyone who was passing by.

My studio was an old residence in the heart of Old Sana'a, as they became accustomed to call it after the revolution of September 1962. When it became a World Heritage Site in 1971 it was called The Old Walled City. Outside the walls of Sana'a was another new city, new in everything, with buildings of cement instead of stonework, with civilised inhabitants who explained that the old city reminded them of a past time when they were victims of oppression, humiliation and deprivation. It was a past they had to forget and even to distance themselves from. So they slipped out from the old city whenever they had a chance to acquire a residence in the new city.

Only the old remained there, bestowing on it warmth with their memories of their lives in the past, preferring to continue there rather than leave it. They carried on their work and their shared rituals at the same time in various places, as if they were one person. They set out for the dawn prayer, regardless of the cold. They were happy to spend the evenings sitting with their friends in the square of the quarter, the wide place overlooked by their houses and their memories about ...

I bought the house nine years ago at a price that was reasonable, compared with the madness of prices these days. It had three floors and a mafraj, a top room looking out through windows in three directions, to Jabal Naqm to the east, Jabal Aiban to the west. I turned the ground floor into an exhibition room for the sale of my art work and also for selling some traditional handicrafts brought to me by some women from the houses around. They appealed to tourists. Though some then were being kidnapped by tribal leaders in order to put pressure on the government to implement demands that were in their interests, tourists would come to the old city in large numbers all through the year. On the first floor I made a studio where I painted with all I had, using colours and fabrics and frames and wooden easels. The second floor contained a permanent exhibition and was set aside for visitors of all kinds, foreign tourists or my own friends and acquaintances.

I spend a lot of time alone in the mafraj, with nostalgia for the few days I had spent in Sana'a as a child before leaving it for ages and having to be content with coming back to it on holidays. I gaze through the wide windows at the most fascinating city in the world with its lofty buildings. The reflection of the light outside on the coloured skylights makes the mafraj glow with romance and calm. I feel a strange numbness as I recall those legends that envelop the city, its buildings and its people in a glittering world.

I open my studio from eight to twelve in the morning. I close it at the time of the noon prayers. The call to prayer goes up in an amazing fugue from the hundred minarets that the old city alone has. The people of the city do not like to be troubled, least of all at the time of prayer. I do not have a fixed time for painting and I leave it for my mood to decide. I leave at five o'clock and go to my home in New Sana'a, while I have someone to stay on and sell work until nine.

I do not often paint obscure surrealist or unreal abstract pictures. I love realism, and am very good at portraits of the faces of old people. I strive to perfection as if I am helping them with a life that is almost fading away. What I really love is to make paintings of these old buildings and to linger over the details, to imagine aspects of them that I have not experienced. Sometimes I am overwhelmed by a sense of sadness as I use my brush, working hard to bring out the wan light that radiates through the windows of a small house or a high house decoration looking down on the old city, leaving the new city as an extensive faint background.

I have no particular rituals in painting, unlike other painters. I do not have unkempt hair, nor do I wear filthy clothes. I do not smoke heavily. But when I have finished a painting I enjoy a weary puff at a special mint-flavoured cigarette. I go back to painting as I might go back to meeting a lover. I keep my hair neat, I put kohl on my eyes and some light make-up on my face. I usually wear a shoulderless dress and short trousers.

Sometimes I have an overpowering wish to carry on working late when I would have to stay overnight at the studio, something that upsets my mother a lot, although she accepts it nonetheless. It is she who insisted on not living in the old city although she never gave me any reason for this. I had implored her to buy a house with more room than my studio so we could live there and I could have my studio at the same time, but she refused absolutely. It is something she does not wish to remember! It is something without a reason, a wound not yet healed. So we remain in our house that we left twenty two years ago. We spent all that time in Cairo and I was able to buy only this small house.

I came back from Cairo with Mother in 2000 after all that long time, exactly one year after my father's death. Father, in spite of his huge love for Yemen and especially Sana'a, never had the slightest intention of coming back, not even for a visit, from his place of exile. He had chosen Cairo with all his heart and lived there from the late 1970s.

Not for a day did Father cease to talk fondly about Sana'a. He spoke of it passionately as if it was his eternal love which he embraced in his arms every night. He closed his eyes on its image in a state of bliss, which he preserved as he wanted it to be; perhaps it was the image of it when he left all those years before. Every morning he would have coffee. He would take the first sip, deliberately crying out loud with the pleasure of its special taste. He would roast the coffee on the fire himself, and divide the coffee beans into three: two thirds would be roasted dark brown and the other third light brown. He then ground in a little cardamom so that the aroma he adored was not lost. I never asked him about what he remembered of the city or what he felt. But I used to sense the same tang and to share the moment with him. I had more hope of returning and building up my own memories there, just as he had done, even though it pained him and left him bleeding to death.

All his love for Sana'a and all his talk about it planted in me a love for the city and also a desire to return there, if not a hope of living there. Sana'a was an enchantress with its history, slumbering beneath the slopes of a mountain bereft of green trees and warm rocks. The city consequently always felt cold and insecure, as he always liked to say. Father would only ask about Sana'a, how the city and its people were, after I or Mother or my only brother had returned from our annual holiday there without him.

After his death Mother could not bear staying in Cairo. She was happy to see my brother marry an Egyptian girl and then leave. Marriage to a non-Yemeni was no problem for my brother or Mother or even Father. But as far as I was concerned it was a real catastrophe. How could I marry a man who was a foreigner, a man who knew nothing of my homeland except by hearsay? A man who had never spent a day with me wandering about the streets of the city, playing in the alleyways and hiding in its nooks and crannies, a man who had not experienced the flavour of my memories whenever I told him about them, telling him of places and people he had not experienced for a day.

I utterly rejected the idea but I did not talk about it to Father or Mother lest they felt disappointment in the education they had chosen to give me, a very civilised education that viewed other people regardless of their nationality, colour or religion. Father did not want me to think like those people who told him one day that he was only born in Sana'a, not a true Sana'ani because his mother was Ethiopian. I was a citizen to the core apart from this. And so I became skilled at inventing excuses for refusing anyone who proposed marriage while I was at the university in Cairo. I always dream of marriage but only to a Sana'ani, yes, a true one hundred per cent Sana'ani, a man who has grown up and been educated in the old city; someone who knows the alleyways and has played in its quarters and has been so moulded by the customs, the traditions and the humanity of the place that he becomes another man. A Sana'ani like Father, with his familiarity with the minutiae of his secrets with Mother, with his deep love for the place, with the details of his daily Sana'ani maleness which comes from I know not where, whether from Sana'a or from his mother. My grandmother, Masarra, was a beautiful Ethiopian woman who gave him his tawny colour and all her affection.

My grandmother, Masarra, told me once something I can never forget about my grandfather. He waited for her with a cup of cold rose water when she was returning from the public Turkish baths. He had prepared it for her the evening before promising her a magical night. This grandfather taught her the distinctive Sana'ani dialect with its ring of letters as they were uttered until she became fluent. He taught her the Sana'ani dances with the coquettish gypsy-like movements he loved until she became familiar with those as well. They spent whole nights happily chatting and dancing until morning without being aware of it. Grandmother Masarra used to say, "I never slept until he was asleep, and I rarely woke up after him. This was so my face was the last one he saw before he went to sleep and the first face he set eyes on when he woke up."

I loved my grandmother and I wanted to love a man who was exactly like Father.

I met Hamid for the first time when he came to an exhibition as an ordinary customer wanting to buy a canvas for his neighbouring Sana'a houses. I was overcome by conflicting feelings, new to me, and felt excited. His relatively large size made me feel I would be like a dove that could be swept away in his arms by his warmth and calm. With some difficulty I escaped from these feelings as we got to understand together the canvas and its qualities. With greater difficulty I tried not to think about him for the rest of the day. But I slept easily at the studio, intoxicated by the sketching of a scenario of a magical Sana'ani night! ...

He did not come after that to collect the canvas as he had promised, and I did not repeat what I had done that night. So for months I avoided spending the night at the studio to escape from that tall broad rotund body and the white face with its honey-coloured eyes.

It is said that washing in the water of the public Turkish baths in the old city of Sana'a guards you against illness. And that the steam coming from the stone walls, with its penetrating nocturnal powers, helps both women and men. This is conditional on going to the baths, one after the other, from the north of the city to the south, from the east to the west, once a month ... from the heat of your body and your intimate parts there grow many strong lads and charming girls after a long time waiting.

Hamid

The jambiya adorns the waist of the Yemeni man as a mark of

honour and manhood. When he fingers its haft in a quarrel, this is a sign of aggression. Taking the knife halfway out of the scabbard is a warning of an attack. But taking the knife right out means war. Blood has to be shed before a man puts it back in its scabbard, his honour satisfied.

Fifty years of my life have passed and I have dreamt of the time when I would go through the alleyways of old Sana'a arm in arm with a lady. I whisper my dreams into her ear, and I tempt her with my desires! ... When this moment actually arrived I could not believe it, even though she was at my side. Did her coming embarrass me? I do not know! Was it beyond my capacity to accept her as a fact of life after she had for ages been a dream? I do not know the answer to that either.

The first time Subhiya agreed to go with me through the alleyways and have Sana'ani coffee in the Salt Suq, I could not believe it. It was not easy for any young Yemeni girl. That was two months after I had visited her studio and bought the painting I had already selected. I said to myself she was kidding me and would not come. Nonetheless I clung to a ray of hope. She was five minutes late and this gave me a sense of despair, ripped apart by forebodings that left me perplexed, wondering whether she would come or not.

But she did come and here I am walking along in her company, making a point of pressing against the corners of buildings in the alleyways and feeling the stones of the houses to prove that I am not dreaming and that she is actually at my side.

I took her first time to the square which knew me when I was a child. I told her what I remembered. Here I used to play football. And here my friends and I used to chase the girls of the neighbours. There is the mosque where I learnt to pray and the school where I learnt how to read and write. Here was I sitting at her side on that long stone bench in the corner of the square as if I had never been in love before and as if my heart was fluttering for the first time.

"For fifty years I have been looking for a woman who would love me." The more these words surprised her, the more they soothed me, because I wanted to tell her about what had happened in my life, about my complicated relationships with women without my knowing whether the fault lay with them or with me! About the passing relationship with a woman every ten years of my life. The fact that she listened amazed me. Not for one day did she give up listening to me with all her feeling. Not for one day did she give up taking in the spiritual crises that I had gone through. She was thus so much above me and I was her wretched inferior.

I told her about Taqiya, the first experience I had with her when I was only seven. I did not understand the secret of my being attracted to her. Was it the kindness she showed towards me and the boys and girls of the Talha quarter? Was it her dazzling beauty that roused us? For she wore no veil over her face when she was playing with us in the quarter. It was as if we were special to her. Or was it my own feeling that I was special to her because she defended me by hitting and threatening anyone who was against me? She said I was "sweet" and no one was going to be against me.

Taqiya was older than me, but I don't know how much. But she was taller than all the boys and girls I used to play with. I never knew what she meant by taking me off with her to the dark corridor in their house after the sunset prayers, and hugging and kissing me to thank me for buying the sweets she wanted from the shop at the end of the street. The feel of her fingers playing over all the sensitive parts of my body was a special pleasure. "Oh God, look after little Hamid." After several such occasions little Hamid enjoyed the feel of her body and the noise she made after each fondle, the noise that has rung in my ears to the present moment. At the end of every encounter she warned me not to tell anyone about our fondlings, otherwise Taqiya would die. The word "die" was a nightmare that haunted me because it meant that I would lose Taqiya, something I did not want but it did happen quickly enough. One year later Taqiya married. With the boys and girls of the quarter I saw her in a white dress waiting for her brother to escort her to the marital home. From afar she noticed me hidden among the other children and gave me a secret smile as she bit her lower lip.

That night I could not stop crying until I fell asleep. The following morning nothing in the quarter had anything to interest me. Taqiya never came back to the quarter, not even to call on her family. She migrated with her husband to Saudi Arabia and I never saw her again. But she came into my fantasies from time to time dressed in a multicoloured cloak and a veil over her white face. She went ahead of me through the quarters and I followed the light that trailed from her without knowing where the trip would end up for us.

The first wet dream I had was when I was fourteen. I suddenly felt the overpowering presence of Taqiya. I relished her fingers and tongue once again; she then disappeared from my memory for ever. When her place was taken by Hadiya, the daughter of a neighbour, I forgot everything that had happened in Taqiya's corridor and I was content with exchanging glances through the windows of our houses that faced one another. We never spoke or even met. All this ended with Hadiya agreeing to marry someone. She slipped out of my consciousness as if she had never existed.

When I was fourteen a third woman passed through my life. I found myself by a prior arrangement unable to answer the examination questions in the university so I would be the following year with Amina, my school-mate with whom I had been in undeclared love for three years. When I did declare my love to her she turned me down because she loved a friend of mine who had not told me anything about her. Maybe he was softening the pain of rejection by a woman of a man's love.

105

The fourth woman was my wife and the mother of my four daughters. We had a traditional marriage. My mother selected her from our relations, describing her to me as being beautiful with white skin, qualities preferred by most men. This was so but after I married her I discovered that I did not care for white-skinned women, nor did I care for women of obvious beauty. I did not dare tell this to my mother because she would say I was too stupid to understand the beauty of women. So for the twenty years I spent with her I did not love her with the love I wanted to love her with. I got used to her so that life could go on. It was difficult for her to respond to the secret call from my innermost heart and to be Taqiya or Hadiya or Amina ...

My meeting with Subhiya was not by chance as she imagined it to be. It was destiny and I have to believe in it. It was not by chance that my father and her father were in that battle for the defence of Sana'a in the war of the 1970s and that one day my father died and her father was saved, and so together we can finish the story. The war that made me an orphan at an early age. I like being by myself and hate anyone who has a father. That war also made Subhiya an orphan with the loss of her homeland and with her sojourn far away for all those years.

It is destiny that my wish has been fulfilled after all these years and as I walk at her side I declare my pride without paying any attention to the looks that follow us whenever we walk out together in the alleyways and quarters of the city. The city never woke up at any time to the tread of lovers' footsteps such as ours, and it never went to sleep to the whispered wishes of the same lovers to be together for the rest of their lives.

Translated by Peter Clark

The Stone of Desire

There is nothing in the place ... apart from heat, cold, dryness and moisture.

The fire is so warm and dry, the water is so cold and wet, the air is so hot, and the sand is so cold and wet.

Out of these properties, Elixir or Red Mercury, that liquid which flows from the stone of philosophers, may grant a bit of immortality and a lot of desire.

An attempt to understand Jābir ibn Hayyān, and the reasons behind stone worship ...

Inside the sculptress's house. Her name has been absent from the minds of the distant neighbours, because of her profession. Her real name was mentioned only by the journalists who rejoiced in festival opening days, or suggested art exhibitions, as if it were a professional duty, or as if they were critics capable of entering the game of sculpting.

The silo, as she liked to call it in her very few joyous moments, was that stone building lying on the edge of the city. He had witnessed long years of hard work serving as a diplomatic agent abroad, a man torn between his government position, his readings, the lack of pleasure, the incomplete family and the torments of a cousin wife, who did not live long.

That house was encircled by a wild garden, which was designed to look like that, to correspond to the impetuousness of the stone, and to the remote alienated place, while her sculptures were scattered in every small corner. Once in a while, you might come across them ... here and there ... near the house, beneath a lighted stained glass window, and in a garden that was like a Catholic cemetery in a small village.

"Stone ... stone ... how wonderful stone is ... who says it is unmalleable? Who says it is a flintstone ... a stone block?! My stone is perfectly shaped and takes possession of my blood veins ... confessing my feelings for him, whispering to him, silently conversing with him, yearning for him, looking for him. Only selected stones enter my house, since the words of the chisel and the hammer, and the dance of the fingers together with the brush, form a meaningful whisper, almost exploring the remote labyrinth soul.

"Now ... the sculpture is readymade, a perfect creature completed that bears both the stone's mightiness and my fanciful dream. The details of its shape are perfectly carved; it stands opposite me like a legendary hero worrying about his triumphs, while I stand in front of him like a temple woman, infected with concealed passion. Only then the stone speaks out while I split into his warmth: my stone has no parallel!"

Thus spoke the sculptress in a moment of revelation when the sculpture has been completed. Rapturously, she felt a great joy while covering her new manly sculpture with a white coverlet, embalmed in her confidential scent.

The sculptress spent her entire day trying to interrogate the stone's emotions, while occupied in itemising the trees of the garden. Nothing shatters the serenity of an artist's morning like an awkward work schedule. That was her decision, despite the insistent pleading of her father's acquaintances, who wished to offer free services to "Youssif Bey" and his respected position.

She was in love with the morning shadow, the scent of lemon

blossom, and the leisurely picking up of decaying dry leaves. She added her own flavour to things, and worked them out in accordance with her own aesthetic philosophy.

During pauses, she moved from corner to corner with her coffee mug, standing either beneath a fig tree, or an almond tree, leaning her back against the stone wall and enjoying its coolness. No one shared their solitude with her and her coffee mug, except the cigarettes that she pulled out of the few packets in that box on the table.

When she started her day in the early light of dawn – after a carefree night – she would carry on working until mid-day. Then she took a shower, had a light snack and slept for an hour. When she woke up, she dressed well, perfumed herself and started work anew, or rather resumed her work on a sculpture that she had been unable to finish in the morning.

She continued until late afternoon, when she would feel a sudden urge to doze. Her eyelids were hidden behind thick corrective lenses, with frames of gold and ivory – at one time very valuable.

She used to turn to her garden at twilight, when the orange sunlight was fragmented in the atmosphere, creating a burning tranquillity with the stone of the house.

When she felt satisfied with her day's work, she would laugh aloud. A special smile played on her lips when things moved leisurely. She smiled when she was about to enter through the door in the house. This was hand carved in her own way, with remnants of a scene that she loved captured through her eyes: a scene for which there was no substitute, in any other city.

At night ... she had a different ritual ... a different routine. After preparing her vegetarian dinner, she would put a carefully chosen bottle of wine on the table, selected from some intimate corners of some airports. The bottle would be by her own glass.

She then took another shower, and dressed in a mischievously bright light evening dress.

She spent her nights reading, enjoying green vegetables soaked in lemon and vinegar, her wine glass filled with the red blood of saints. When the body shivered in rapture, she turned the music up to amuse herself, her lonely house, plunged in the darkness of the night. She went on with her pleasures, until she felt her body was anaesthetized. Her mind was stimulated and she was overjoyed. It was like when she was a little girl, thrilled with her maturing body, the first symptoms of femininity, with small adventures toward her innocent coming of age.

Today, she is stirred, as if things had never gone away all these years. Only the blazing light could dispel them. They have been invoked by the cold gale of the night, and the glitter-filled wine glass. When the glass is emptied, her body is already exuding sweat. She is utterly exhausted, weary of rapture, paying the tax on her life, with her incomplete fading beauty heading towards decay.

Like some primitive piece of stone, she threw herself over the old sofa. Nothing could wake her from the dreams that attacked her mercilessly, though her cough occasionally disturbed her on midwinter nights. When the bones moaned of the stone's coolness and the silence granted by the night with blackness of evil, she dragged her legs and went and lay down on the large bed. She plunged into its soft warmth, as her hand searched for a man's ghost. She wished he was there that moment.

Morning light revealed the features of a woman in her fifties. She had been tall and thin, but age had brought on obesity and a flabbiness that girded her waist and rump, and caused her breasts to sag.

The receding henna-dyed hair made her twice her age. There were more freckles all over her face and breasts, but few on her hands. These hands had long fingers, like those of a trained pianist and were adorned with silver and majestic gem stone rings.

In two things you would find no gleam; her fragile and damaged hair, and the teeth accustomed to daily doses of coffee and nicotine. Only her skin maintained its freshness.

She had always searched for her crude stone, looking for complicated things in people, creating that complication between woman and existing things. Man's body was her real pleasure. She dealt with every single muscle in that body with a woman's body strength, a woman haunted by thirst for passion. The dance of the fingers seemed as if she had soaked them with attar or bay leaves. As she sculpted, all her senses connected her to communication, though she was never satisfied until the mouth had granted her the feeling of an absent kiss.

When the sculpture was completed, she made passionate love to her new idol, with a nocturnal pagan wedding ceremony. She dignified its presence by uttering old ritual prayers. Like a temple priestess, she writhed around to the hymn of the god of fertility and growth, confronting his rain, and waiting for his herbs to grow and go green around her. In those nights, she would light a fire with the remnants of a Zoroastrian fire, and recall talismans from the earliest hymns of guidance. She continued pacing round the fire, giving birth and spontaneity to her body before it sunk into filth!

After performing this pagan prayer ceremony, she would wake up, purified from the spirit's wounds, as if she were a new bride of fertility, rejoicing at the moment of possession, wishing that this moment would only last in a different form ... any different form in life ... even if it was that atheist workman who, when she was still a child, came to install the gate of the big house. She was fascinated by his sweating hands, and the blue suit that concealed the details of his tall body. She had watched the ductility of the steel and the process of heating that melted everything. It had been a moment of a child watching things that she would love in the future. But the blacksmith's look had hurt her and affected her eager wish to watch the hand at work.

If only he would come now, with all his satanic desire!

Let that guy who stole her youth and the pink school-day letters live with his wife, subdued under the responsibility of providing for his children, and pursued by the curse of diabetes that has turned him into a haunted greenish ghost. It was he who had run away from her that day, dumping her and all her gifts, using his unemployment as a pretext for not marrying. The truth was that all he cared about was trying to find at any price an opportunity to travel to the Gulf. At that moment, she took money from the box which she had inherited from her mother, and gave it to him. He took the money and went to Kuwait, and came back to marry a divorced woman who had already worked there as a teacher, with a girl and a five-year-old boy. He made her his wife, urged by both a steady internal avarice and a masculinity from days in the merciless coast cities!

On that day, she sculpted the bust of an effeminate man, one half a face, the second half fragmented, carved as if beasts were eating it, living on it for days on end.

She placed it outside the house and kept glancing at him whenever she had a chance. After the affair she had with this fugitive semi-man, she spent all her life advancing towards success, gaining celebrity through newspapers, magazines, exhibitions, critical acclaim, non-stop travel, and participating in activities. She also hosted occasional guest intellectuals who attended conferences, and lovers of her art. These visits usually ending up with helpless drunken kisses, with the guests claiming they had to go back to their impatiently waiting wives.

Indeed, those nights started joyfully, yet the house was soon free of visitors, and the dinner plates remained upon the dinner tables. Like a lioness fed up with satiety and mating, she wished they did not belong to her at that moment. These nights rapidly faded away, filching that unconsummated feminine happiness she had always longed for. Nothing remained after those intimate gatherings but painful memories of a mother who had been unable to raise her, and a father who was lost in the cities of politics – and his second wife. Long years of absence were enough to gratify his wish for lukewarm meetings with his only child, meetings that soon ended up shortly with complaint and counsel from his second wife.

Thus she passed a life that imposed new measures of love, and the kind of affair she should have. Day after day, her condition deteriorated, and she was unable to give her transformed body to anyone anymore. Then one day, a blind beggar led by an eleven-year-old boy knocked on her door. She gave him what was left over from breakfast, and wanted to give him a lot more.

At first, she felt he was her new art project ... that he could rudely heal her old virginity. She watched him as he ate, drank, rubbed his moustache and groped at things; she looked at the body's details, his wakeful ears, his leaping nose, his unkempt beard that looked like wild night plants.

She looked at him stealthily, as he entertained himself inside his void, engaging in a dialogue with her; and conversed with him just by asking questions.

The boy noticed her glances, and she became almost confused. She threw him an orange, to appease and distract him, seeking to silence him.

The blind beggar burped and prayed for her, as he usually did when he was happy with the food he had been served. He prayed that God may grant her a long life, good health, a livelihood, children and a blessed house.

She felt he was sincere, or imagined him so. She asked him

to stop over, and tried to explain to him that he was her next art project, that she wanted to make a sculpture of him.

As a professional beggar, with street begging skills, he did not really understand her words, nor was convinced of what she said. He replied:

"Ma'am ...", he replied. "I'm only a poor dervish ... pray for our generous all-giving God".

"I'll pay you 100 dinars for a month of work," she said like an apprentice prostitute. "In addition, two meals a day, and a quarter bottle of arrack are guaranteed ..."

"Fine," the blind beggar replied, "just throw in a daily packet of cigarettes."

"I wouldn't have agreed if you'd asked for a quarter hash joint," she laughed.

The blind beggar's eyes shone in the dark. His front teeth stuck out as he laughed, "Ma'am ... you're a woman of inherent generosity ... I swear by God ... and I deserve your compassion."

At that moment, she wished she could explore his body. The blind beggar pretended to be plunged in dark blindness, and made a suggestive movement that he had learned early in his blindness. Did that cunning beggar make this gesture intentionally, in order to get her, or was it spontaneous? She was not convinced of the latter; however, she was assured of her next art project. He accepted her kind offer, and was thus guaranteed a month of pleasures: food, wages, no walking, and no more scuffles with his wife that usually ended up in violence.

Only one question worried him: was her offer worth it? What was so special about him?

There was a brief conversation between the beggar and his son. The boy, who used to answer his father's vague questions, himself asked many questions. He was his father's two eyes, but this time, he wished he were the black stains under the eyes!

It seemed that there was something relating to masculinity. The blind man hoped that the boy did not understand it and reveal it to his mother who was forever cross during her customary uneventful evening.

The blind man said to the boy, "Son, let's eat two meals a day, cash the one hundred dinars, and tell your mother that we have earned only fifty dinars. We can get a whole packet of cigarettes and you can smoke one cigarette alone after each meal. What do you say? Let's enjoy this month without telling your witch of a mother. Don't tell her anything if you really want to eat good food, and oranges, and try a cigarette, and not walk so much".

The boy murmured agreement, wishing he had known everything sooner.

Like all blind people afraid of their livelihood being snatched away, he came with his son regularly to her house even before the appointed time. This began to annoy the sculptress, upsetting the rhythm of her day, which she liked to flow like a stream.

The boy had in mind the daily fresh orange, the breakfast at half past eleven, and the shadow of the large fig tree that brought on a noontime drowsiness, and the woman's glances that his adolescent mind tried to understand, and also her sweet words. He even tried to visualize her female form which he could drag into his wet mattress. Late at night in his miserable camp the image of her nakedness came to him.

After these days of anxiety, the father and his son spent the evenings at their home sitting together. The father wanted to know something he had forgotten or maybe he wanted to reveal something. When there was no response from his son, he slipped out feeling his way with his fingers and groped through the dark. He was content with the silence, and flirting with a woman he knew only by touching her, in search of ecstasy with the effortless union of their hands. Desire was roused, dispelling the pain of daily weariness of hassle, chatter about details of the children, the harassment of the overcrowded neighbourhood, whose poverty-stricken inhabitants had to make their own days and worlds. Even small things in life added a liveliness that was otherwise absent.

At night, he could not forget the sculptrrss's voice, and tried to create a sculptured image of her in his blindness, as he made love to his wife. The new image worked, like the night itself, and his wife's laugh and form turned into soft hands caressing his back and stiff limbs, and he briefly fell asleep.

Of course his daily visit to the sculptress's house with his son disrupted her plans, and her pleasant idle way of life. However, she adjusted her life to him as much as she could, very conscious of him and his son.

She finally managed to fit them into her daily routine, determined by her work.

The son kept close to his father until she devised some games that were appropriate to his passage toward early adulthood. This way, she ensured his silence with an amazing television set which she usually switched on to watch documentary programmes or disagreeable reports or news items that reminded her of the old homeland and the villages scattered along the other forgotten bank. The television was a sedative for the boy. The black and white films it showed gave him pleasure and made him laugh, and even stirred him.

At first, the blind man thought that the attention given to the boy was an excuse to get to him personally, and that the boy's presence was insignificant to her. He tried to explain this to her, saying that he was a man who wanted answers.

"This wasn't our agreement, Ma'am," he said. "The boy is still young, he hasn't grown a moustache yet. What are your demands? If you still want something from me, I'm ready."

He was overwhelmed by doubt like any blind man. The sculptress understood his intentions, and tried hard to prove to him that he was only an art project, and that was what he had to stick to and not disturb her work with his private affairs. As regards his basic needs, she was ready to meet them all.

He cried out, "But, Ma'am, the boy is still young. He hasn't grown a moustache yet. I'm ready to meet all your needs. May God have mercy on your parents' souls."

"Try to understand, man! Let the boy be diverted, and let's get on with our work."

"Ma'am, I am under your orders. Whenever you want. You have showered us with kindness."

"Listen, try to understand me. I just want to make a cast of your shape."

"Whatever is your command, Ma'am. Though I don't really get the point. Whatever, just stay away from the boy."

"Listen to me now. You're driving me crazy with talk of your boy. I don't need him. You are my chief concern. Do you understand?"

"As you wish, Ma'am. I am at your disposal."

"There's no need to call me Ma'am."

"As you like."

"Come with me. I want to make a cast. But don't say a word."

"Yes, Ma'am. May God bless you with all success."

"God! Grant me patience. Follow me and hold your tongue."

"And the boy, Ma'am?"

"Let him watch TV. Do you want him to be blind like you?"

"Have mercy on us, Ma'am ... we are wretched people. Begging dervishes."

"Enough chatter! Let's focus on our work."

He submitted to her like a boy rebuked for making a mistake. However, everything inside him made him cross about life's cruelty in creating mankind. He also felt he was receiving a new light that would make his days much happier. Then he felt as if his bladder was about to burst.

She treated the beggar's body as raw material that differed from stone. It was more like a dead skin – and she was a vegetarian – and lacked the solidity of marble and the plasticity of stone. It was a shape that did not relate to her – she never paid attention to its creation process. She waited for the moment of readiness, as if she had to do something she did not like doing, but did it nonetheless. That wearisome night, she had to defeat the fugitive man, the fugitive life, and just be content with her handiwork.

She became exhausted with the beggar and his son, and their incessant demand for food. She wished she could be alone with the rituals that granted her a sense of nostalgia.

Words of thanks could have been enough, but not for a blind beggar and a son on the outset of a begging career. She had better open up the fridge, and empty it of food, which was soon due to expire.

She stood still, not knowing why she thought about the idea of expiry. This thought caused the muscle in her face to twitch unceasingly. Soon she surrendered to her solitude again, realizing that the heart cannot always have a place for many people.

Only the son stayed attached to that door. He had felt happy ever since coming to the house. He also felt attached to the sculptress who was like a feminine sculpture that was fixed in his mind. She did not look like his mother; and he did not know how to hold fast to her. He remained attached to her many sculptures, and to details that he got to know outside the rotten camp. He spent his night feeling lost. How could he get all these things back again? Most of all he recalled the orange that he had had, now almost a month ago!

Twenty-one years, seven months and seventeen days later, at the corner of the street with a new name, Ahlam al-Majeedi Street, in the little yard of the square a sculpture was set up, and was unveiled by the governor of the capital earlier that day. I had before taken the path, barefoot, to the house for the first time in my life. Today I left some lemon blossoms that would brighten up this new empty place, and remind her of a flower she always loved. I lit a pipe, and wrapped my Kashmiri shawl round my neck. I did not wait for the rain to stop. I was there, and her soul was there too, and the city needed that rain on that exceptional day – exceptional at least for me, a man who had changed as soon as he entered the sculptress's house, leading a blind beggar, amazed and full of questions.

I passed my hands over the sculpture's freckled face, and touched the thick glasses, realizing then the value of ivory. I looked for a long time at the slightly bare forehead, and then planted a kiss of consent on the lips of the sculptor, a kiss that meant nothing but celebration of her anniversary, and love for a woman in every detail of whose daily life I had been familiar. She was a woman who had taught me much during her last years. There was satisfaction at what his hands had worked at on this stone.

Translated by Reem Ghanayem

Contributors

Ali Azeriah is Moroccan. He has degrees from the University of Bath and SUNY at Binghamton, USA. He taught at the King Fahd Advanced School for Translation at Tangiers and currently teaches at Al Akhawayn University, Ifrane, Morocco.

Alice Guthrie is British. She studied Arabic at the University of Exeter and at IFEAD in Damascus. She is a literary and media translator, and has recently translated work by the Palestinians, Atef Abu Seif and Ala Hlelel.

Inaam Kachachi is Iraqi. She is the Paris correspondent of *Asharq al-Awsat*. Her novel, translated as *The American Granddaughter*, was shortlisted for the International Prize for Arabic Fiction in 2009.

Jabbour Douaihy is Lebanese and Professor of French Literature at the Lebanese University. His novel, translated as *June Rain*, was shortlisted for the first International Prize for Arabic Fiction in 2008.

Kamel Riahi is Tunisian and is Head of the Translation Department at the Higher Institute for Translation in Algeria. He has published one novel, two collections of short stories and three works of criticism.

Lana Abdel Rahman is Lebanese, resident in Egypt. She has degrees from the Lebanese University and the American University of Cairo. She has published two novels and two collections of short stories, and works as a cultural journalist.

Mansour el-Sowaim is Sudanese and was born in Darfur. He works as a journalist in Khartoum and has published two novels and collections of short stories. His work has been translated into French and into English.

Mansoura Ez-Eldin was born in a village in the Delta in Egypt, and has worked in journalism and television. Her novel, translated as *Beyond Paradise*, was shortlisted for the International Prize for Arabic Fiction in 2010.

Mohammed Hassan Alwan was born in Riyadh, Saudia Arabia. He has an MBA from the University of Portland, Oregon. He has published three novels as well as short stories. He writes a weekly column for a Saudi newspaper.

Mohammed Salah al-Azab was born in Cairo and has published novels and collections of short stories. Among several awards he has won the Suad Al-Sabah Award for the Novel.

Nadiah Alkokabany was born in Taiz, Yemen, and has degrees from Yemen and Egypt. She is Professor of Architecture at the University of Sanaa. She has published three collections of short stories.

Nasser al-Dhaheri is an Emirati and was born in al-Ain in the United Arab Emirates and has studied in the UAE and in Paris. He has been editor of *al-Ittihad* newspaper. He has published nine volumes of short stories and of articles.

Nassir Alsayeid Alnour is Sudanese, and was born in Darfur. He has worked as a freelance journalistic writer, researcher and translator, mostly in literary and political matters, and currently works as a translator in Saudi Arabia.

Paul Starkey is British and is Professor of Arabic Literature at the University of Durham. He has written on Tawfiq al-Hakim, is author of *Modern Arabic Literature* and has translated several volumes of contemporary Arabic literature.

Peter Clark is British and has translated fiction, history, drama and poetry from Arabic since 1980. He has lived and worked in seven Arab countries, is a Trustee of the International Prize for Arabic Fiction and a Contributing Editor of *Banipal*.

Reem Ghanayem is Palestinian and has degrees from the University of Tel Aviv, including a PhD in Comparative Literature. She has translated Palestinian poetry and written articles on literature.

أصوات عربيّة جديدة

أصوات عربيّة جديدة

ندوة ١

تحرير
بيتر كلارك

SAQI

بالتعاون مع
الجائزة العالمية للرواية العربية

الطبعة الأولى ٢٠١٠

ISBN: 978-0-86356-414-7

الجائزة العالمية للرواية العربية
www. arabicfiction. org

مـــؤســـسة الإمـــارات
www. emiratesfoundation. ae

SAQI
www.saqibooks.com

المحتويات

مقدّمة

تأسّست الجائزة العالمية للرواية العربية عام ٢٠٠٧. وارتبطت، منذ
البدء، بعائلة جوائز البوكر. وتُمنَحُ جائزةُ مان بوكر سنوياً، منذ عام
١٩٦٨، لعمل روائي لكاتب من المملكة المتحدة، وجمهورية أيرلندا،
ودول الكومنولث. وقد كانت "مان بوكر" بمثابة الإلهام لجائزتين
أخريين، هما جائزة بوكر الروسية، التي تأسّست عام ١٩٩٢،
وجائزة كين للأدب الأفريقي، التي تأسّست عام ٢٠٠٠.

وقد اعتمدت الجائزة العالمية للرواية العربية الهيكلية ذاتها الموجودة
في جائزة مان بوكر، حيث يديرها مجلس عالمي من الأمناء (معظم
أعضائه من العرب) يقرّر استراتيجية العمل، ويعيّن المحكّمين، كما
أنه مسؤول عن مناقشة التمويل وإدارة الميزانية. ومنذ البداية، تكفّلت
مؤسسة الإمارات، في أبو ظبي، بدعمها مالياً، حيث إدارتها المتمركزة
في لندن، وهي شركة خيرية مانحة، مسجّلة في لندن.

يقدّم الناشرون روايات ثلاثاً، في الحد الأقصى، سنوياً، نُشرت في
السنة الفائتة. ويتمّ اختيار هيئة محكمين مستقلّة، تعلن، في غضون

ستة أشهر، القائمة الطويلة للمرشّحين، وتكون مؤلَّفة من ستّة عشر عملاً، ثم القائمة القصيرة التي تقتصر على ستّة أعمال مرشّحة. تنتهي الدورة السنوية بمنح جائزة مالية لكتّاب القائمة القصيرة، وجائزة مالية أكبر للفائز. وقد مُنحت الجائزة الثالثة في أبو ظبي، في شهر آذار/ مارس عام ٢٠١٠.

إن هدف الجائزة هو تكريم الكتّاب، وضمان الاعتراف بهم، وتشجيع القراءة، فضلاً عن أنها جائزة عالمية، ولهذا يُصار إلى إعلام دور النشر العالمية بها في الخارج. وقد حظيت الرواية الفائزة في الدورة الأولى، "واحة الغروب"، للكاتب المصري بهاء طاهر، باهتمام نقدي في كلّ أرجاء العالم. ودُعي الكاتب إلى مؤتمرات وندوات من إندونيسيا إلى الولايات المتحدة.

وقد دأبت جائزة كين للأدب الأفريقي، خلال السنوات العشر الماضية، على تنظيم ورش عمل وندوات للكتّاب الشبان، وفي عام ٢٠٠٩، أقامت الجائزة العالمية للرواية العربية ملتقى للكتّاب الشبّان العرب. وكان الاقتراح أن يُقام في أبو ظبي. ولكن، ما إن سمع سموّ الشيخ حمدان بن زايد آل نهيان بالفكرة، حتى بادر فوراً إلى تبنّيها، ليكون الرّاعي والمضيف في آنٍ معاً. وهكذا، باشر بكل سخاء، الإعداد للندوة التي أُقيمت على جزيرة صير بني ياس، بين الثامن والسابع عشر من شهر نوفمبر، ٢٠٠٩.

وقد دُعي المحكِّمون خلال الدورتين الأوليين إلى اقتراح أسماء الكتّاب الشباب، الذين كانت أعمالهم مدرجة بين الروايات المئة والعشرين، التي تقدّمت إلى الجائزة، خلال عامي ٢٠٠٨ و٢٠٠٩.

وقد اختار مجلس الأمناء الأسماء استناداً إلى هذه المقترحات، آخذين في الاعتبار التوازن الجغرافي، والتنوّع بين الذكور والإناث. وفي النهاية اختير ثمانية كتّاب مشاركين في الندوة ـ خمسة رجال وثلاث نساء. اثنان من هؤلاء من جمهورية مصر، قياساً للعدد الضخم من الروايات الذي يُنشر سنوياً في ذلك البلد. أما البقية فهم من لبنان والمملكة العربية السعودية والسودان وتونس والإمارات العربية المتحدة واليمن. وكان ثمّة كاتبان (عراقي وسوري) كنا نأمل أن يشاركا، لكنهما، في اللحظة الأخيرة، لم يتمكّنا من ذلك. وتراوحت أعمار المشاركين بين السابعة والعشرين، والواحدة والأربعين.

دُعي الكتّاب للمشاركة. وجميع هؤلاء نشروا كتباً، وحظوا باهتمام نقدي لا بأس به، إما داخل بلدانهم، أو خارجها. والأكيد هو أنّهم جميعاً لفتوا انتباه المحكّمين الذين رشّحوا أسماءهم.

وعلى غرار الندوات التي كانت تُنظّمها جائزة كين، دعت الجائزة العالمية للرواية العربية كاتبين مكرّسين لإدارة النقاشات وتقديم المزيد من المشورة الفردية والتشجيع، وهما اللبناني جبور دويهي، والعراقية إنعام كجه جي. وكلاهما روائيان لهما تجربة واسعة، ويحظيان بالاحترام، وكلاهما وصلا إلى القائمة القصيرة للجائزة العالمية للرواية العربية.

اجتمعت الندوة على مدى تسعة أيام. ولأننا كنا نقيم على جزيرة، كنا معزولين عن ضوضاء المدينة الكبيرة، ولهوها. في كل صباح، كان المشرفون يعقدون جلسةً فرديةً مع كل كاتب على حدة. وفي السابعة مساءً، كان الكتّاب والمشرفون يجتمعون معاً، لمدة ساعتين، ويستمعون

إلى قراءات من مشاركين اثنين. وتُناقش الكتابات، وتؤخذ التعليقات على محمل الجدّ، بعيداً عن المديح المجاني أو التجريح الشخصي.

ووفت الندوة بكلّ وعودها، بل وتجاوزتها. ويشهد المشرفون على ذلك. هذا الكتاب هو ثمرة هذه الندوة، وخلاصة تلك القصص أو الفصول من الروايات التي كُتبت ونوقشت خلال الندوة. إنها تجربة غير اعتيادية لجميع المنخرطين بها، وتأمل مؤسسة الجائزة العالمية للرواية العربية أن تجعل منها حدثاً سنوياً.

وقد أسهم العديد من الأشخاص في هذا النجاح. فبالإضافة إلى سمّو الشيخ حمدان بن زايد آل نهيان، أودّ أن أشكر بيتر كليفز، وستيفن مكورميك، وأحمد عرشي، ومهنا المحيري، من مؤسسة الإمارات، وزكي نسيبه وبيتر هيللر، في أبو ظبي، ونيك إلام من جائزة كين للأدب الأفريقي، إضافة إلى المشرفين والمشاركين في الندوة لجعلهم إياها مناسبةً إيجابيةً بامتياز.

بيتر كلارك

منسّق ندوة صير بني ياس، نوفمبر، ٢٠٠٩
أمين الجائزة العالمية للرواية العربية

مدخل

حين هبط صديقنا الروائي السوداني منصور الصويم من طائرة
"السيسنا" الصغيرة على أرض جزيرة "بني ياس"، صفقت أشجار
القرم المزروعة في الأرض المالحة احتفالاً بوصول أول رجل من دارفور
الى هذه الجزيرة المنعزلة في الخليج. ولم يكن منصور وحده. كنا مجموعة
من الكاتبات والكتاب من ثماني دول عربية، حملتنا طائرتان "جو/
بر/ مائيتان" من أبو ظبي إلى هنا للمشاركة في ندوة عن الكتابة
الإبداعية. وفي هذه الجزيرة أمضينا عشرة أيام... لم تهز العالم لكنها
وفّرت لكل منا أفكاراً جديدة وصداقات جديدة.

هل هناك روائي لم يحلم بأن يجلس متفرغاً للكتابة في جزيرة منعزلة
وسط البحر؟ كانت "صير بني ياس" في غاية الهدوء قبل أن يفد إليها
معنا كمال الرياحي. هذا البركان التونسي الجامح الذي يبدو كأنه يريد
أن يفكك العالم ويعيد تركيبه على هواه الروائي. لكن منصور وكمال،
وصحبتهما نادية كوكباني الآتية بخفر وتصميم من اليمن، ومنصورة
عز الدين ومحمد صلاح العزب حاملَين معهما خفة الروح والقاهرة

بأبهى حللها الروائية، ومحمد حسن علوان، السعودي اللطيف والساخر بامتياز، ولنا عبد الرحمن العاشقة للكتابة من لبنان، وناصر الظاهري الإماراتي الواثق من أسلوبه وخياراته الجمالية، لم يكونوا سياحاً عاديين في الجزيرة التي تبعد ساعة طيران عن اليابسة، بل كانوا مستكشفين يبحثون عن فكرة جديدة يؤثثونها ويلبسونها كلمات تجعل منها نصاً يلفت النظر. ولم تكن تلك المهمة سهلة.

كتاباتهم التي جاؤوا بمسوّداتها الأولى كانت فاكهة متنوّعة المذاقات. وكان علينا، نحن المشرفين على الندوة، إنعام كجه جي من العراق وجبور الدويهي من لبنان، أن نقوم بما يقوم به كبار الطباخين في مدرسة للطهو، أي أن نتذوق ونصحّح نسبة السكر أو درجة الاستواء. لكننا، منذ اليوم الأول، أدركنا أننا إزاء زملاء لنا يملكون تجاربهم الخاصة، وأننا سنتبادل الرأي، الند للند، وسنعمل معاً على ألا تحترق أي طبخة. وبهذا ألغينا فكرة الأستاذ والتلميذ وعملنا بروحية مجموعة من الكتاب الشباب، والأقل شباباً. وهنا لا بد من الإقرار بأن أكثرنا حيوية كان منسّق الدورة، الكاتب والمترجم والمستعرب البريطاني بيتر كلارك، الرجل النشيط الذي تحمّل كسل البعض منا أو ما يسمّى "نزوات العباقرة".

عشرة أيام. يلتقي المشرفان في صباحاتها اثنين أو ثلاثة من الكتاب، ويقرأون نصاً قصصياً أو فصلاً من رواية، ويناقشون الأسلوب واللغة والشخصيات واقتراحات تطوير الفكرة. وخلال هذه الفترة يكون الآخرون في غرفهم، كل واحد يشتغل على نصه الخاص، مستفيداً

من التسهيلات التي يوفرها له السكن في منتجع مريح وهادئ. وفي السابعة من كل مساء، يحين موعد التقاء الجميع حول طاولة الاجتماعات للاستماع الى ما قارب الاكتمال من فصول روائية أو قصص قصيرة. إنها ساعة تبادل الأفكار بحرية، والتطرق إلى المشكلات العملية للكتابة والبحث عن حلول لأسئلة تفرضها التجارب التي بين أيدينا.

طبعاً، كان يمكن هذا "الالتصاق" اليومي في السكن والكتابة وتناول الوجبات وحتى سهرات السمر الليلية في المقهى المكشوف، أن تسبّب انفجارات مزاجية صغيرة. لكن من بركات هذه الندوة أنها ضمّت أشخاصاً نجحوا في التعايش والانسجام، يتقبل كل منهم ملاحظات زملائه بصدر رحب، ويلتزم بما يراه مناسباً منها. أما ما كان غير ذلك فقد كانت الفكاهة كفيلة بتمريره. حتى البركان التونسي كمال، القادر على قصف أعتى النصوص برشاش انتقاداته، لم يفلح في زعزعة أحد، بل كان الملح الضروري للندوة.

ويوماً بعد يوم، بدأت ملامح النصوص تتضح والفصول الأولى من الروايات تكشف لنا عوالمها. ولعل أجمل ما لحظناه في هذا اللقاء هو خصوصية كل واحد من الكتاب الثمانية. إن نصوصهم نابتة بطريقة طبيعية من الأرض التي يعيش فيها كل منهم، محمّلة بشخصيات محلية وجغرافيا موصوفة وروائح متفردة ولغة لا تتردد في الاستعارة من المفردات العامية حين يكون ذلك ضرورياً في الحوارات. وهكذا كتبت نادية كوكباني رواية تحتل فيها صنعاء وأحداثها القريبة دوراً رئيسياً. ورسم منصور الصويم ملامح "فرنساوي"، ذلك الرجل الدارفوري

الذي يقارب الأسطورة. وجعلت منصورة عز الدين من بطلة قصتها امرأة من القاهرة "اللي فوق" فكشفت عن عنف النفوس المهزومة ومعاناتها، كما كشف ناصر الظاهري عن معاناة النحاتة الجائعة للحب. أما كمال الرياحي فقد وجد موضوعه في واحد من "أبناء بورقيبة"، أولئك اللقطاء الذين حملوا هذه الصفة عبئاً مدى الحياة. واندسّ محمد حسن علوان، كما يندسّ القندس، بين أفراد عائلة من الرياض لكي يكشف تناقضاتها ويروي لنا، بموازاتها، حكاية حب ملتبسة. وبقدر ما كانت بطلة لنا عبد الرحمن مرهفة وهي تكتب هواجسها في رسائل إلى فرنسي بعيد لا تعرفه ولا يعرفها، كان بطل محمد صلاح العزب فذاً وهو يموت عدة ميتات أسطورية ويعود إلى الحياة ليسحرنا بحكايته.

هل مرّت على عرب بني ياس هلوسات مشرقية ومغربية مثل هذه من قبل؟ أتخيّلهم سعداء، تحت خيامهم الخافية على الناظرين، وهم يشهدون ولادة روايات لكتّاب شباب يطرقون بوّابة الأدب العربي بقبضات واثقة. شكراً لهم.

كامل الرياحي

الغوريلا

آخر أطفال الزعيم

وحده الغوريلاّ كان يتدلّى في يتمه لا يشبه أحداً، عارياً مثل جرو على
الإسفلت. تُنبت جمجمته غرباناً تطير لتأكل الأسماء وتبتلع العوالم.
الرواية

العصيان

عند الساعة الواحدة ظهراً تقريباً، كانت الريح تدحرج علبة جمعة منهوبة
الروح في الشارع المقفر. سكون كبير يصل قوس "باب بحر" ببرج
الساعة العملاقة عند تقاطع شارعي محمد الخامس والحبيب بورقيبة.
العاصمة الخالية يشوّش سكونها معتوهها الشّهير: رجل من ظنون
يطوف بالساعة طوافه الأخير، قبل أن يأخذ في إبعاد النّاس وتحذيرهم
من سمّ العقارب العالية، ثم يبدأ في رجم أعداء وهميين بالحجارة
والحديد والبيوت والأشجار والغربان والتيوس. أشياء لا يراها غيره،
يتوهّم أنه يلتقطها من القاعدة الرخامية لساعة الفولاذ المتبرّجة كعاهر
في آخر سنوات النضال. الناس كانوا ينعمون بقيلولة شهر أغسطس

المقدّسة. الحرارة تعدّت الخمسين درجة وشيطان منتصف النّهار يفلي عانته من بقايا لذّة هاربة.

فجأة ذبحت أصوات سيارات الإسعاف والشرطة القيلولة النائمة فهرع الجميع ببقايا نعاسهم وما تيبّس عليهم من منيّهم إلى شارع الشوارع. كان الحدث هناك، عند السّاعة الشاهقة. أحزمة من الشرطة تسيّج المكان. رجال فرق "التدخّل السّريع" يختفون وراء خوذاتهم الباردة، يدفعون بعصيّهم المتفرّجين الذين هطلت بهم أبواق السيارات من كل مكان. بشرٌ بلا عدد يرفعون رؤوسهم إلى قمة السّاعة القاسية. كائن صغير بحجم الإصبع، يتراءى للجميع من بعيد، يتسلّق بسرعة الصرصور الساعة أمام دهشتهم ليعلن القيامة.

اشرأبت الأعناق نحو المتسلّق الجَسور الذي انتهى إلى رأس السّاعة مُمسكاً بأحد عقاربها. سحب من جيبه الخلفي قارورة. شرب ثم أفرغ ما بقي منها على فروة رأسه. استل حزامه الجلدي، ثبّت به نفسه إلى حلقات الحديد والتفت نحو الجماهير التي تكاثرت تحته مثل النّمل. حاصرتها الشّرطة المتوتّرة، ركض أعوانها في كل اتّجاه يكلّمون أجهزة اللاسكي ويطلبون بإشارات متوتّرة من الرّجل العالي أن ينزل من الممنوع. بينما كان هو يغمغم بكلام تتمزّق أحشاؤه في الأجواء فلا يصل منه إلاّ فتات كبعر الأكباش. تشي حركة يده اليسرى، التي يلوّح بها يميناً وشمالاً بأنه يرفض النزول. عادت الشرطة تدفع الناس المتحلّقين مثل الخنافس حول الساعة، تحاول منع التصوير وإخراس الأصوات والهواتف المحمولة المرفوعة نحو عقارب الساعة. حركة المرور شُلّت ومحركات السيارات تنبض مثل عروق عدّاء المئة متر.

أمر خطير ما كان يحدث، فلم يجرؤ أحد على الاقتراب من الساعة منذ سنتين بعدما سقط منها أحد مشجّعي كرة القدم فرحاً بفوز فريقه بكأس الجمهورية. يومها، تحوّلت مياه تلك النافورة التي تضخّ مياه الزينة تحت الساعة إلى بركة حمراء. منذ ذلك المساء أصبحت الساعة تخضع لحراسة مشدّدة، وهي التي تحتلّ موقعاً خطيراً في قلب العاصمة، زيادة على ما يرويه عنها المعتوه أحياناً.

ازداد الزّحام وانتعشت الصفوف الأمامية بالسيّاح الذين تدفّقوا من الشواطئ ومن الفنادق القريبة. خفتت عصيّ أعوان الشرطة قليلاً لكن توتّرهم ازداد. كانوا يركضون في كل مكان، يسيّجون الأرصفة ويوسّعون المنطقة المحظورة بينما الرّجل متمسّك بلسان العقرب في أعلى الساعة مثل وزغة.

قبل سنوات كان ينتصب في مكان هذه الساعة تمثال أخضر لبورقيبة على حصان يرفع إحدى قائمتيه الأماميتين في وجوه الناظرين إلى السماء. قيل إنّه يرفعها في وجه ابن خلدون الذي زُرع تمثاله مثل الكابوس أمامه، وبطلب منه. بعد إطاحة حكم الراكب اقتلع التّمثال ونبتت مكانه ساعة عملاقة بجذع إسمنتي بارد سرعان ما توالدت ونبت لها صغار في كل مدينة وفي كل قرية. بينما طُوردت تماثيل الزعيم في كل أرض.

استبدلت السّاعة بأخرى سويسرية أو إنكليزية أو أميركية، أخبار متضاربة حول جنسية الساعة الجديدة وجذعها البرونزي المزيّن على طريقة الرقش العربي. كلام بلا دليل ولا برهان عن ساعة مجهولة

النسب غُرست في قلب المدينة اللاهية بأبنائها. لا أثر للزعيم الذي رُحّل تمثاله إلى "حلق الوادي" ليظل ينظر إلى البحر المرّ.

ظل الرّجل العنكبوت يتجوّل فوق المحظور مستعيناً بحزامه الجلدي الذي ينقله من مكان إلى آخر مثل متسلّق جبال محترف. وتحته العالم مُرتبكاً. اشتد الزحام بعدما خرج الموظفون من مكاتبهم. مضت ساعة كاملة والشرطة تأكل عصيّها، عاجزة عن إقناع رجل السّاعة بالنّزول. في الزّحام كانت تجري أمور غريبة. نشطت السّرقة ونشل الهواتف المحمولة والعقود من جيود النساء وامتدت الأيادي إلى النهود المشدوهة والعجيزات المنسية.

الصّعود إلى أعلى الساعة جرم كبير ومعصية لا تُغتفر، وما حدث يومها مسألة تمسّ الأمن، والشرطة في مأزق. كيف يمكن أن تسيطر على الأمر والفضيحة تحدثُ أمام الجميع: أهاليَ وأجانبَ، والبلاد في عزّ الموسم السياحي؟

يكاد الضابط يأكل وجه شرطي مهزوم وهو يسأله للمرة الألف: "كيف وصل إلى هناك؟ أين كنتم؟ كيف تسمحون له بأن يقترب من السّاعة وأن يتسلّقها؟".

في الجانب الآخر انقضّ أحد أعوان الشّرطة على سائح وانتزع منه آلة التّصوير التي صوّبها نحو السّاعة. اجتثّ الشرطي البطارية منها وأعادها له بعصبيّة محذّراً إياه من استعمالها مجدّداً. هكذا صارت المنطقة المسيّجة منطقة أمنية محظورة.

بدأت الجماهير تتململ من تصرّقات أعوان الشّرطة الذين جعلوا بينهم وبين موقع الحدث مسافة كبيرة. ازداد تذمّرهم عندما شاهدوا

رجل السّاعة يلوّح بيده موجّها خطابه نحو رئيس فرقة التدخّل السّريع. فهموا أنّه يطلب ماءً فقد أخذ يلوّح بالقارورة الفارغة في الهواء. جاءت قارورة الماء. صعد بها شرطي إلى أعلى السلّم الداخلي للسّاعة. رمى إليه بالحبل الذي عُلّقت به القارورة. اختطف الحبل آمراً الشرطي بالرجوع من حيث أتى بعدما همّ بمفاوضته.

لم نسمع شيئاً من حواره مع الشرطي. فقد كنّا مشغولين بما يهذي به أحد الشبّان صائحاً فينا: ”إنّهم ينقلون الأحداث في التلفزيون وصوت الرّجل مسموع. انظروا لقد جاءتني رسالة هاتفيّة قصيرة تعلن الخبر مع رقم ترّدد القناة“.

سحبوا هواتفهم. كانت الرّسالة قد وصلتهم جميعاً في الوقت نفسه. ازداد أعوان الشرطة اضطراباً وبدأوا يبحثون بيننا كالمجانين عن شيء ما. وصلت فرقة أخرى شُغلت بالبحث في البنايات المقابلة والمجاورة عن مكان البثّ وعن الكاميرا التي تصوّر الحدث.

هرول البعض إلى بيوتهم بينما ظل الجمهور يتكاثر حتى ضاقت به أرصفة الشوارع وفاضت به الطّرق.

الجنازة

أتذكّر الآن ذلك اليوم. بدت فيه السماء الفسيحة مثل صدر أرملة عجوز. قشرة سميكة من الجلد الميت. النجوم كانت تأكل نفسها والقمر جثة مشنوقة في الظلام وأشجار الطريق غانيات في ماخور ضيق يصطدن التائهين.

وحده الغوريلاّ كان يتدلّى في يتمه لا يشبه أحداً، عارياً مثل جرو على الإسفلت. تُنبت جمجمته غرباناً تطير لتأكل الأسماء وتبتلع العوالم.

كم حاول أن يقلّده. خصمه كان ساحراً أمام الضوء. خفيفاً كان،
يلعب بالعبارة مثل لاعب موهوب ينقل الكرة من قدم إلى أخرى دون
أن يسقطها أرضاً، "يجنقل" بالجميع مثلما يشتهي. يثبّت الكرة أحياناً
فوق رأسه ويترك الجميع مشدوهين، أفواههم مفتوحة أمام البهلوان.

لم يحبّ بورقيبة يوماً لكنّه تحوّل إلى ضرورة. كان هدفه وملاذه
وعدوّه وذريعته لارتكاب أي شيء. ينام اليوم هادئاً في قصره الأرضي
بينما الضجيج يمزّق الغوريلا. عمل المستحيل حتّى يكون بجانبه.
يحرسه من العفاريت ومن الديدان والذكريات.

بدلة نظامية. لم يكن هناك طريق أخرى إليه غير تلك البدلة الزرقاء.
حارساً للمرقد. كان يجب أن ينفرد به وحيداً. وجهاً لوجه. الغوريلا
الذي أنجبه الإله الأبيض ذو العينين الزرقاوين.

في ذلك اليوم، تغيّر كل شيء. تبعثرت الأحاسيس وازدحم الغوريلا
بالمتناقضات. كان جثمان الزعيم في المقدمة يسير ممدوداً على العربة
العسكرية مغطّى بالعلم، يجرّ خلفه العالم راكضاً، مثل إله ممدود
على العربة العسكرية يسير نحو قريته المتمدّنة وهو في آخر الطابور
الطويل يتلقّى الأكتاف والركلات. تتدافع الوجوه والأجساد من حوله
لتعبره نحو الجثمان. تغرقه الشتائم واللعنات أحياناً. كان يعطّل حركة
الركض الأخير خلف جثمان الإله الراحل. كان الغوريلا يرى نفسه
يصرخ في الخلق الراكض: "أنا طفله، طفل بورقيبة العظيم، هلمّوا إليّ،
هلمّوا إلى عزائي". يغرقه دمع اليتم والجحود وتُعميهم عنه المعميات.

وحيداً يسير خلف الجثمان مثل الحقيقة الخجولة. تفصله عنه
الأكاذيب الضارية. تأكله حمّى الهزيمة فيتذكر نفسه في المعطف الألماني

الثقيل في السجن، يحتمي به من برد زنزانة مارس، تتلبّسه فجأة صورة بورقيبة في جزيرة جالطة يقضي شهور النفي بالمعطف نفسه.

كلاهما وحيد. كلاهما مسجون. يأكلهما البرد، تسير الجنازة مثل ناقة النبي، وخلفه القافلة تسير كما أرادها، وخلف القافلة غوريلا من صلبه يتركه فجأة للظلام.

يومها فقط أحبّه ونقم على السائرين في الجنازة، عندما أخذت السيارة السوداء المسجّى، تفرّق الوجهاء وتبخّرت دموع المراسم برحيل كاميرات الأخبار ليبقى الغوريلا وحيداً يحتمي بالوبر الأسود وإسفلت الطريق.

يحاول أن يصرخ صرخته القديمة، تخونه كفّاه، تنهالان على صدره كجثّتين، تنهار صورة الغوريلا ليتصاغر إلى قرد منسيّ في الصحراء يبحث عن شجر أو غصن أو حبل أو كوبرا تلدغه حتى ينهي عذابه. يخيّم عليه السواد ويضمحلّ في الحزن القديم. كرة أخرى كان يجب أن يتصدّى لها بشجاعة. كرة أخرى مزّقته لترميه وبقايا العمر على "دكة" الاحتياط.

ها هو الآن يتجوّل فوق الساعة مثل نمر مسعور يبحث بين جماهير النمل تحته عن فريسة. كان قد اختفى منذ سنتين ولم يُعثر عليه أبداً حتى ظهر فجأة فوق الساعة في هذه القيلولة المميتة من يوم ٣ أغسطس. عيد ميلاد صاحب العينين الزرقاوين الذي نسيه الجميع بسرعة. ليته، وهو المعلّق هناك فوق الساعة، يغمغم منذ ساعة بكلام لا يبين، يحدّثهم عن ليلته تلك.

الهروب

لم يكن الغوريلا، في تلك الليلة قبل سنتين، يتوقّع أن يحدث معه ما حدث، فالهستيريا التي انتابته وجعلته يطلق كل رصاص رشّاشه في مرقد بورقيبة، سرعان ما انقشعت مثل سحابة سوداء ليدفع بنفسه إلى رحلة الفرار. ركض بألف قدم نحو العراء بعيداً عن الشوارع والأنهج متحاشياً الزحام. انحرف به الركض خارج المدينة. اهتدى إلى سكّة قطار مهجورة. صدئ حديدها ولم يعد يذكر آخر قاطرة مرت به. الحديد يموت أيضاً، هكذا فكّر الغوريلا وهو يركض بين الحديدتين الممدودتين إلى الأفق المجهول.

هجم على أذنيه من جديد صراخ النساء وصياح الرجال وهلع السيّاح في ساحة القبر وهو يطلق رصاصه الحيّ في جنون مثل جندي مهزوم.

"كلّكم من صلبه، كلّكم هو".

لا يدري كيف ضغطت أصابعه على الزناد ليطلق الرصاصة الأولى ولم يتوقّف بعدها كأنّما كان هناك شخص آخر يمسك بذراعه ويدفعه إلى إطلاق المزيد من الرصاص.

كانت رحلة فراره من مدينة قبر الرئيس أوّل عهده بالخوف. كان ينبطح على بطنه كلما سمع سيّارة شرطة أو طائرة أو بوم أو هدهد زاهد في شجرة خروب ميتة.

ركض وركضت معه الأفاعي والفئران والسحالي والعقارب. الكل يشارك الغوريلا هروبه.

بعد ساعات باغتهم الظلام جميعاً، انقضّ عليهم من محجره،

فانقلبت السحالي والأفاعي والثعابين والجرذان على ظهورها كأن سمّمها السواد. جفّ العرق على جسد الغوريلا. نزل البرد مشفوعاً بالصقيع المدمّر، تسلل الغوريلا داخل قناة إسمنتية مطروحة قرب السكّة من بقايا مشروع حفر مصرف المياه، كحبة أسبرين في الماء ذابت جفونه المتعبة في النعاس. غير بعيد عن السكة كانت سيارات الإسعاف تعوي طول الليل. لا بدّ أنها تنقل الجرحى من القبر إلى مستشفيات العاصمة.

الكوابيس لا تترك فريسة جاهزة. كان الغوريلا يطارد في نومه كرات مستحيلة تمزّق قفصه الصدري مثل الرّصاص لتتدفّق قناة الإسمنت على السكّة المهجورة بدماء خاثرة.

ينهض من الكابوس يعاود الهروب على إيقاع صفّارات سيّارات الشرطة التي لم تتوقّف.

وصل مع الفجر إلى تجمّع سكّاني. اندفع نحو كشك للسجائر. طلب علبتين من سجائر ٢٠ مارس'. ابتاع حزمة من الجرائد. نظر إليه البائع بريبة وهو يسأله: "أنت لست من هنا؟".

لا أنا من الجنوب جئت أزور أهلي.

في هذا الوقت؟

لا أنا مغادر الآن. أنتظر الحافلة.

لا حافلات هنا. عليك بسيارات الأجرة. هناك. أشار الرجل إلى مكان عند الهضبة.

شكراً.

---

١. نوع من السجائر يحمل اسم تاريخ استقلال تونس .

احتضن الغوريلا حزمة الجرائد وهرول باتجاه المحطة. وما إن ابتعد عن الكشك حتى غيّر اتجاهه نحو الخلاء. انزوى وراء بقايا بيت مهجور وفتح صحيفة. أصابه الهلع وهو يجد صورته تتصدّر الصفحة الأولى. يفتح الثانية والثالثة والرابعة، صورته في كلّ الصحف. أخبار تعلن إفشال عمليات إرهابية في العاصمة وفي المنستير من جماعات متطرّفة. تقول الأخبار إنّه وقع الاستعانة بالجيش لملاحقة المتطرّفين وإنّ بعضهم فرّ إلى الجبال والأودية وإن البحث عنهم ما زال جارياً. وتحت عنوان الخبر كانت صورته وصور أخرى لبعض المشتبه فيهم ودعوة للإدلاء بأي أخبار عنهم. صحف أخرى نشرت صوراً لبعض الجثث وصفت أصحابها بالمتطرّفين الذين أبادتهم السلطات. كانوا بملابس غريبة وبلحى طويلة وشعور كثيفة. كانت أفواههم فاغرة وعيونهم جامدة تنظر إلى المشهد الأخير قبل الرصاصة.

ركض الغوريلا بحزمة من الخوف الجديد مبتعداً عن البلدة، مستحضراً نظرة صاحب الكشك المريبة.

عاد إلى سكّة التّيه. كان وحيداً هذه المرة، بلا كائنات، يركض في طريق الخوف. حتى ظلّه اختفى كما لو أنه انتحر أو سقط منه مثل طمأنينة زائفة. رمت به السكّة عند المساء أمام سياج عال لمزرعة مجهولة. ظلّ ساعات يطوف بها منتظراً حلول الظلام. باغتت ظهره فوهة رشّاش وصوت يأمره أن يرفع يديه إلى رأسه. هكذا انقلب الغوريلا من قانص إلى قنيص. كان ذلك قبل عامين.

دفعه الصّوت لوضع الانبطاح. برك عليه. أحس بركبتيه الثقيلتين تهشّمان ظهره وهو يقيّد يديه إلى الخلف قبل أن يرفعه من كتفيه.

وجد نفسه أمام رجل مقنّع غارق في السواد يحمل رشّاشاً غريب الشكل. دفعه أمامه إلى داخل المزرعة التي ظهر لها مدخل فجأة.

كانت المزرعة مزروعة كلاباً في كل مكان. كلاب متوحّشة لا تتوقّف عن نباح عدواني. بدت مهيّأة لتمزيق الدنيا لو انعتقت من سلاسلها. عادت ماسورة الرشاش تُغرس في ظهر الغوريلا تأمره بالتقدّم. مد الخطى نحو المجهول على ضوء مصباح كهربائي خافت يوجهه صاحب الرشاش من خلفه يتحسّس به مسلكاً دقيقاً يشق حقل القمح إلى شطرين.

لا يدري الغوريلا أين وقع. أمره رجل الرشّاش أن يتوقّف أمام كوخ من القش بعد دقائق ثقيلة من المشي. رطن بكلام غريب لم يتبيّنه الغوريلا. خرج من الكوخ رجل آخر ملثم ثبّت عصابة سوداء على عينيه وقاده إلى الداخل. أحس بقدميه تنزلان سلّماً ما وتغزو أنفه رائحة تربة ندية. بدا المقنّع الجديد الذي يدفعه أكثر عنفاً فقد كان لا يتوقف عن دق مقدمة سلاحه في ظهره. الغوريلا المغلوب على أمره لا يدري أين هو من العالم. لم يعد يفكر في ما خلفه من ضحايا رشّاشه المجنون الذي أفرغه في مرقد الزعيم. لقد أصبح مطارداً لسبب آخر.

ها هو الغوريلا، اليوم، فوق الساعة. مكان تمثال بورقيبة تماماً. يلقي بقميصه ليلوذ بالعري. وصلت سيارة المطافئ، اخترقت الجمهور وبدأت ترفع سلّماً باتجاه قمّة الساعة. انفتحت درجاته حتى اقتربت من الغوريلا الذي تمسّك بحزامه الجلدي. خاطبه الشرطي في مضخّم

الصوت يدعوه إلى النزول ويعده بأن يستمعوا إليه. لوّح الغوريلا بيديه
يميناً وشمالاً.

ملقوط

هل تراه ما زال يذكر ذلك اليوم الذي حمل فيه لقب الغوريلا؟

منذ أكثر من ثلاثين سنة كان الغوريلا يقف أمام صورة بورقيبة
المبتسم، هناك في أعلى الجدار عند محلّ الساندويتش. كان يبتسم له
ملوّحاً بكفه البيضاء وبالكفّ الأخرى يمسك مشموم الياسمين، في
الأسفل كان الغوريلا الطفل، يقضم نصف الخبزة بالهريسة والسردين.
الزيت يتقاطر على قميصه وهو في الأعلى يبتسم كالجرح. أبيض
ناصعاً. شعره أبيض. ابتسامته بيضاء. كفه بيضاء. بدلته أيضاً كانت
بيضاء والزيت برائحة السردين يتقاطر على قميص الغوريلا الصغير.

إحساس فظيع بالفخر والهوان معاً في اللحظة ذاتها يتصارعان
داخله مثل ثورين هائجين وهو يقلّب هويّته على جنبيها مثل عملة
غريبة، وجه يقول إنه سليل أهم رجل في البلاد فترفعه الفكرة إلى
أعلى الجدار ليطلّ من خلف صاحب الصورة على القصور والحدائق
والزرابي واللحوم والثمار، ووجه يقول إنه مجهول النّسب وإنه ليس
ابناً حتّى لجرذ أو حمار، فيسقط من جديد في التّبن ويغرقه الزيت
والسردين والعار. يذوب في ابتسامة بيضاء كجمجمة لرجل لم يسمع
عنه. فليس سوى طفل من أطفال بورقيبة الكثر.

عندما عيّره أطفال القرية لأوّل مرة بأنّه من "أطفال بورقيبة"[2]
ابتسم ابتسامة عريضة مثل ابتسامة بورقيبة تماماً وكأنه يؤكد النسب.

---

٢. عبارة تطلق على الأطفال اللقطاء في تونس الذين بلا أب محدّد.

لكنّه لم يبتسم بعدها أبداً عندما انهالت عليه مترادفات العبارة: كبّول،
ولد حرام، ملقوط، batard، ابن زنى. رأى ساعتها أسنان بورقيبة مثل
قواطع وحش يتقدّم نحوه ليفتك بعظامه. هرب يومها من الملعب إلى
المقبرة، وأمام قبر والده وقف يصرخ ويشتم ويصيح حتى ضاع صوته
في بئر سحيقة. هل تراه اليوم يذكر أنّه أنزل سحابة السّروال وأغرق
قبره بولاً ساخناً؟ كم شعر بالعار بعد ذلك!

جلس عند ذلك المساء يشاهد مع أخته البيضاء والده "الجديد"
وهو يلقي خطابه اليومي: "توجيهات سيادة الرئيس"٣ من خلال
شاشة التلفزيون الأسود والأبيض. كانت الشاشة تُشبههما تماماً:
أبيض/ أسود. علم بعدها أن أخته هي الأخرى ابنة بالتبنّي فهي بيضاء
كالحليب بينما هو أسود كالفحم. عندما سألها "هل نحن فعلاً من
أطفال بورقيبة؟" دمعت عيناها وتركته إلى غرفتها. كانت أكبر منه
وبالتأكيد لاحظت الأمر أو سمعته. الأسرة التي تبنّتهما لم تترك لهما
فرصة للافتراض. وكان طفل بورقيبة وكان بعدها الغوريلا.

ها هو يُلقي بقارورة الماء وقد ملأها ببوله على الجماهير راطناً بكلام
لا يُفهم. سقطت القارورة في يدّي أحدهم. لم يكن غير "الجطّ" الذي
التحق بالساحة منذ دقائق. وقف تحت الساعة في الصفوف الخلفية
وأخذ يمخر أنفه كعادته وهو يتطلّع إلى السماء. وصله الخبر من حبيبة
التي تقف بعيداً في الجانب الآخر تدافع عن عجيزتها المنتهكة في
الزحام. تأمّل الجطّ الرجلَ الأسودَ المعلّقَ وغمغم: "هو. هو لا شك
في ذلك. أتذكّره جيداً". عادت به الذاكرة إلى سنوات الطفولة. كان

---

٣. برنامج شهير كان يبثّ خطاباً قصيراً لبورقيبة يومياً يتوجّه به الرئيس إلى
الشعب في شكل توجيهات.

الغوريلا يلعب معه وأترابه كرة القدم. وكانوا يرغمونه على حراسة المرمى التي لا يقبل بها أحد. كان يتّجه كل يوم إلى طرف الملعب ليقف بين حجرتين يطارد كراتهم. يسدّدون وهو يلتقط ويلتقط ويلتقط الكرة تلو الكرة ويرجعها إلى المنتصف الملعب بيده. ما زال الجط يذكر نظرته الغريبة التي رمقه بها يوم وقف أمامه يريد أن ينتزع منه الكرة. لاحظ أن ذراعيه قد طالتا بشكل غريب حتى أدركت كفّاه الركبتين. قال الجط "غوريلا. تبدو يا صالح مثل الغوريلا. انظر يديك". ضحك الأطفال وتصايحوا باللقب الجديد لصالح الذي ارتجفت وجنتاه. تكوّرت قبضتاه مثل ملاكم شرس قبل أن يمسك بالكرة ويرميها إلى آخر الملعب ويغادر البطحاء بالغوريلا على كتفيه.

خبر عاجل

كرة أرضية في شاشة الفضائية الناطقة بالعربية تدور بشكل جنوني على إيقاع موسيقي متوتّر معلنة جينيريك الأخبار.

يظهر مذيع بارز الجبهة بربطة عنق سوداء منقّطة. يفتح عينيه الواسعتين جيّداً. يترك لحظات من الصمت تحبس أنفاس مشاهديه الذين خبروا أسلوبه المميّز، قبل أن يقول بجدية:

ارتبك الشارع الرئيسي للعاصمة التونسية إثر تسلّق شاب أسمر ظهيرة اليوم برج ساعة ٧ نوفمبر بتونس العاصمة البالغ علوّه خمسين متراً. واعتصم الشاب بقمّة البرج ولم تنجح، إلى الآن، المحاولات الحثيثة من الشرطة والحماية المدنية في إنزاله.

وتتضارب الأقوال حول هويته ومطالبه، حيث يروج بين الجماهير

التي تتابع الحدث أنه يعتزم الانتحار. وقد اغتنم الشاب فرصة مدّه بحبل لمساعدته في النزول ليديره حول رقبته مستميتاً في رفض إنزاله.

وقد عمدت السلطات الأمنية التونسية إلى منع وسائل الإعلام في عين المكان من تصوير الحادث، كما لاحقت كل من حاول التصوير بالهواتف الجوالة وغيرها من وسائل التسجيل البصري.

ووصلنا أن الشاب يرفض النزول من مكانه منذ ساعتين فأسقط المظلة العسكرية الصغيرة التي قذفها إليه رجال الحماية المدنية قصد مساعدته على النزول.

وسنوافيكم بالمزيد من التفاصيل في نشراتنا المقبلة.

عادت الكرة الأرضية إلى الظهور وأخذت في الدوران في سماء مجهولة قبل أن تتحلل في رغوة صابون اللوكس التي كانت تداعبها كف أنثوية في حمّام ما.

لانا عبد الرحمن

رسائل إلى يان أندريا[1]

بيروت، تموز ٢٠٠٦

يان...

قطرات الماء على كتفيّ العارية منثورة كنمش خفيف على وجه أبيض. أتركها لتجف وحدها.

أنت تحب هذه القطرات. في أيام البرد تلسعني ملامسة الهواء لها، لكن الحر خانق الآن، والعثور على ماء للاستحمام في وقت الحرب أمر يرتبط بالقدر الذي قد يرمي بك لأن تكون في خيام النازحين، أو في قلب بيت.

ونحن الآن في بيت مغلق، لا يأتي إليه أصحابه إلا أياماً قليلة في صيف كل عام.

الكلمات التي أكتبها لك في العتمة، هذه السطور التي سأكرّر

---

١. يان أندريا: هو الحبيب الأخير للكاتبة الفرنسية مارغريت دوراس، عاش معها ١٥ عاماً، كان كاتباً شاباً في الـ٢٥ من عمره وكانت في الـ٦٥ حين بدأت قصة حبهما. كان معجباً بنصوصها في بداية العلاقة ثم وقع في غرام الكاتبة، وبعد موتها كتب عن علاقته بها كتاباً بعنوان «هذا هو الحب».

كتابتها غداً على جهاز الكمبيوتر لأرسلها إليك، تمدّني بالقدرة على المقاومة، وعلى البقاء وسط هذا العبث.

ربما وجدت مارغريت دوراس مكانها في الكتابة. ربما يكون هذا صحيحاً. لذا أكتب إليك لأكتشف ماهية علاقتي بها، وبك.

إذ طالما فكرت... لماذا أحبّتك مارغريت دوراس وعاشت معك حتى لحظاتها الأخيرة؟

ظللت قربها، تساعدها على الرحيل بهدوء، وظلت تحبك.

الانتقال إلى مكان أكثر أماناً لم يفرحها، على الرغم من وجود ماء، وكهرباء، وهاتف، وتلفزيون يتابعون عبره الأخبار. عندما غادرت البيت لم تأخذ معها سوى بعض ملابسها، وجهاز الكمبيوتر، وروايات مارغريت دوراس، وكتاب يان أندريا عنها. لكن حين وصلوا إلى منطقة "الصنايع" نظرت الأم باستخفاف إلى أغراض ابنتها، وإلى انشغالها بوضع الكمبيوتر في مكان مناسب، ولم تعرف زينب هذه المرة ما إن كانت تلك النظرة بسبب الليلة الطويلة التي أمضوها تحت أصوات الصواريخ، أم هي النظرة المستخفة شبه الدائمة نحوها. الأم تكاد تفقد عقلها بسبب الحرب، وتفكر في الرحيل إلى الجبل حيث كانت أختها تمضي أيام الصيف. لكنها لم تجد دعوة صريحة من الأخت، واعتزازها بنفسها لا يسمح لها بأن تفرض حضورها هي وأولادها بحجة الحرب المباغتة.

رغبة الأم في البحث عن مكان أكثر أماناً من شقة خالها الخالية طوال العام في منطقة "الصنايع" يشعرها بالخزي، يظهر هذا على ملامح

وجهها كلما تحدثت الأم عن ضرورة مغادرة بيروت كلها. تنظر زينب من النافذة إلى جموع النازحين الذين ينصبون خيامهم في حديقة "الصنايع"، كيف يتعايشون مع الحرب، ومع نقص الماء والطعام، السجائر وحليب الأطفال. ينامون في الخيام، وعلى الأرض، أطفالهم يستحمون في العراء، أما النساء والرجال فيلجأون لتدابير مختلفة، كأن يغتسلوا في طرف الخيمة مداراةً لأجسادهم العارية.

تتلفت الأم في أرجاء المنزل، تتحسّر بنقمة على الحياة المرفهة التي ضاعت منها، لأن زواجها نقلها ـ من وجهة نظرها ـ إلى طبقة اجتماعية أقل، وجعلها تظل طوال عمرها من سكان "بير العبد" في "الضاحية الجنوبية"، بدلاً من أن تسكن في قلب بيروت، حيث تربّت وكبرت. الحضور مع الأم بالنسبة إلى زينب، لساعات طويلة، ولأيام متواصلة، أمر مزعج جداً، وخاصة أنها تبيت معها في الغرفة ذاتها. تسبّب لها أمها إحساساً بالتوتر، تحديداً حين تضطر زينب لتبديل ثيابها في وجودها وهذا ما تتجنّبه دوماً، لأن الأم لا تفوّت فرصة لانتقاد جسد ابنتها غير المتناسق، والشعر الكثيف الذي يغطي ساقيها وأعلى فخذيها، وفي بعض الأحيان لا تتأخر في تذكيرها بأنها لم ترث جمالها الأرستقراطي، وأن بشرتها سمراء، وفيها بثور لأنها أخذت ملامح عائلة أبيها القروية. كلما نظرت زينب إلى أمها أحسّت باستفزاز، كان شعر الأم بنياً فاتحاً مصبوغاً بإتقان، شفتاها مطليتان غالباً بلون خمري غامق، عيناها يتطابق لونهما مع لون شعرها، أنفها رفيع وصغير كما لو أنه يحتقر العالم، بالإضافة إلى أنها تصرّ على ارتداء ثياب أنيقة داخل المنزل حتى في زمن الحرب، هناك أيضاً تبرّمها الدائم، نظرتها

الساخرة، تحسّرها على ترمّلها المبكر، وعلى عمرها الذي ضاع هباءً في تربية أولادها.

تتحوّل الأم إلى كائن ضعيف ومستسلم أمام ابنها الأكبر وسام. حين يأتي ليطلب منها المال، تمنحه إياه وهي تشعر بالسعادة لأنها تحسّ بحاجته المستمرة إليها، تتظاهر بالاعتراض في بداية الأمر، لكنها تقوم بالتصرّف ذاته في كل مرة: الاعتراض ثم المنح. وهو سيظل محتاجاً إليها ما دامت تملك المال، وسيمنحها بعض الاهتمام والعطف لقاء ما يأخذه، يأتي وسام ليأخذ المال كي يختفي لأيام عدة، ثم يعود للإقامة في البيت وهكذا. أما الآن في أيام الحرب، فهو مضطر للاستقرار مع العائلة في البيت المستعار، يتنقل بين الصالون وغرفة النوم مبدياً انزعاجه، ثم يعود إلى غرفته التي استقل بها، ومنع أخيه الأصغر عامر من المبيت معه، لأنه يجب أن يحظى بغرفة مستقلة، بما أنه الأخ الأكبر. غرفة مستقلة، ليخفي علب البيرة، وزجاجات الويسكي تحت السرير.

لكن أكثر ما هو مزعج بالنسبة إليها أن تمسك علبة الثقاب، لتجد أنها تحتوي على سيجارة مسحوقة وعود ثقاب استُخدم من قبل، أو حين تأخذ أمها آخر سيجارة من علبة سجائرها، وتتجاهل تماماً حاجتها للسجائر، تعرف الأم أن زينب لن تقدر على مواجهتها بهذا أبداً. كانت الأم تدخن في الليل سراً، وتضع السيجارة ورمادها وعود الثقاب في علبة الكبريت الفارغة، لكنها تنسى أن تلقي بها بعيداً، أو تتكاسل وتؤجل الأمر حتى الصباح، لا تشعل سيجارتها أمام أولادها، لأنها تريد أن تكون أماً مثالية دوماً، في بيتها كانت تدخن في غرفتها الخاصة، لذا لا يمكن ملاحظة هذه التفاصيل

الصغيرة. وبما أن علبة الثقاب الفارغة موجودة في الغرفة المشتركة، فليس هناك مجال للشك في أحد آخر.

يان..

إنه تشابه مضنٍ يرهقني، أبحث عنها، وعنك. أنت تعرف ما لا أعرفه، لكنك لا تعرف شيئاً عنّي. سأثق بك كي تضع حداً للشبه الذي يرهقني، للشبه الذي ربما يكون وهماً، أو هروباً من الحقيقة.

في صباحي الباكر هذا، أنظر إلى سقف الغرفة التي أنام فيها. تتمدّد في زاويته رقعة مجعّدة، تنزّ بقايا الدهان الأبيض على سريري. أسمع صوت أمي في الصالون، تثرثر على التلفون عن الحرب، مع خالي المقيم في الخليج، الذي استعرنا بيته لنسكن فيه خلال الحرب.

أصوات الأطفال النازحين في حديقة "الصنايع" ترتفع وهم يصدحون بأغنية للمقاومة، ويرسمون على الحيطان بنادق وإشارات النصر. ومن النافذة أشاهد مذيعة من إحدى الفضائيات أتت لتسأل الأطفال وأهاليهم عن الحرب. هكذا يصير التهجير مادة إعلامية ينبغي أن يعرفها العالم عن كثب ليساعد في إنهائها. البارحة كانت هناك مذيعة أخرى من فضائية مختلفة، شاهدناها أنا وساندرا حين كنا في الحديقة نسأل الأمهات عما يمكننا فعله لمساعدتهن. إحداهن طلبت منا وهي خجلى حبوب منع الحمل، فيما أخرى توسّلت إلينا كي نحضر سجائر لزوجها، امرأة ثالثة طلبت أوعية لطهو الطعام، وإبريقاً لتسخين الماء وغلي الحليب.

تفاصيل صغيرة لم أكن لأنتبه لها لولا الحرب.

لماذا أستمر في الكتابة إليك فيما لم يعد يتذكرك أحد؟ أفتش بين

أوراقك، أعبث بذاكرتك، وأسألك عنها، مضت على رحيلها أعوام
كثيرة. كان عالمنا يتسع أكثر وأنت تحكي عن شغفك بها، تلك العجوز
الساحرة بأي إكسير تمكنت من أسر قلبك حتى الآن.

سأستمر في الكتابة، لك، عنك، عنها، وعني، لأصل إلى يقيني
الخاص الذي يمنحني الخلاص.

في البيت، داخل غرفتها في الطابق العلوي تكون مارغريت وحدها.
في البيت فقط تكون وحدها وتحس بالضياع المخيف الذي تكتب
عنه، في الحديقة كائنات تشاطرها الوحدة، عصافير، حشرات، قطط،
فأر صغير يعبر سريعاً في لحظة خاطفة، لكن هنا في هذه الحجرة ـ التي
تحتوي على طاولة، سرير، وخزانة زرقاء ـ حين تكون ستارة نافذتها منفرجة
قليلاً ليبرز منها شق من الضوء، خيط طولي رفيع لا يكفي ليهدّد الوحدة
والعتمة، تدرك أنها مكثت هنا عشر سنوات وحيدة تؤلّف رواياتها،
وتصوغ حكايات جارحة عن ألم عتيق، كان من المفترض أن يُنسى منذ
زمن طويل.

البارحة تشاجرت معه، صدّت الباب في وجهه، طلبت منه
الرحيل، ظل هو جالساً عند حافة البوابة ينتظر عبور نوبة اغترابها
ووحدتها. كانت ثملة وهي تطلب منه الذهاب بعيداً، وكانت تفكر
بما يريده منها هذا الشاب. قلب باريس كرنفال من المسرات، يتركه هذا
الأحمق ليطرق باب امرأة عجوز، هي نفسها لا تظن أن كونها كاتبة
يعطي مبرّراً لهذا الشاب لكسر عزلتها والبقاء إلى جوارها.

نظرت من شق النافذة نحو الحديقة، العصفور يقف على غصن
الشجرة الصغيرة، سيطير سريعاً لو أحس بحركتها عبر مسافة بعيدة،

تكره أن تكون سبباً لفرار العصفور، إذ برغم طول زمن بقائها في هذا البيت، وفي تلك الحديقة، لا يزال العصفور الصغير يسارع بالطيران حين يحسّ باقترابها. مرّرت يديها على شعرها وهي تفكر بالنزول إلى الدور السفلي لإعداد قهوتها. في هذا الركن الصغير كتبت "انخطاف لول ف. شتاين"، هنا انخطفت لول إلى مكان مجهول ولم ترجع قط، لم ترجع سوى للتحاور معها. منذ "انخطاف لول ف. شتاين" أدركت أنها وحيدة تماماً مع كتابتها، مع صور أبطالها الهاربين والضائعين. كانت وحيدة دوماً، لكن مع كتبها الأولى تختلف عنها الآن، لكنها الوحدة ذاتها في الأماكن كلها، هنا ظهرت لها "لول فاليري"[٢]، وفي هذا الوقت أيضاً لمع اسم يان أندريا في حياتها. لماذا انخطفت "لول" وبقي "يان" هنا.

والآن لماذا يأتي يان أندريا ليفرض حضوره على هذه العزلة؟ اعتادت منذ وقت طويل أن لا تحسب الزمن. الزمن مثل رذاذ المطر نظنّه كثيراً لكنه لن يلبث أن يتوقف.

تدرك مارغريت بعمق أن محنتها الكبرى مع الزمن السائر. لذا لم تعد تقربه، تجاهلته تماماً، وقررت الحياة من دون ساعات وأيام، رفضت هذا التقسيم الأبله للأيام والأعوام، وفي دورة هذا التجاهل ضاع من ذاكرتها اليوم الواقعي، كانت تقول "لماذا لا يكون اليوم هو الثلاثاء بدلاً من السبت، لماذا لا يكون هذا العام هو العام السابق أو التالي، لماذا عليّ الرضوخ لتقسيمات ابتدعها الآخرون وجعلوا منها

---

[٢]. لول فاليري هي بطلة رواية لمارغريت دوراس بعنوان "انخطاف لول. ف. شتاين".

قانوناً يسري على العالم كله". هي لن ترضخ لهذا القانون وستعيش زمنها الخاص.

في عزلتها تعرف الصمت، تقترب من السكون، ترى وجه الإله شفافاً مثل غلالة غيم، نقياً، وبريئاً، فرحاً كما لم يكن الفرح. لذا كانت تخشى الاقتراب أكثر، تشيح ببصرها بعيداً متواطئة مع صمتها الكثيف. تعرف هي أن هذه العزلة تمنحها غبطة قدوم أبطالها الهاربين، عليها أن تصمت طويلاً كي تتيح لهم مجالاً للوصول، للكلام، للبوح بحكاياتهم، لتكتب.

في تلك العزلة، ماذا كان عليها أن تفعل سوى أن تكتب. أن تقلب أقلام الحبر الكثيرة السوداء الموجودة على طاولتها وتختار أي قلم ستكتب به هذا اليوم. أوراق الكتابة بيضاء تماماً، خالية من السطور، هناك أقلام حمراء وخضراء، لتضع خطوطاً بجانب الكلمات التي ينبغي عليها العودة لها.

بينما كانت زينب تكتب على الكمبيوتر، وتتابع مع أمّها مشاهد الحرب على التلفزيون، فاحت من غرفة وسام رائحة سيجارة حشيش. تميّز هذه الرائحة جيداً، والأم أيضاً، لأن وسام حين يضطر إلى الإقامة في المنزل لأيام لا يتورّع عن إشعال سيجارة حشيش في غرفته، هو متأكد من أن الأم لن تجرؤ على إغضابه، وستغض الطرف لأنه سيهدّدها بمغادرة البيت نهائياً.

وقفت الأم وهي ترتدي قميص نوم من الساتان الأزرق وادعت أنها ذاهبة للنوم كي تتخلص من الموقف، ناولت زينب ورقة مكتوباً عليها لائحة من الأطعمة والخضار التي ينبغي عليها إحضارها في اليوم

التالي. لاحظت زينب أظافر يديْ أمها التي بهت لون طلائها الوردي، كما لاحظت نقاط نمش قليلة على ظهر اليد تظهر مع التقدم في العمر، تناولت منها الورقة وهي تسمع تنبيهها أن لا تتأخر صباحاً في إحضار الحاجات المنزلية.

بدا لها أن وقت الحرب مهم بالنسبة إليها، لأنه أبعد عن ذهنها التفكير بالانتحار. فالموت مجاني ومتوافر بكثرة، الموت لم يعد حدثاً، أي إنها لو ألقت بنفسها الآن من هذه النافذة، من هذه الشقة، ومن الدور الثاني، في مبنى يطل على حديقة الصنايع، التي يسكنها النازحون، فلن يكون ذلك سوى خبر غريب، لكنه لن يكون حدثاً مهماً.

فكرت أن موتها سيكون مجانياً، لكن ليس هذا السبب فقط هو ما يبعد فكرة "الانتحار" عن ذهنها، بل الموت قبل الوصول إلى فكرة الخلاص الذي تبحث عنه.

موتها في وقت السلم، حين كانت حياتها تعج بالفراغ والوحدة قد يؤدّي بها إلى الخلاص. أما الآن فإن الحرب تمنحها الإحساس بأنها كائن يستحق الحياة. الآن صارت تفهم إحساس المقاتل بأهمية دوره في زمن الحرب، ولماذا يحسّ بالهزيمة بعد انتهائها، حتى وإن كان منتصراً، لقد انتهى دوره، ويصير عليه العودة للحياة كأي رجل عادي، حينها تبدأ معاناته. ولو حدث وقام نزاع مفاجئ بين طرفين، فسيبتهج لأنه قادر على تحويله إلى حرب كبيرة، لأنها تعيده إلى دائرة الحياة، التي همّشته في زمن السلم.

يان

عند الصباح الباكر.

أحب المرور ببطء أمام عربة بائع الخضار، أحب رؤية وجهه المتفائل رغماً عن الحرب، يرش رذاذ الماء البارد على النعناع والبقدونس والزعتر البري. ينادي على بضاعته بلهجته التي تكشف عن مكان قدومه، هكذا يعلن أن كائنات العربة ستتفرق بعضها عن بعض بعد قليل وتتوزع في بيوت كثيرة، وتصير يقظتها الصباحية في الشارع مجرد ذكرى تنتشر في كل بيت.

برغم قيامي بالأعمال المنزلية منذ أعوام، غالباً أنسى حبّات الطماطم في درج الثلاجة حتى تذبل، وحتى أعرف وخز الضمير لأي كنت مشغولة بحل نزاعات أبدية تبدأ داخلي مع كل صباح.

"لماذا لم يطرقوا جدار الخزان؟".

هذه العبارة لم تسمع بها أنت، ولم تقرأها، أليس كذلك؟ لقد أخذتها من رواية لغسان كنفاني أعطاني إياها مازن، سأحكي لك في يوم ما عن مازن، وعن حكايتي معه.

وأنا متى سأطرق جدار الخزان؟

ماذا كنت تفعل حين كانت مارغريت تسقي ورود حديقتها، ولماذا كنت ساهماً في كآبتك إلى هذا الحد؟

حين يكون زمني مائلاً للغيم، سأمر بيدي اليسرى بين خصلات شعرك الشتائية، وأترك أصابعي ترسم بكريما الفانيليا تجاعيد جبهتك.

العابرون في الشارع عند المساء يكونون مثقلين بكل حكايات يومهم، لذا لن يصدقوا أن الفجر قد يحمل حباً جديداً، صافياً كماء النبع.

ثمة روح قُبلة مُعذبة ظلت معلقة في الفضاء، فلا هي ظلت في سمائها العليا، ولا نزلت إلى جسم لطيف.

سأتجاهل هذه الحقيقة. لا يمكنني التصديق أنك تهت عني، وأحببت الطمأنينة أكثر مما أحببتني. لكن هذا ما حدث.

كانت طاولة مارغريت وهي تجلس في المقهى، تواجه الباب المطل على شارع السان ميشيل. تتأمل مارغريت الفتاة التي تسير في الشارع وتتشبث بمعطفها وتتكلم بانفعال مع الرجل الذي يسير برفقتها، تعاتبه، تتشاجر معه. كان يان منهمكاً بالحديث عن نص مسرحيته الجديدة، قالت له فجأة:

ـ كل هذا سيصبح ذكريات في وقت ما، مجرد ذكريات منسية...

بدا يان متفاجئاً من كلماتها، سألها بخيبة:

ـ ما الذي سيصبح ذكريات؟

مررت كلتا يديها على خصلات شعرها الذي طغى عليه اللون الرمادي، ثم قالت:

ـ كل شيء، كل شيء سيصبح ذكريات، جلستنا هذه، أنا، أنت، اليوم، هذه اللحظة، مسرحيتك التي تحكي لي عنها، تلك الفتاة التي تتشاجر مع الرجل الذي تحبه، كل هذا سيصير مجرد ذكريات قد لا يعرف بها أحد.

خفضت مارغريت رأسها، وظلت تنظر إلى الطاولة لثوان عدة، قبل أن تقول وهي تضرب بيدها بخفة على يد يان الممدودة على الطاولة:

ـ أكمل ما كنت تحكيه عن مسرحيتك، أسمعك.

نظر إليها يان، حدّق في وجهها، في التجاعيد الرقيقة حول عينيها، في خطي العمر حول وجنتيها الشاحبتين، أحس كم هي

هشة، وكم يحبها. هذه المرأة التي يراها الآن لا تختلف كثيراً عن البنت الخائفة في روايتها العشيق٣.

حين تكتب زينب، تكتشف مدى عزلتها داخل حلقة واحدة لن يكون فيها سواها، تكتشف هذه العزلة في تشبثها باستمرار الكتابة إليه. الكتابة لا تدخلها إلى مكان آخر، لكنها تجعلها على تماس مع حلقته المجهولة التي ينعزل فيها هو. في هذا الشغف للتماس بين حلقتين، بين عزلتين تحدث الكتابة، عندما تقترب منه، وتحس أن حلقة حديدها البارد تلامس حلقة أخرى يختفي هو وراءها.

ربما يكون البشر معزولين في حلقات يتفاوت حجمها، لذا يبحثون عن الحب، وربما هم يعيشون من دون اكتشاف عزلتهم الحقيقية، ويظنون أن كل ما يقومون به من نشاط يومي مكثف، هو جدار ضد العزلة.

اكتشفت كل هذا في وقت مبكر، منذ حكاياتها الأولى مع حامد. عرفت أن الأحاسيس الإنسانية تكون حقيقية في وقت ما، وفي ما بعد، بنسبة من النسب، بشكل أو بآخر، تتبدّل. لا بد أن يحدث ما يوقف ديمومة أي استمرار، فقط كي تستمر الحركة الدائرية الأبدية للحلقة الأكبر. فالموت، والميلاد، والحرب، وكل هذا الرعب، والألم، كلها ليست سوى وسائل تمنح للحلقة الكبرى ديمومة الاستمرار الذي يُنهي في دورانه كل الحلقات الأصغر.

لقد غيّرتها هذه الحرب. كما غيّرتها ليلة "عيد الفصح" الوحيدة التي حضرتها، ليلة العيد أدركت عزلتها. وفي الحرب عرفت أنها أكثر حرية وقوة. فالحرب تختبر قدرتنا على الفقد. في البداية تختبرنا

---

٣. رواية "العشيق" من بين الروايات الأكثر شهرة لمارغريت دوراس.

الحرب في الأشياء ثم في البشر، في الحرب تعلمت التمسّك بالبشر والأحلام، ثم تعلمت ممارسة لعبة التخلي، إسقاط كل ما صرفت ببذخ لجمعه، بروفة للرحيل، بروفة للفقد، ثم بروفة للموت أيضاً.

يان...

هل تعرف كيف يكون طعم الموت، هل أخبرتك مارغريت عنه؟ جاءت الحرب عندما كنت أحضر لك هدية، دي.في.دي لفيلم (End of the affair). الفيلم الذي حكيت لك قصته ثلاث مرات. لكنك كنت مأخوذاً بصوت "أديث بياف" وهي تغني عن باريس، حنينك الأول.

ليس وزني الخفيف هو الذي يشعرني بأنني كائن غير ثابت على الأرض، بل إحساسي المستمر أنني كائن غير مرئي.. أحياناً كان من الممكن أن يصطدم بي أحد العابرين في شارع أيامي، ثم يتركني ويعبر من دون كلمة "اعتذار" أو "أسف" هذا ما حدث أكثر من مرة، الذنب ليس ذنبي. اقتناعي بأني كائن غير مرئي. لكن الآن من الممكن أن أموت، أن يتناثر دمي على الأرض، أن أكون رقماً في سلسلة الضحايا. هل سأتأكد حينها أني كنت مرئية، كنت حية، وكان لي جسد لم أعرف كيف أحبه؟

الظلال تمنحني قدرة أعمق على الإبصار، لذا أدرك أنك تعرف بقلبك ما أعنيه، كما كانت مارغريت تعرف بقلبها سبب إصرارك على البقاء معها.

الآن، في هذا الوقت المهدّدة أنا فيه بالغياب، تمنحني كتابتي لك يقيناً للبقاء. أقلب روايات محبوبتك وأبحث عن ظلك النحيل بين

السطور، ثم أقرأ كتابك عنها، وأفكر هل حقاً "هذا هو الحب"[٤].

تمنّت مارغريت لو كانت متسولة غير مشغولة سوى بالبحث عن معيش يومها، أو غجرية، غير مطلوب منها تذكر الأمكنة، والوجوه، والأسماء. أكثر ما يعذبها هو ذاكرتها الهرمة المثقلة بتفاصيل لا يمكن التخلص منها إلا بعد زمن من العزلة والصمت. منذ سنوات حين كانت تدعو أصدقاءها من باريس إلى أمسية عشاء في منزلها، تظن أنها ستهرب من ثقل العزلة الكثيفة، لكن حين يحضرون، بعد أن يبدأ الصخب يطفو في المكان، وينتشر الأصدقاء في المطبخ والصالون، متنقلين بين البيت والحديقة، تجد نفسها أكثر عزلة، تجلس في مقعدها ذي الغطاء البيج المشجر بألوان من البني والكريم، تتكئ على هذا المقعد وفي يدها كأس من الويسكي المثلج، هي وكأسها، منذ سنوات معاً.

يان... يان أندريا، "يا له من شاب ذي عينين مشعتين ووجه فيه براءة شاحبة". تردّد هذه العبارة في داخلها وهي تلمحه يتحرّك بين الضيوف، ويبتسم لها عن بعد وهو يدير جهاز التسجيل على موسيقى تحبّها، ثم يتجه نحوها ليمسكها من يدها ليرقصا معاً. كان ثلاثة من الأصدقاء يناقشون سياسة ميتران، بينما صديقتها الصحافية إيرما التي بلغت الخمسين قبل شهر تشاركهم الحديث بحماسة شديدة عن السياسة الجديدة لحزب العمال. تطوف نظرات مارغريت بينهم فيما يد يان تحيط بخصرها، تحس كم هي بعيدة، ليس هناك

---

٤. "هذا هو الحب" كتاب يان أندريا شتاينر عن علاقته مع مارغريت دوراس، وقد كتبه بعد رحيلها.

ما يدفع الحماسة بداخلها لأي مشاركة في الكلام، تود الاستماع بصمت، تود الرقص أيضاً بين ذراعي يان.

هي وهو يشكلان لوحة غريبة، لوحة عبثية مجنونة، تكسر كل الأفكار الثابتة عن خطوات الحب، والسن، والزمن. في العلاقة مع يان، كما في العلاقة مع جسدها، لا تنتظر سوى عطاء آني، آني فقط. ليس بينها وبين يان سوى "الآن" و"الآن فقط"، ماذا تريد أكثر من ذلك. لو حدثت معجزة استمرار "الآن"، فسيحصل الكثير من الفرح، لكن هذا لن يحدث لأن الزمن يمضي، لأن الأصدقاء سيذهبون، وهي مع مرور كل يوم ستكبر يوماً، ويان أندريا أيضاً سيزداد توهجاً قبل أن يبدأ بالأفول، هو أيضاً سيكبر مثلها، هو أيضاً سيرتكب جسده نحوه خيانات مختلفة. إنها معادلة الزمن الأبدية نتقدم كي نصل، نتوهج كي نأفل، نكبر كي نموت، محاصرون بهذا الرعب رغماً عنا، ولا نملك أمامه أي سبيل للنجاة. لو منحها جسدها بعض الصمود، الوقوف عند حد معيّن من الخيبة، يمكنها أن تستمر أكثر، وأن تكتب أكثر، الكلمات لا يصيبها الهرم، لا يزال لديها الكثير لتقوله، كتابتها لا تزال فتية وقادرة على الحركة بنشاط وسط هذا الركام. الكتابة هي الشيء الوحيد الذي ظل معها طوال الوقت... طوال الوقت، وفي كل أنواع الأحزان والمسرّات.

تذكرت عبارة دانيال حين كان يقول لها: "إن ميزة الحياة في قدرتك على رؤيتها من أكثر من وجه، وإيجاد أسباب دائمة للفرح". كانت تقاطعه لتقول: "وأسباب للحزن". يتمّم عبارته المبتورة قائلاً: "فرح وجودك في الحياة، ثم فرح استمرارك بها كل يوم شيء عظيم".

في الليل، وقفت مارغريت طويلاً أمام المرآة. نظرت إلى نهديها، كانا صلبين، ومتماسكين في وقت ما. كانت على ثقة بأنهما أجمل جزء

في جسدها، لكنه لم يعد كذلك، هي لم تعد هي، هاتان الساقان اللتان تظهر عروقهما النافرة، غريبتان عنها، هذا الجلد المتغضن ليس جلدها، متى حدث له كل هذا التحول، كيف تم في غفلة عنها. لكن الانهيارات لا تحدث فجأة، ثمة تصدّعات داخلية تبدأ بالتجمع تحت الطبقة السطحية، وحين تظهر يكون كل شيء قد انتهى، ويصير الترميم أمراً شكلياً لا يطال الجوهر الأصلي. هي ليست البنت الشابة التي كانت تركض سراً للقاء العاشق، هي ليست المرأة التي تندفع بنهم نحو الحياة، الحب، الشهوة. ثمة أشياء تفتر مع الوقت. أما يان أندريا وحضوره الذي يكسر عزلتها، فلا يسبّب لها سوى ارتباك يفجّر أسئلة عن شتى أنواع الحقائق التي أفنت عمرها بحثاً عنها.

خيانة الجسد تبدأ سريعاً، تحس بالعجز، أسرع بكثير مما تتوقع. ومع خذلان الجسد وخيانته، تبدأ الحاجة للعزلة والصمت، الحاجة الملحّة للكتابة، للتخلص من ذاكرة تنز تفاصيلها وتختلط مع الأحداث اليومية. لقد وعت أنها بحاجة للفصل بينهما: بين اليومي والمتذكر، ومن أجل هذا الوعي فرضت على نفسها اعتياد العزلة والتآلف معها. الكتابة لن تأتي إلا مع صمتها الطويل، حينها ستتحرك الأشباح القابعة في داخلها بحثاً عن الحرية، عن حياة جديدة عبر كلماتها. وحين يحصل كل هذا تنتبه مارغريت للخيانات اليومية التي يرتكبها جسدها. هل هناك أبشع من خيانة يدك حين تنوي الكتابة، ارتعاشة المفاصل، تمرّد الأصابع عن إمساك القلم، أنت ضعيف، واهن، لا تملك كلمة آمرة على أعضائك، مع مرور الوقت عرفت "ماغي" ـ هكذا كان يناديها دانيال ـ أنها تهدهد جسدها، وتحايله، تتوسّله سراً أن لا يصل في خياناته حداً لا رجوع منه.

منصور الصويِّم

أشباح فرنساوي
فصل من رواية

لم يكن فرنساوي حاضراً في الحكاية، لم يكن جزءاً من نسيج
الأحداث، تشابكاتها وتداخلاتها، انبهاماتها وانفصالاتِها؛ فرنساوي
حينها، حين تمفصلت الوقائع، وحين تمظهرت المصائر واستبانت
المآلات، بجناحي غمام، كان يحلق في برازخ انعتاقه الأبدي، ومن
هناك، من عمق الروح يشير؛ ويقول: نعم، هكذا يا ولد، تناسجت
الأشياء ... هكذا، بدأت رحلة البرازخ ... رحلة الأرضي، السماوي،
رحلة اللاانفكاك، اللاعودة، اللاصلح، اللاسلام، اللانوم، اللاراحة،
اللاشيء ... هكذا يا ولد انسج الحكاية، وتذكر أنه لا حكاية، لا
فرنساوي، لا دفاق وأرز خلا، لا إوزات رمادية ولا حبارات شائخة، لا
كسار بمياهه الكاسرة، لا قضاة سكارى ولا نساء راقصات، لا رقيب
أو عقيد أو جنود يلوّحون بأقدام تعبة، لا زمن مضى ولا زمن آتٍ، لا
أنا لا أنت ... يا ولد، طارد الخيوط، ألصق الرقاع ورتّب الألواح ...
وتذكرْ في زمنه كان فرنساوي وكانت الحكاية ... لا تنس، لا تَسْهُ،
لا تَحِد، هو الطريق يا ولد، فامضٍ ... يا ولد امضِ، امضِ.

... يمضي الولد، تقوده نداءات البرازخ، التماعات ذاكرات تعبة، شائخة ومشروخة ... في الدروب القديمة، مقتفياً الآثار الثملة، متشمّماً الروائح الحذقة ومترنحاً كما ترنّحت الطرقات والأزقة وقش البيوت في زمانه؛ مترقرقاً كما تترقرق الدموع في مآقي الذاكرات المتهالكة، التي باتت تنسى كل شيء وتتذكر كل شيء ... كما الصدف تقتنص أوقاتها، والأقدار ترتب لموضع ضرباتها؛ يمضي الولد، أعمى تقوده بصيرة، أصمّ تقوده غريزة، مقعد تقوده ريح، وغائب تقوده برازخ ... يمضي.

إلى أي مصير تجرّه يا فرنساوي، إلى أي أشراك ومصائد تقوده وأنت تتزاول أمامه بأنفك الراعف وسطوع عينيك، فأنت، يا فرنساوي، حرقت حتى الآن سبع أرواح، أتراه يكون ثامنهم؛ ذاك الذي راوغك وانسحب باكراً، ربما ليسخر منك هناك وأنت تحلق بين برازخك ... انظر إليه في وحل عمله اليومي، غارقاً وسط تفاهات الكلمات وقذاراتها مما يدفع به صحافيو السطحية والسلق السريع. المحتالون يغرقونه في مستنقعات لغاتهم الهزيلة وأفكارهم المترهلة، لكنه بك يلوذ وأنت تتشابح أمامه على شاشات الكمبيوترات وبين طيات أوراق الأصول، ولحظة مراجعة أولى الـA3 ... لك مهمة حقيقية الآن، فهو بك يقهر سخف أخبار الرياضة وسماجة أعمدة الرأي والسذاجة المبثوثة في صفحات الثقافة والفن، الولد المدقق اللغوي، يتشبّث بك، خاصة بمشهدك المثالي والرياح اللامحسوسة ترمي بك في قلب دوامات الكسار؛ يا فرنساوي، تذكر، حين سبحت والرصاصات تنزلق من جسدك اللامع تحت أشعة الصباح مثلما تنزلق عنه قطرات الماء وأنت

تفر صوب الدغل الصغير، حيث الجنود المختبئون بنقيبهم ورقيبهم وغزالهم المشوي ومؤنتهم من مريسة وبغو تكساس البااااارد ... بهذا المشهد السحري، خاصة يكافح بك محمد لطيف إعلانات المحاكم وشركات الاتصال وصفحات رؤساء التحرير، التي لا تموت أبداً ... يستحضرك عند هذا المشهد مثلما أفلته وتركه منزلقاً حضرة الرقيب بشير. نعم عاد بشير الآن وصار ينثر في ليالي انفلاتاته المتجدّدة حبات الحكاية، فتأمّل يا رجل، بعد كل هذه السنوات يعود بشير لنبش الماضي، متحجّجاً بزياراتك الدورية، وانصباب الشلة من جديد في متاهات مدينة أخرى، أكبر وأوسع وأكثر قساوة: حليل نيالا. هكذا يبدأ بشير هذياناته ثم ينداح كما انداحت مياه الكسار تحت وخزات الدوشكا وأنت تفر صوب الدغل الصغير؛ يا فرنساوي ...

إذاً أين محمد لطيف، المدقق اللغوي، السكير، الحزين، من فرح بانبثاقاتك الموسمية وتحليقات أطيافك التي لا تفتر ... إنه وسط بحيرة قرفه الصحافي يمد يده فانتشله يا برزخي.

نعم، ذاته الرقيب بشير، الذي يطلق صرخاته الشلة كل خميس برفقة محمد لطيف، المصحّح والقاص السكير، نعم ذاته الرقيب بشير، أطلق صرخاته هذه قبل خمس وعشرين سنة، داخل عنبر الجراحة والكسور بمستشفى نيالا الملكي، في سكون الفجر وهدوء المرضى داخل العنبر. أطلق بشير صرخاته، في الحقيقة هي صرخة واحدة بعدها سكن وهمد ودفن رأسه بين يديه. كانت مهمته مرافقة المصاب عوض فرنساوي حتى المستشفى، لم يكلفه أحد بملازمة الجسد المحطم المكسور العظام، وحده ودون استئذان قادته، اختار بشير مرافقته من القسم الجنوبي

لشرطة حيّ تكساس جنوب وحتى مستشفى نيالا الملكي، ثم اختار بعد ذلك ممارضته بعنبر الجراحة، مرتدياً زيّه الرسمي مضفياً على أجواء العنبر مسحة من رهبة بوجهه المتجهم وعينيه المحمرتين.

ـ لقد تحطمت أضلاعه وثقبت رئتاه.

هذا ما قاله الطبيب ثم أضاف:

هناك شق في جمجمته وربما يعاني من نزف داخلي.

لم يكن بشير منتبهاً لحديث الطبيب بقدر ما كان مدهوشاً لمرأى الدموع التي أخذت تنهمر من عيني فرنساوي مبللة شاربه الخفيف ولضمادات وجهه البيضاء ثم سائلة على عنقه النحيل.

ـ قد يفيق، كل شيء على الله.

قال الطبيب ذلك، ثم ربّت بيده شرائط الرقيب بشير. ثلاثة أيام بلياليها جلس بشير أمام الجسد المحطم الأضلاع والمشقوق الجمجمة، ثلاثة أيام لم ينم خلالها إلا لماماً، ثلاثة أيام وانهمار الدموع لم يتوقف من عيني فرنساوي المغمضتين في حزن وأسى، ثلاثة أيام والطبيب يمر ليمسح بمنديله سيلان الدموع ويأمر الممرضات بإبدال الدربات وحقن المريض بالمهدئات، ثلاثة أيام والرقيب بشير يناجي ربّه الذي لم يناجه من قبل لشفاء كسور فرنساوي وسلامته وعودته من جديد لنثر ضحكاته ونصب فخاخه وأشراكه. في اليوم الرابع، في فجر اليوم الرابع نام الرقيب بشير، دهمه تعب الأيام الثلاثة وحاصره النعاس، رمى عنقه على مسند كرسي البلاستيك وانزلق في سبات عميق، لم يدر متى وكم من الوقت استغرق في النوم، لكنه استيقظ ويد رقيقة تهزه برفق. كمن يخرج من غيبوبة شرع عينيه، ظنه حلماً

وهو يبصر فرنساوي يحدّق به مبتسماً ممسكاً بيده، حاول النهوض،
همس عوض فرنساوي:

ـ اقعد، ارتاح يا بشو.

ابتسم وهو يمسك بكفه، ظنه قد شفي، ابتسامته الوضيئة ترتسم
على وجهه الوسيم، اقترب بجسده من الفراش، أحس بألم يعكر وجه
فرنساوي، نزل على ركبتيه وهو يحتضن بكفيه يديه. قال فرنساوي:

ـ تعبت يا بشير ...

قال ذلك ثم حاول الارتفاع قليلاً عن الفراش، نهض معه بشير
مقترباً أكثر بوجهه من وجهه، أضاف فرنساوي:

ـ سأرحل الآن يا بشير، لكن ...

تأوّه وهو يقلّب عينيه اللوزتين في ألم، بينما بشير يضغط بكفيه على
اليد الصغيرة محاولاً إلهاء عينيه عن دموعهما الحبيسة، قال بشير:

ـ ستصحّ يا عوض، بس ارتاح.

قاطعه بابتسامة ناحلة وهو يقول:

ـ لا تحزن يا بشير، سأزورك كثيراً.

تقلب في توجع وأضاف:

ـ كما سأزورهم أولاد ...

ترقرقت الدموع من جديد بعينيه، لكنه همس محاولاً الارتفاع
بجسده:

ـ تعال با بشير، في هدية ندي ليك.

اقترب بشير أكثر حتى لامس بوجهه وجه فرنساوي الملفوف
بالضمادات والمبتل بالدموع، بيده الطليقة علق عوض فرنساوي حول

عنق بشير حجاباً جلدياً صغيراً ثم مرر يده على صفحة وجهه وهمس:
هذا سيحفظك في السنوات المقبلة، فقط لا تنزعه أبداً عن عنقك.

في ذلك الفجر الهادئ، أسلم عوض فرنساوي الروح، تاركاً الرقيب
بشير ينشج وجسده يرتج بأكمله من البكاء. في فجر ذلك اليوم خرج
الرقيب بشير لأول مرة منذ ثلاثة أيام من بوابة مستشفى نيالا الملكي؛
هواء بارد لفح وجهه، تقدم من أشجار النيم الشبحية في ظلام ذلك
الفجر، لمح أجساد المشردين والمشردات مكوّمة تحت جذوع الأشجار
وأسفل سور المستشفى، التفت بجسده صوب الغرب وأخذ يحدق
بأنوار قسم الأوسط، أبصر من مكانه ذاك ديدبان الحراسة منتصباً أمام
البوابة، شرطيين يتجولون داخل القسم وخارجه، أبصر عربة كروزر تعبر
ببطء من البوابة ثم تنطلق باتجاه الجنوب، وصلته صرخات جنودها
وهم يزعقون ويهللون ويكبرون، من مكانه ذاك أمام بوابة المستشفى،
أخذ بشير يرقب انبلاج الصباح؛ الأنوار المتقطعة لباصات المواصلات
الهرمة، بائعات الشاي المثابرات وهنّ يشرعن في إعداد قهاويهن المرتجلة
تحت أشجار النيم وقرب سور المستشفى، عمال يومية وعتالون
وسماسرة وصغار تجار السوق الجنوبي ينزلقون نحو السوق الكبير،
أسراب من جنود القسم الأوسط، يعتلون الإسفلت، بأزيائهم الرياضية
يركضون صوب الشمال، ممرضات وممرضون يخرجون من بوابة
المستشفى ويصطفون بانتظار الترحيل. الرقيب بشير يحدق بعينين
مغمومتين، يشعل سيجارة، يمرر أصابعه على القلادة حول عنقه،
حجاب نجاته في السنوات المقبلة، هدية مريضه الميت التي سيربطه به
إلى الأبد. يهمس، لنفسه، لهواء الصباح البارد، للشماسة والمشردين،

لبائعات الشاي، للتجار والعتالين، لصفوف الممرضين والممرضات، للجنود الراكضين والديدبان المنتصب بعيداً، للملازم ياسر الغائب وسيادة العقيد ووكيل العريف فريني، لعفاف؛ يهمس:

ـ مات فرنساوي، مات هذا الصباح.

يغلق محمد لطيف جهاز الكمبيوتر بعد تأكده من إخفاء الملف وتمويهه جيداً، يراقب الشاشة وهي تلج ظلامها، لكنه يتسمّر بمكانه وهو يبصرك من جديد، يراك يا فرنساوي وأنت مُسَجّى على فراش المستشفى ولا أحد قربك، مضى الرقيب بشير وتركك وحدك تعانق موتك، يعرف محمد لطيف بصورة ما أنك ستُغْسل بغرف غسل الغرباء بمقابر الكنغو، وأنك ستدفن بمساعدة نفر قليل من عمال المستشفى، يعرف هذا كما أنه يعرف أن ملف موتك المغلق والمنسي لن يفتح صفحاته بعد أعوام طوال أحد سواه، حين تجمعه ليالي سكر مدمّرة مع رقيب مثقف منسحب من البوليس اسمه بشير، يقضيان الليالي يصرخان وهما يناديانك ويعتذران؛ نعم يعتذر محمد لطيف لأنه جاء إلى العالم بعد انصرافك، ويعتذر بشير لأنك تركت العالم وأودعته العذاب.

يخرج محمد لطيف الآن، يقطع المسافة بين الجريدة وموقف المواصلات ماشياً، يستعيد في مشيته سرد الأحداث المنثورة في عشوائية. يتذكر أن فرنساوي قبل أن يسلم الروح ذكر للرقيب بشير شيئاً عن حسرات وندم ستعصف بسيادة العقيد وزمرته من وجهاء المدينة، عن شرارات نار ستحاصره ولن تتركه إلا رماداً، ثمة شيء آخر ينسبه لك يا فرنساوي، ويثق بأنه سمعه من فم بشير الثمل: حرائق وموت وزخات

رصاص تخترق الأجساد وتفجر الرؤوس، هروب وفناء ودمار كامل ...
بقدمه يشوت محمد لطيف حصاة صغيرة، يشعل سيجارة، الليلة لن
يذهب إلى السامراب شمال ليسكر ويهذي برفقة بشير وأصدقائه من
السكارى الملاحيس، سيقضي ليلته في القراءة أو نائماً أو في حضن
أول امرأة من الشارع تصادفه ... يحاول التحرر من شبحيتك الخانقة
يا فرنساوي وهو ينسل وسط زحام موقف المواصلات، لكنك تبرز
له كالجان وتحاصره. داخل الحافلة المتجهة إلى الفتيحاب؛ يتكئ بعنقه
على النافذة ويستدعيك، يبصرك مترقرقاً على سطح مياه النيل الأبيض
والعربة تعبر الجسر ... في دُفّاق على حدود أفريقيا الوسطى، تنتشلك
فرقة ضالّة أو مُضللة من فرق الشرطة، تقودهم من رهد إلى رهد[1] ومن
واد إلى واد ومن دغل إلى دغل، خمسة عشر يوماً تجولون في الخلاء البكر،
تصطادون الحباري والغزلان والأرانب البرية، تسبحون في مياه الرهود
والأودية، تشوون البفرة وعيش الريف وتمصون أعواد العنكوليب[2]،
تجربون طلقات بنادقكم في تفجير ثمار البطيخ والتبش[3] وإسقاط
حبات الباباي والدوم ... تريهم قدراتك في اصطياد أبشوك[4] وسلخ
شوكه وهو حيّ يفرفر بين يديك ... خمسة عشر يوماً يا فرنساوي
وأنتم تضللون النهابين ورجال القبائل الملثمين، تتحاشون مسالكهم
ودروبهم. كنت تقودهم بذكاء وحنكة يا فرنساوي وأنت تُراطِن قائدهم
النقيب ياسر بفرنسية طريفة ...

---

١. الرهد مجرى مائي خريفي.
٢. نبات أشبه بقصب السكر من حيث الطعم، يزرع في الخريف.
٣. نوع من الخضروات المحلية.
٤. حيوان صغير يتميز بجلد يكسوه الشوك ولحمه يؤكل.

وهو يرتمي تعباً ومتهالكاً على فراشه بمنزل الأم بالفتيحاب،
يتخفف من أحمالك الثقيلة، ينزلك بتكساس، أمام منزل البطلة،
يدفعك من الباب، باب الزنك بصريره المزعج ثم يسمعك تنادي:
بشير يا بشييييير. يتركك هناك وينام.

لكنك، أيها الشبحي المراوغ، ما تنفك تزوره في أحلامه
وكوابيسه، في نوماته القصيرة المتقطعة يبصرك، تتراءى له معلقاً على
فروع شجرة نِيمْ، مربوط من قدميك، شخص ما؛ يرتدي الكاكي،
يقترب منك، بمحاذاتك يقف ثم يصرخ: الآن استعدوا. يدفعك بكلتا
يديه ويبتعد، تتطوح كالأرجوحة، بعينيك الغاضبتين، من أعلى
لأسفل، تمسح أجساد الكاكي وهي في وضع الاستعداد، عشرات
الأجساد ترتكز على ركبها وتسند على أكتافها بنادق الكلاش،
ثم يصمّ الدوي أذنيك، مئات الطلقات ترشق جسدك النحيل في
تأرجحه السريع، البطيء، المتلاشي ... وأنت تتدور معلقاً تسمع
ضحكاتهم وقهقهاتهم، تحس بأيديهم تحصي الثقوب على ثيابك
الممزقة ثم إظلام ... يستيقظ الولد: اللعنة يا بشير.

هكذا إذن يقضي محمد لطيف أيامه معذباً بك، منذ أن تلقفك
هذيانات متشنجة من فم الرقيب بشير، منذ أن أقسم على أن
يلتقيهم واحداً واحداً وإن مكث باقي عمره يبحث عنهم، من خلال
هذيانات بشير حفظ الأسماء: العريف فريني، درس الهندسة وهو الآن
نقيب بالشرطة الهندسية، مولانا عصمت، ترك القضاء، وهو الآن محام
بالسوق العربي، الملازم ياسر، يمثل الآن شيئاً ما عظيماً وكبيراً بشرطة
الجمارك، تاجر البن خليل، يعمل الآن خفيراً مع منظمات الإغاثة بنيالا

(الوحيد الذي بقي هناك)، العقيد، سيادة مدثر الجاك، سيادة العقيد،
يا فرنساوي ... حفظ لطيف الأسماء وتمسّك بأهداب الهذيانات
وكوابيس الليل وما يخطه على جهاز التصحيح بعد ذهاب إدارة
التحرير، الولد المُصحّح حرفاً حرفاً سيسكبك يا فرنساوي، حرفاً
حرفاً سينثر حبات البن، وينتزع نجوم الأكتاف ويبعثر أوراق القضاة
والمحامين وموظفي الضرائب ... أشباح من تطارد من يا فرنساوي.

في الصباح، قبل أن يغسل وجهه، وقبل أن يرمي للأم بتحية الصباح،
وقبل أن يربط حذاءه ويرمي على كتفه حقيبة كل المهام، في الصباح قبل
كل شيء سينكفئ على كرّاساته ويسوّدها بكوابيس الليل وبسيل من
هذيانات بشير ومجتزآت من تاريخه المقبور، يكتب محمد لطيف:

ذات عصر فاتر يمسك الرقيب بشير بخرطوش الماء ويبدأ برش
رمل القسم الجنوبي بتكساس، متجولاً داخل باحة القسم يجر
خرطوشه وينثر رذاذ الماء على ذرات الرمل الناعم، هدوء ذلك العصر
حفزه على التفكير بحماسة في أمسية اليوم؛ كل شيء معد وفق
ما خطط له، عند العاشرة بالضبط ستحضر رملة وصويحباتها من
بنات حيّ الثورة، أمر العرقي البكر محسوم، فإلى جانب المُصادَر
بالقسم، هناك كمية محترمة محجوزة لدى البطلة، كما أن هناك
ثلاث زجاجات ويسكي أرسلها تاجر البن خليل، الخراف المشوية
جاهزة، سيحضرها أبكر بيلو صانع الأقاشي الرشيق، المدعوون
سيبدأون بالتوافد منذ التاسعة، سيادة العقيد كالعادة سيحضر
متأخراً جداً مما سيتيح لهم التلذذ بالأقاشي والعرقي وبعض
الويسكي، والأهم أن رملة وصويحباتها سيندلقن دون مفاجآت،

كما في أمسية اليوم ستدار المباراة المنتظرة بين الملازم ياسر والقاضي عصام، ستكون ممتعة وخاصة أن عصام مولانا لا يسكر أبداً وإن تجرع برميلاً من الشراب المرّ والمعتق ... وهو يجر خرطوش الماء دائراً في الباحة ومدوراً للأفكار في رأسه، وجد بشير نفسه يقترب من البوابة الرئيسية للقسم، ومن مكانه أسفل شجرة الليمون المُزهِرَة أبصرهم قادمين، ستة أو سبعة، كالحين ومغبرين، اقتربوا من القسم في ثبات، لكنهم توقفوا قرب البوابة وتركوا أكبرهم سناً يقترب من شجرة الليمون المُزهِرة ويصافح حضرة الرقيب.

أهلاً في شنو؟

يقول بشير، ويجيبه شيخ الريفيين:

جنابك بَقُرنا اتنهبت، جايين نفتح بلاغ.

يرمي بشير خرطوش الماء على حوض الليمونة المُزهِرة ويسأل الشيخ بلؤم:

لماذا لم تذهبوا للقسم الرئيسي.

يقول الشيخ:

قالوا لينا بنتبع للقسم دا.

قال هذا وأخذ يحدق بوجه الرقيب باللؤم ذاته، أشاح بشير بوجهه، ثم أشار بيده صوب مكتب البلاغات:

امشوا المكتب داك بتلقوا الضابط.

تحرّك الشيخ الريفي ومن ورائه رهطه من الريفيين ... وقف بشير في مكانه وهو يسُبُّ الريفيين وأبقارهم وأوساخهم وكل نهابي الإقليم وصعاليكه، حاول استعادة سلسلة تأملاته حول سهرة اليوم لكنه فشل،

ماذا لو دفعوا به في عملية جديدة من عمليات النهب المسلح، لقد سئم المجازفة ومطاردة نهابين لا يهابون الموت، يود لو يتركونه يستمتع قليلاً بالحياة، رملة وعفاف ورمال تكساس الباردة، أوقف سيل أفكاره وهو يبصر الملازم خارجاً من مكتبه ومن خلفه الريفيون المتسخون، لا بد أن المهمة راقته؛ هذا المستجد المتعجرف، حدّث نفسه وهو يشد قامته تحية للملازم الصغير، قال الملازم وهو يضع كابه على رأسه:

سنمضي للرئاسة لفتح البلاغ، كن مستعداً.

ثم أضاف وهو يفتح باب عربة اللاندروفر المركونة قرب البوابة:

في كل الأحوال كن مستعداً ... السهرة أو الخروج في مهمة طويلة ...

ابتسم الملازم بخبث وهو يغمز بعينه للرقيب بشير، الذي تصلب بمكانه وأخذ يتابع العربة وهي تخرج عبر البوابة والريفيون الأجلاف معلقون عليها. جلب كرسياً من داخل مكتب البلاغات، غرسه في طين الليمونة المزهرة ورفع رجليه على جذعها الصلب، لن يحتاجوا إلى أفراد من قسمنا، أخذ يفكر، القوة بالرئاسة كافية، ثم إنه من فترة لم تخرج أية قوة لمطاردة النهابين، ركن للفكرة، القوة ستكون كافية بالرئاسة والقسم الأوسط ولن يحتاجوا لإمداد من الأقسام الطرفية والبعيدة، لكن قد يُكلّف الملازم بالمهمة، الملازم فقط، قائد الفرقة الجديد، المنقول حديثاً من العاصمة ... ابتسم في حبور وهو يُقصِي نفسه عن المأمورية ويبصر الملازم متورّطاً في أوحالها وحبالها ... نهض نشطاً واتجه صوب مكمن السهرة خلف الحراسات، وجد وكيل

العريف فريني والجندي صالح منهمكين في لعب الكوتشينة، سألهما
وهو يحرّك عينيه في المكان:

كلو تمام.

أجابه فريني:

تمام جنابك.

التلج، الكولا، الترمس، المدمس ...

قاطعه صالح:

والجراد والزيتون والجبنة المضفورة ...

قاطعه فريني:

قلنا نطلع الكراسي والترابيز قريب للموعد.

قال بشير:

جميل، ما عايز أغلاط، الناس الليلة مهمين وسيادة العقيد
بنفسه موصينا.

لم يكن هناك فعلياً ما يوّديه الجنود الثلاثة وضابطهم الجديد الصغير
السن، كانوا يقضون نهاراتهم في لعب الكوتشينة والليدو، بلاغات
صغيرة وتافهة ظلت ترد إليهم أحياناً وتحسّسهم بمهامهم كشرطيين،
سرقات مخجلة داخل الحي؛ أغنام منزلية، ملاءات وملابس قديمة، رجل
سكران مزعج، مشاجرة في عرس ... أشياء مملة أغرقت الجنود في بحيرة
من الكسل والخمول، فقط خميسات العقيد هي التي كانت تخرجهم
من رتابة أيام القسم الجنوبي بتكساس وسكونيتها، تلك الخميسات
المنتزعة من صلب الجنون والمغمسة بالنزق والترف السلطوي. بشير فكر
أكثر من مرة أن سيادة العقيد هو من اقترح زرع القسم الجنوبي بأطراف

حي تكساس البعيد أصلاً عن المدينة، أمسيات مجنونة وسهرات ماجنة أقامها العقيد برفقة أصدقائه من كبار رجالات المدينة. قضاة ومحامون وسياسيون محليون، موظفو المحافظة وموظفو بنوك وضرائب وزكاة وتجار محليون ووافدون، ثمة نساء كذلك، زوجات متعهرات، بائعات شاي، بائعات فواكه بسوق الملجة، مغنيات محليات، عاهرات، قوادات، سحاقيات، كل الغريب والمنفلت كان يجمعه العقيد ويفرغه في أمسيات تكساس ... تلك الخميسات متنفس العقيد وبطانته، تلك الخميسات، مجرى فصامات العقيد، انفجارات غضبه المجنون، أمسيات فرحه الهستيري ... تلك الخميسات، الجنون، الصراخ والبكاء، المشاجرات العنيفة، محاولات القتل ومحاولات الانتحار ... العقيد المجنون اختار بعناية جنوده للقسم الجنوبي بتكساس، حتى رئيس القسم، الضابط الجديد، الملازم المنقول حديثاً من عاصمة البلاد، أبصر فيه سيادة العقيد ثقوباً تسد احتياجاته، لذا أرسله إلى هناك، إلى تكساس، القسم الجنوبي، قائداً على قوة تتكوّن من ثلاثة جنود.

نسي بشير مع نهايات عصر ذلك اليوم أمر الريفيين وأبقارهم المنهوبة جنوباً وحضرة الملازم الذي خرج برفقتهم، حمّى السهرة كانت قد بدأت تجتاحه وهو يقلب الاحتمالات: احتمال أن يغش الجميع في لعبة قمار مضروبة، احتمال أن يتلقى ورقة صغيرة من ضابط إداري البلدية تكفيه مؤونة قرية من السكر، احتمال أن يبيعهم مخزون القسم من العرقي المصادر بأضعاف ثمنه، احتمال أن يعتصر رملة وحيداً بمكتب الملازم الصغير ... احتمالات متعددة تعتمد على مدى سكرهم وحجم انفلاتات العقيد أخذ يديرها بشير برأسه، أشعل

سيجارة، جر كرسي البلاستيك وخرج من البوابة، عند ناصية القسم الخارجية وضع كرسيه؛ لكنه قبل أن يضع مؤخرته عليه لمح مقدمة الكروزر الأولى تخرج من بين زقاقات بيوت القش والطين ... استند بيديه إلى الكرسي وهو يرقب العربات الثلاث بجنودها ودوشكاتها المنصوبة تقترب من القسم، منه تقترب وحضرة الملازم من مقدمة إحداها يحدق به مبتسماً.

قفز الملازم الصغير، البهي الطلعة، ممسكاً بيمينه كلاش العمليات وبيسراه كابه الحربي، قال لبشير وهو يجتاز البوابة إلى الداخل:

جهز نفسك ح نطلع قبل الغروب.

ممسكاً بمسند كرسي البلاستيك بيديه كان بشير يحدق مغتاظاً بالجنود الصغار على ظهور الكروزرات، يحتضنون رشاشاتهم الخفيفة ويهزون أقدامهم المدلاة خارج الظهريات ببطء ورتابة. لم ينتبه للريفيين المنحشرين وسط الجنود في إحدى الكروزرات إلا بعد أن لمح كبيرهم وهو يرتفع بهامته ويصدمه بنظراته المتحدية.

في ذلك الخميس البعيد فكر بشير بعصيان أوامر حضرة الملازم، بل فكر في شكواه لسيادة العقيد، لكبير ضباط إداريي المحافظة، لمدير قسم مكافحة التهريب ولاختصاصي الباطنية الوحيد بالمدينة، إلى مولانا عصام قاضي محاكم النظام الخاصة، إلى البطلة بائعة العرقي ... إلى أميرة أميرة العاهرات، إلى كوجن كبير قوادي المدينة إلى ... لكنه وجد نفسه مع انسدال عصر ذلك اليوم ملتصقاً بجسده مع جسد الملازم، في المقعد الأمامي لإحدى كروزرات وحدات مكافحة النهب المسلح، يدخن سيجارة ماركة برنجي ويتابع

في مرآة العربة الجانبية مجموعة أطفال عراة يجرون خلف الكروزرات فرحين وضاحكين. تلك كانت البداية لاستعادة أبقار الريفيين المنهوبة؛ التي لن تستعاد أبداً.

منصورة عز الدين

Déjà vu

لمع المشهد في ذهن سميحة فجأة بينما تقف بسيارتها في ذلك السوق الشعبي للخضار!

كانت تقود بسرعة كبيرة على الطريق الدائري آتية من مصر الجديدة إلى حدائق الأهرام حيث تقيم، وبينما تدندن بكلمات أغنية لنجاة الصغيرة، سهت ونزلت من منزِل "صفط اللبن" بدلاً من "المريوطية"، فوجئت بنفسها في منطقة غريبة تماماً عنها للدرجة ظنت معها أنها في مكان غير المدينة التي ولدت فيها.

منطقة شعبية، شوارعها ضيقة وغير معبدة، يتوسطها سوق صغير للخضروات يجعل العبور بالسيارة مستحيلاً دون الاصطدام بفرشات الطماطم والباذنجان والبصل المتناثرة هنا وهناك. منطقة تشبه كثيراً وصف كريم لمكان سكنه.

بدأت تشعر بالارتباك فقللت من سرعة سيارتها، وفجأة أحست أنها مرت بهذا الموقف من قبل، كأنها ليست في هذا المكان بالفعل بقدر ما تتذكر أنها كانت كذلك في الماضي، كانت بكل ما يجري

حولها كأنها مجرد ذكرى مختزنة في عقلها، ذكرى ظلت مأسورة لسنوات ثم تحررت فجأة لتبدو كلحظة حاضرة.

لم تكن المرة الأولى التي تختبر فيها حالة "Déjà vu"، غير أنها الأكثر غرابة، في المرات السابقة اعتادت أن تحس فقط بأنها مرت باللحظة من قبل، وتجبر نفسها على التفوّه بكلمات معيّنة كي تتطابق مع ما تتذكر أنها عاشته قبلاً، ثم فجأة يتلاشى كل شيء من ذاكرتها، تصبح الذكرى مجرد بقعة خافتة الإضاءة في صحراء شاسعة من العتمة.

أما الآن فتشعر بأن هذا المكان الذي تراه للمرة الأولى قد فتح باباً لمنطقة معتمة بداخلها، لحياة ربما عاشتها في السابق. رأت نفسها وكأنها تناضل للخروج من حطام حادث مروّع، ثم تلاشى كل شيء من جديد، وعادت مرة أخرى امرأة تناضل لتخرج بسيارتها من هذه المنطقة المزدحمة والضيقة.

خرجت إلى شارع مواز لشارع السوق لكنه أوسع منه، ثم وجدت نفسها في النهاية في منطقة المريوطية التي اتجهت منها إلى حدائق الأهرام، فبدأت تشعر بالهدوء.

وكما انبثق المشهدُ في رأسها من العدم، انبثق أيضاً وجهُ امرأة شابة بعينين واسعتين ذواتيْ نظرة عميقة، وجبهة بارزة قليلاً للأمام، امرأة تشبه خادمتها نورا تماماً.

كانتا تسيران معاً في مكان مشابه للسوق، نورا تسعل بشدة، وسميحة تربت كتفها محاولة أن تشغلها بثرثرات لا تنتهي.

رن صوت سعال نورا في أذنها كما لو كان حقيقة حاضرة، كأنها تراها وجسدها يرتعش قليلاً من أثر السعال المتواصل، غير أن المكان

الذي كانتا تتحركان فيه ظل غامضاً، هو فقط يشبه سوق الخضار بضوضائه وزحامه، لكنه يبدو كما لو أنه غارق في ضباب كثيف.

حاولت تجاهل الأمر والتركيز فقط على الطريق أمامها، لكنّ جسد نورا المرتعش ووجهها ذا العينين الواسعتين استمر في التراقص أمام سميحة حتى وصلت إلى بيتها.

كانت تشعر بانقباض لا تفهم مبرّره. دخلت إلى حجرة نومها، تمدّدت على الفراش وعيناها مثبتتان على السقف. ومن دون مقدّمات جاءتها الأحداث كما لو كانت تحلم: نورا تتألم بجوارها بصوت مجروح من دون أن تبصرها، فيما هي محشورة في مقعد السائق غير قادرة على تمييز أي شيء حولها سوى صوت الأنين المختلط بضجة مزعجة وطنين يكاد يشق رأسها، وخبط متواصل على أبواب السيارة. من بين هذه الضجة ميّزت جملة "دي ماتت" قبل أن يتلاشى كل شيء.

غرقت في النوم، وحين استيقظت كانت ما تزال مرتدية ملابس الخروج وتعاني من صداع شديد وشعور بضيق بالغ تخلّفه عادة ليلة مليئة بالكوابيس برغم عدم تذكرها لأي منها. ذهنها فقط مشبّع بشذرات مبهمة تبعث على كآبة غير مفهومة. أخذت جملة "دي ماتت" ترن في رأسها بلا توقف.

بدت نورا كأنما تختبئ منها في ظلام مبهم للحظات قبل أن تعود لتظهر لها من جديد. سعال وجسد مرتعش وعينان واسعتان ... امرأتان تسيران معاً في ما يشبه سوقاً شعبياً قديماً ولا شيء أكثر.

سحبت الهاتف الموضوع على الكومود بجوارها، واتصلت بكريم.

كانت موقنة بأنه لم يفق من نومه بعد، لذا لم تستسلم حين لم يرد من المرة الأولى، عاودت المحاولة بإلحاح لن ينفع معه أي تجاهل.

خرج صوتها متوتراً رغماً عنها: تعال فوراً ... الحقني!

أنهت المكالمة كعادتها قبل أن تستمع لرده. خافت أن يواصل نومه متجاهلاً إياها، فكرت أن تهاتفه مرة أخرى، لكنها لم تفعل لتذكرها جملته، التي صفعت أذنها في نوبة من نوبات غضبه النادرة، بأنه ملّ من مكالماتها المماثلة، وأنه يحضر فقط خوفاً من دوامات الشكوى والنحيب التي ستغرقه بها لو تجاهلها، لم يعد يخشى كثيراً أن تكون في ورطة فعلية.

تتخيّله ينهض ببطء من الفراش بعد أن أيقظته هي، وتتخيّل أخرى شابة راقدة بجواره. تزعجها الفكرة، فتضع "سيناريو" بديلاً، تراه يزيح الغطاء عن جسده بنشاط، ويقوم مسرعاً، تتعثر قدمه، فيقع بقوة على كوعه الأيمن، يلعن حظه العاثر. يتذكر أنه لم يرها منذ عشرة أيام، فيعرف أن حظه ليس عاثراً لتلك الدرجة، يكفي أنها هي من اتصلت به، بدلاً من أن يزورها هو فجأة، أو يلح عليها كي تقابله.

يترك هذا السيناريو هو الآخر كآبة لا تنقصها، تتساءل: كيف لم يتصل بها طوال عشرة أيام؟!

في العاشرة تماماً سمعت رنّة جرس الباب، أنصتت لصوت نورا ترحّب به بحماسة، وتقوده إلى حيث تجلس هي في الشرفة المطلة على الأهرام.

جلست سميحة شاردة وحزينة وقد رفعت شعرها الأسود كله لأعلى وهى ترتدي فستاناً بلا أكمام من الكتان الأزرق وأمامها على المنضدة

زجاجة نبيذ وعدة أطباق مليئة بـ"المازات". لم تعتد أن تشرب مبكراً هكذا، لكنها اليوم غير قادرة على تحمّل مزاجها الكئيب دون شرب.

صبّت له بعض النبيذ في الكأس. بمجرّد أن رأته، ومن دون أي كلمات ترحيب، أشارت إلى الكرسي المواجه لها كي يجلس. لم تتكلم معه لمدة ... فقط تنظر بشرود نحو الأهرام القريبة أو تراقب نباتات الحديقة من جهنمية وياسمين وقرنفل باهتمام، تتناول المكسّرات، وترشف رشفة من كأسها بين آن وآخر. تشاغل عنها بأكل الكاجو واللوز فتذكرت مصطفى حبيبها السابق الذي عرّفها على كريم، اعتادت أن تقارن بينهما، أحبّت مصطفى كثيراً، تحمّلت نزقه وشكها الدائم في إخلاصه لها، لطالما تساءلت: هل عرّفها على كريم حين بدأ يضجر منها؟ أكان واثقاً من أنها ستعجب بصديقه، وساعتها يمكنه التخلص منها دون تهديداتها المتواصلة بالانتحار؟ ندمت فجأة على هذه التهديدات، وتمنّت لو تمسحها من حياتها ككل لا من ذاكرتها فقط. هل أخبره كريم أن علاقته بها بدأت قبل أن يهجرها هو؟ لا تعرف لماذا هاتفت كريم في اليوم التالي مباشرة؟ ولا كيف انتهى الأمر بهما معاً في الفراش؟

استدارت إليه أخيراً، وقد عادت لها ابتسامتُها الساحرة، كأنما ضغطت زراً مسح عنها الحزن والتوتر وأحضر ابتسامة موظفي العلاقات العامة.

سألته:

تفتكر إني ممكن اقتل؟ أو على الأقل أكون اتسببت في موت حد؟

أجابها بلا تفكير:

لو ممكن تقتلي كنتي قتلتي مصطفى.

انزعجت بشدة.بمجرد أن نطق باسم مصطفى، بينهما اتفاق غير
معلن على تحاشي ذكر اسمه ... ككل قواعد علاقتهما، كانت هي
من سّن هذه القاعدة من غير أن تقولها صراحة.

اعتادت أن تشير إلى حبيبها السابق بـ"هو". تقول إنها مدينة له
بالكثير ... علمها كيف تستمتع بأغاني أم كلثوم بعد أن قضت
عمرها كله في الاستماع للأغاني الأجنبية وحدها. وتسهب في كيف
جعلها تستسيغ الروائح الشرقية بعد أن كانت لا تطيقها. يمكنها أن
تتحدث لساعات عن أفضال تافهة له عليها، دون أن تشير إلى أنه
استولى على جزء كبير من ثروتها. مثل كريم كان يصغرها بأكثر من
عشرين عاماً وينتمي لأسرة فقيرة. اعتاد أن يرافقها كظلها في كل مكان
تكون فيه. وهو معها لا يبدو على الإطلاق كحبيب لها، كان يشبه
مساعداً شخصياً أو سكرتيراً يتودّد لأصدقائها وصديقاتها. وهو ما
يفعله كريم حالياً كأنه تحول إلى دوبلير أو وريث له. وريث أقل مهارة
وجاذبية.

انتقل انزعاجها إلى كريم، وندم بشدة على نطقه باسم مصطفى،
غير أنها لحسن الحظ عادت لتجاهل ما يقوله، مواصلةً كلامها:

كريم أنا شفت كأني اتسببت في موت نورا. هل ممكن أكون آذيتها
في حياة سابقة وراجعة تنتقم مني؟

لمحت ارتباكاً سرعان ما نجح في قمعه قبل أن يسألها ساخراً:

حياة إيه حضرتك؟!

نظرت له بريبة، كأنها تفكر في وضعه مع نورا في خانة أعداء

٦٨

الحيوات السابقة. إلا أنها مسحت فجأة نظرة الريبة، وبدأت مونولوجاً طويلاً لا علاقة له بما كانت تقوله.

تكلمت عن تقلبات الطقس وأخلاق الرعاع التي سيطرت على المجتمع، وزيادة الفقر والأصولية. كانت تتحدّث كأنها تدلو بآراء خطيرة في برنامج تلفزيوني، ومن وقت لآخر تنظر حولها بخفة كأن هناك متفرجين غير مرئيين يتابعونها باهتمام.

كلمات كثيرة قالتها دون أن تلاحظ أن كريم لم ينتبه إلى حرف واحد منها، لأنه انشغل بمراقبة شفتيها المكتنزتين، وتأمّل تفاصيل جسدها الذي بدأ يميل للترهّل، ونظرة عينيها المغلفة بطبقة كثيفة من الغموض الموحي المتحدّي لبصمات السنوات القاسية على بشرتها. وجّهت بصرها إليه، فتعرفت على نظرته حين يشتهيها. وودّت لو يمارس الجنس معها الآن.

حتى أثناء الجنس كانت لا تتنازل عن ابتسامتها المرسومة بعناية على شفتيها. تغمض عينيها فتبدو كما لو أصبحت في عالم آخر، وحين ينتهيان يبدأ توتّرها. تنغلق على نفسها وتبكي في بعض الأحيان، أو تتعامل معه بحدة غير مبرّرة، قبل أن تعتذر باكيةً بعدها بساعات أو في اليوم التالي.

التقطت عيناها انحسار الشهوة العابرة عن محيّاه، ليعود محاولاً الإنصات، فواصلت مونولوجها الذي يجعلها تبدو كما لو كانت تصدّق كل كلمة فيه.

هذا الصدق البادي عليها في كل تصرفاتها خاصة حين تكذب كان أكثر ما يميّزها. لم يكن تمثيلاً، أو على الأقل كان ذلك النوع من

التمثيل الذي يتماهى فيه الممثل مع الشخصية التي يؤديها بحيث تكف شخصيته الأصلية عن الوجود. غير أن المذهل في حالتها أنها كانت كل يوم بشخصية مختلفة، تتقمّصها، ثم تهجرها في اليوم التالي لشخصية أخرى. كانت أحياناً تتحول من شخصية لأخرى بسرعة مزعجة، في جلسة واحدة تكون المرأة المثالية، داعية المحبة، فالضعيفة الواقفة على شفا انهيار عصبي حاد، ثم الأنثى الخطرة القوية الشخصية المهووسة بالسيطرة، إلى آخر الشخصيات المختلفة التي تدور بينها دون أن تتنازل أبداً عن طابعها الأرستقراطي أو الابتسامة الرقيقة المرسومة على شفتيها والتي تضفي عليها مزيداً من الغموض.

ظهرت نورا فجأة. مرّت بالقرب منهما، ونظرت لها، فارتبكت لبرهة. غادرت نورا الشرفة، فتبعتها هي بسرعة بعد أن استأذنته لدقيقة. عادت من جديد وابتسامتها المغوية تتألق على شفتيها، غير أن حزناً عميقاً بدأ يسكن نظرتها.

بدت شاردة، وتساءلت هل وصلت همهماتها الغاضبة مع نورا إلى أذنه؟ حتى هذه اللحظة لم ترد أن تخبره بالسبب الحقيقي وراء اتصالها الصباحي به وإصرارها على حضوره فوراً. بعد أن قررت أن تناقش معه كل شيء بهدوء، عادت وترددت.

بات صوتها أكثر خفوتاً عما سبق، ومن وقت لآخر كانت تنظر نحو المكان الذي وقفت نورا فيه منذ قليل.

رجعت نورا بخطوات صاخبة، تحمل في يدها باقة من القرنفل البلدي، يبدو أنها قطفتها لتوّها من الحديقة. خصّته بنظرة

متفحصة في طريقها إلى المزهرية الموضوعة على طاولة صغيرة في طرف الشرفة. أخرجت الورود المتفتحة من المزهرية ووضعت باقة القرنفل بدلاً منها، ثم حملت الورود وغادرت وهي تدندن بكلمات أغنية مبهمة. في هذه الأثناء كانت سميحة صامتة تماماً، تعتريها رجفة خفيفة.

بمجرد خروج نورا من الشرفة، انتفضت سميحة قائمة، فقام بدوره.

قالت بصوت خافت:

مش هنعرف نتكلم هنا، إيه رأيك نخرج سوا بالليل؟

رد بخفوت مقلداً إياها:

— مش هينفع، أنا مفلس ومحبط.

قامت بنشاط، واختفت لدقائق، عادت بمبلغ أعطته إياه مبتسمة، ثم قادته إلى الخارج. وما إن أصبحا في الحديقة، يقفان بين شجيرات الجهنمية والقرنفل البلدي، حتى طلبت منه عنوانه واعدةً إياه بمفاجأة مفرحة.

فور ابتعاده، أخذت تتجول وحدها في الحديقة، اقتربت من شجيرة ورد بلدي، مدّت يدها نحو وردة حمراء لم تتفتح بعد، فنغزتها شوكة حادة، تراجعت للخلف قليلاً وقد طفرت الدموع من عينيها. مسحتها بسرعة واستدارت في طريقها للداخل، خيّل إليها للحظات أن نورا تراقبها عبر النافذة من وراء الستار، إلا أنها حين دققت النظر لم تجد أحداً.

بعد الرابعة عصراً أخبرت نورا أنها ذاهبة لمقابلة صديقة لها ولن تأتي إلا متأخرة. تركت سيارتها، واستقلت سيارة أجرة، طلبت من

سائقها أن يوصلها إلى عنوان كريم ... نظر الرجل إلى ملابسها الأنيقة وطلتها الأرستقراطية محاولاً تبيّن سبب توجّهها إلى هذا المكان، لكنه لم يتكلم.

تذكرت فجأة أن نورا وضعت الورد البلدي في المزهرية، وعادت بعد ساعة لتضع باقة القرنفل بدلاً منه بلا مبرّر. أبعدت الفكرة عنها وحاولت استدعاء كريم إلى ذهنها، أزعجتها نظرة معيّنة لمحته يختلسها إلى خادمتها الشابة. كانت سيارة الأجرة قد وصلت إلى منطقة "صفط اللبن" بشوارعها الترابية الضيقة ... تأملت الفوضى المنتشرة، والبيوت القديمة شبه المتلاصقة، فشعرت بالمسافة التي تفصل كريم عنها، وتضايقت لذلك. فكرت أن الإحساس نفسه لا بد أنه يصله حين يسير بجوارها في نادي الجزيرة أو حفلات الكوكتيل في بيوت صديقاتها.

توقفت سيارة الأجرة، وأشار السائق إلى بناية قريبة. خرجت من السيارة لتجد نفسها في سوق مشابه للذي تاهت فيه أمس. سارت متصنعة الهدوء والجميع ينظر إليها باندهاش. أدركت أن دخولها شقة كريم سيلفت الأنظار حتماً، فتراجعت عن الفكرة ووقفت في ركن منزوٍ تتأمل المكان الذى يعيش فيه. فكرت أن نورا لو جاءت هنا وأرادت التسلل إلى شقة كريم فستكون مهمتها أسهل. لن تبدو غريبة مثلها هكذا عن المكان.

استدارت عائدة إلى السيارة التي كانت لا تزال في انتظارها. حين وصلت إلى الفيلا، لم ترن الجرس، فتحت الباب بمفتاحها الخاص، لأن نورا معتادة الخروج حين تخبرها هي أنها ستتأخر.

دخلت فسمعت صوت كريم آتياً من الشرفة، اتجهت إلى هناك لتراه جالسا مع نورا يتشاركان حديثاً قطعه وصولها. غادرت نورا المكان بسرعة، فيما أخبرها كريم أنه عاد للاطمئنان عليها لأنها بدت متوترة صباحاً فلم يجدها.

جلست تستمع إليه يتكلم طويلاً دون أن تسمع فعلياً أياً من كلماته، فقط تتابعه متظاهرة بالإنصات محاولة أن ترسم ابتسامتها الدائمة. انتظرت بصبر حتى انتهت زيارته، فقصدت غرفة مكتبها ... أغلقت الباب عليها، أخرجت ألبوم الصور، وأخذت تتأمّل صورها القديمة: واحدة وهي طفلة بالزي الرسمي لمدرستها "رمسيس كولدج"، وأخرى ترتدي فيها ثوب سباحة يكشف معظم جسدها المشدود بفعل اليوغا وهي في العشرين من عمرها، وثالثة في الستينيات مع أبويها في رحلة لإنكلترا ... مرت على باقي الصور سريعاً، وعندما وصلت لصورها الأحدث طوت الألبوم. وهي تغادر الغرفة تحاشت النظر في المرآة المجاورة للباب.

لم تسأل نورا عن سبب جلوسها مع كريم، ولم تنهرها لسماحها له بالدخول في غيابها، فقط طلبت منها أن تسافر معها بسرعة إلى شاليه الساحل الشمالي. لم تحمل سوى حقيبة يدها التي التقطتها بسرعة وهي تسحب نورا وراءها.

كانت تقود على طريق مصر الإسكندرية الصحراوي بسرعة كبيرة وهي تدندن، من جديد، بكلمات أغنية نجاة ... أحست بخفة لم تشعر بها منذ سنوات، عادت شابة جميلة تزهو بحسنها وقوامها الممشوق، ارتفع صوتها أكثر وزادت من سرعة سيارتها. يلسع الهواء

٧٣

البارد وجهها فلا تنتبه، تسألها نورا عن سبب السفر المفاجئ فلا
تردّ عليها، وفجأة لم تستطع التحكم في عجلة القيادة، اختل توازن
السيارة منها، ثم لم تعد واعية بالعالم من حولها، يأتيها فقط صوت
أنين مجروح، طنين يكاد يشق رأسها، وضجة تغلف كل شيء.

محمد حسن علوان

جزء من رواية "القندس"
رواية لم تنشر بعد

عائلتي بكماء في ما بينها ثرثارة في محافل الآخرين. كلنا اخترع
فضائحه بكتمان رهيب حتى لا يعرف أحدنا ماذا يحاك في الغرفة
المجاورة. أتساءل إذا كنا فعلاً نفهم بعضنا أكثر مما يفهمنا الآخرون؟
لا يبدو ذلك ممكناً وفق ظروفنا الثابتة التي لم تتغيّر منذ أقرّها جدي،
وثبّتها أبي، وانتقلت عدواها في جينات العائلة بعد ذلك.

وما دمنا لا نقول صار لزاماً أن نتقوّل. تلك هي محاولاتنا العشوائية
لفهم بعضنا بعضاً، أن نتواصل حسب افتراضاتنا عن كل واحد منا
لا حسب ما نحن عليه فعلاً.

وحسب هذه الافتراضات، فشقيقتي الكبرى، هند، ليست فقط
مشرفة تربوية مزمنة في كلية البنات، بل هي هند التي استأثرت بأكثر
جينات القندس الشكلية، ويتضخم ردفاها كل سنة. كلما التقيتها
أشعرُ بأنهما أضخم مما كانا عليه في المرة الأخيرة، وأجدها تلوم
الكورتيزون والهرمونات والعظام العريضة، ولا تقول أكثر من ذلك.

إنها شقيقتي الوحيدة، ولهذا كان يجب أن نقول لبعضنا أكثر عن بعضنا، وهذا ما فعلناه كثيراً ... و لم نصدّقه أبداً.

هي أكبر مني بسنة، ولكن فرنسيس بيكون يقول إن الإنسان يكبر في اليوم الأول من زواجه سبع سنوات دفعة واحدة، ولأنها تزوّجت مرتين وأنا لم أتزوّج قط، فهي تكبرني بخمس عشرة سنة إذن، وتتصرف كذلك فعلاً.

لولا أن هند تزوجت مرة ثانية لظلّت طويلاً تلومني على طلاقها من زوجها الأول. برغم أنها زيجة لم تكتمل أصلاً. كانا عاقدين، وكنتُ في السابعة عشرة، وعندما عدتُ إلى منزلنا في حي الناصرية آنذاك وجدتُ سيارته الكاديلاك الحمراء تقف أمام الباب، ببجاحة الكاديلاك التي كانوا يصنعونها في أوائل الثمانينيات طويلة مثل قارب صيد وعريضة مثل منكبي مصارع. هرعتُ فوراً إلى هراوتي الصغيرة التي كنتُ أخبئها تحت مقعد سيارتي بلا مبرّر، وقررتُ أن أتخذ موقفاً يسرّع انتقالي من المراهقة إلى الرجولة كما ظننت، وهشمتُ زجاجها الأمامي تماماً.

أتذكر أن أبي بصق على وجهي ليلتها عدة بصقات متقنة، وأن هند التي دفعتها أمام زوجها الوشيك ذاك وأنا أصرخ بهستيرية مصطنعة "اطلعي فوق يا بنت" لم تطلع قط، يرغم أني ظننتُ أنها فعلت ذلك عندما عبرت جواري باتجاه الدرج بينما أنا أحدق في عينيْ زوجها بنظرات صارمة وهو يبادلني بنظرات مستخفة. عادت هند من ورائي فجأة وسدّدت لي لكمة عمودية أعلى ظهري، وصفعتني على قفاي مرتين، قبل أن أتعارك معها عراكاً غير متكافئ، وزوجها يتفرج.

حدث بعد ذلك أن عادت الكاديلاك الحمراء لتقف أمام الباب عدة ليالٍ أخرى، بزجاج جديد، وأنا لا أملك لها دفعاً. وتعمدت هند الاختلاء به في المجلس مقفلاً إمعاناً في الاستهزاء برجولتي المرتبكة، وحدث أن أجبرني أبي على تقبيل رأس زوجها مرتين، واصطحاب كبشٍ ذي قرنين إلى بيته على سبيل الاعتذار، ولكن الزيجة لم تكتمل برغم ذلك. ولا أعرف التفاصيل المؤكدة حتى الآن.

يبدو أن مشهد عراكنا الوضيع أمامه لم يجعل هند تبدو جميلة كما يريد زوجته، ولا رزينة كما يتوقع، وأنها كانت أخت الفتى المتهور الذي لا يجب أن يكون خالاً لأبناء لم يجيئوا قط. شيء يشبه القدر ويشبهني جعل هند تنفصل عن زوجها وهي عذراء ونصف مجنونة! ولو أني كنتُ متهوراً فعلاً كما ظنّوا لأتقنتُ الحكاية وهشمت رأسه بدلاً من زجاج سيارته، ولكني لم أكن إلا شاباً يمارس الدور العمريّ الذي وجدتُ أبناء حيّي يمارسونه ويتحدثون به، ولبسته على روحي المرتبكة الصائمة عن الثقة منذ ولدت، ووجدتُ أخيراً جدوى لهراوتي الجبانة التي كلفتني الكثير من الكبرياء. هل نملك أكثر من الكبرياء عندما نكون في السابعة عشرة؟

أن أتذكر هذه التفاصيل الخشبية وأنا في الأربعين الآن يشبه أن أحارب الغبار برئة مستعملة وقديمة. يستعصي عليّ استفهام الحالة التي كنتُ عليها، والدوافع التي خلقت تصرفاتي، فأجدني أحيلها إلى تبريرات لا أصدّقها أنا نفسي. الحزن الذي أنا عليه الآن، كعاشقٍ مبهوت، يجعلني أنظر إلى حياتي كمشروعِ خرب ليس إلا، رغم أني

٧٧

متأكد من أنها كانت حياة لا بأس بها. صحيحٌ أنها لم تنوّلني هيفاء كما أريدها، ولكن نوّلتني منها ما يكفي للكتابة.

أحياناً أفكر أن هنداً ربما كانت أهم امرأة في حياتي، رغم أنها بعيدةٌ جداً عن روحي هذه الأيام، ولكنني اقتسمتُ معها كوباً من العمر المهمّ، ورغيفاً من الذاكرة المملحة لم يكن ممكناً أن اقتسمهما مع غيرها. أحياناً أتعجب من قلة ما هو مشتركٌ بيننا ومن سطوته وقوة تأثيره. لا أظنني كنتُ سأختارها أختاً لو أنا نختار ذلك ولا أظنها كانت ستفعل أيضاً. ولكنا تورطنا في رحم واحد، أنجبنا تباعاً من أبٍ غير مرغوب فيه. ونشأنا في كنفٍ ضيّقٍ احتوى طفولتنا الجافة على مضض.

أقول هذا وأنا على يقين الأربعين التي لا تفتعل المعاناة لأني أعرف أن أمي لم تكن تريد أبي ولا هو يريدها، وأنها طارت بعد إنجابي بسنواتٍ قليلة إلى رجلٍ آخر أنجبت منه أطفالاً أفضل. وبالتأكيد أن هنداً لا ترى ما أراه، وتصرّ على أنها كانت وسوسة شيطان تستعيذ من أن يعودها هي وزوجها بعد حين، ويصيرها إلى ما صارت أمنا إليه.

كانت هند الطفلة باردة العينين، خاويتين من كل ما في الأعين عدا الإبصار الوظيفي فقط. عندما أتأمل حياتها أشعر كأني أطالع فيلماً وثائقياً عن طفولة سفّاحة محتملة ولكن الحياة، لحسن الحظ، لم تمنحها غضباً كافياً. تدحرجت بها العناية السماوية إلى مصير هادئ ومقبول ولكنها ما زالت غريبة عن كل الأشياء، فلا تكاد تتعلق بشيءٍ، ولا تفضّل شيئاً، ولا تميل لشيءٍ، ولا تشتهي شيئاً ... أو أنها لا تقول. إنها تعرف أنها تحتاج: فتندفع إذا استطاعت، أو تنكفئ إذا عجزت.

وُلدت على طرف سجادة قديمة مليئة بالأتربة، وولدتُ أنا بعدها بسنة واحدة في مستشفى جديد، وفراش ناصع البياض. هذا ما منح هند أسباباً أكثر لكراهيتي كلما ذكرت أمي ذلك في أحاديث العائلة التي تتكرر كثيراً. والحقيقة أن ولادة هند في مجلس عتيق على سجادة مثربة كانت شأناً عادياً يمكن أن يتكرر في الكثير من بيوت الرياض تلك الأيام لولا أن خيالي كان خصباً.بما يكفي لأن يخترع من تلك الحالة آلاف النكات الصالحة لمناكفتها.

كانت ليلة برد تضاعفت معها آلام الولادة، وكادت هند تختنق عدة مرات لولا حنكة تلك القابلة الحبشية العجوز التي استوصت أمي بها خيراً قبل شهرين من ولادتها لهند حتى تضمن خدماتها العجيبة. حدثتنا أمي، دون مبالاة بصفاقة التفاصيل، أنها اضطرت إلى أن تربط إحدى قدميها بقضيب معدني يمتد من إطار النافذة مستخدمةً خمارها الأسود بينما تربط القدم الأخرى بحبل قصير وتوصي عمتي أن تبقيه مشدوداً، لتفرج بين الرجلين اللتين أبت أمي أن تفرج بينهما كما يجب. ذلك الحوض الصغير لفتاةٍ في السادسة عشرة من عمرها لم يكن يتحمّل انفراجاً كهذا، قالت أمي: "كل آلام حياتي ... تلاميذ ألم تلك الليلة!"، حتى الإغماء كانت عاجزةً عن السقوط فيه لفرط الألم. وصرخت هند في النهاية، وسحبتها القابلة بسرعة، وسقطت أمي إعياءً، وانطبق فخذاها على الجرح الكبير، وخرجت عمتي هاربةً بغثيانها بعيداً بعد أن طوت طرف السجادة لتغطي بها أمي وتلملم ارتجافاتها من برد تلك الليلة.

ولأنها جاءت قطعةً ضئيلةً من لحمٍ وردي لم تحتمل أمي منظرها،

ولم تعرف كيف تحملها وترضعها وتعتني بها. ولهذا رضعت هند من مرضعتين غريبتين، إحداهما يمنية كانت تقيم في الحي نفسه أرضعتها دون مقابل شرط ألا يطول ذلك لأنها كانت ترضع توأماً، ولا يوجد حليب كاف لتلك الرضيعة المتطفلة، أما المرأة الثانية فكانت مرضعة مستأجرة أفريقية الأصل جاءت بها القابلة ضمن خدماتها المتعدّدة. وانتهى الأمر بهند أن تكون أختاً بالرضاع لسبعة أطفال يمنيين وأفارقة، وأختاً بالنسب لي أنا الذي سخرتُ بكل عنصرية مما فعله ذلك الحليب القديم بها، وما صيّرها إليه. وطالما وصفتها بـ"العبدة" و"الزيدية" حتى عهد قريب.

أتراني أكتبُ هذا اليوم كتأنيب متأخر على وقاحة الماضي؟ من المحيّر أن تربّي في داخلك ذنباً عنيداً لأختٍ لا تعرف كيف تعتذر لها، ولست متأكداً إذا ما كانت هي في حاجة لهذا الاعتذار وإذا ما كان سيجعلها امرأة أفضل.

لو قلتُ لهند اليوم إني أعتذر عن منابزتي لها لربما سخرت مني، ولربما استيقظ في داخلها حيوانٌ لئيمٌ يمتصّ روحي التائبة حتى آخر قطرة. المشكلة أن منابزاتي لها كانت تغوص في داخلها كأسهم مسمومة، بينما ما تفعله هي بي في المقابل كان يسقط قريباً مني كسرب من الذباب الفاشل. لا يمكن للفتاة أن تكون أجرأ لساناً من الفتى ذي الخيال الجامح. الفتى الذي كان يبتكر لأخته إهانات شائكة في طفولته، ويكتب لحبيبته كتباً أنيقة عندما كبر. وعندما يقف عند مفترق الأربعين يتمنى، ولو للحظة، أن ينقلب سلوكه بين المرأتين لتنال كل واحدة ما تستحقه فعلاً!

لا أدري ما إذا كانت الأثداء الغريبة التي رضعت منها هند تختلف عن ثدي أمي الغريب أيضاً والذي أرضعتني منه على عجل لأنها انفصلت عن أبي مرةً أثناء حملها بي ففطمتني في شهري السابع ورحلت. وبعد أشهرٍ عادت لتمكث سنوات قليلة مع أبي في علاقة لم تكن أفضل من ذي قبل، ثم انفصلا انفصالاً أخيراً تسنى لها بعده أن تتزوج رجلاً آخر. هكذا كان الحليب الذي صبّته أمي في جسد هند متأخراً، والحليب الذي صبّته في جسدي مستعجَلاً. ولهذا تبدو لنا أمي مجرد كائن غائب أسري يحمل هوية أمومية لا أكثر. ثمة عاطفة ورقية تشدنا إليها وتجعلها أمنا وتجعلنا أبناءها، ولو شددناها قليلاً كما تشد العواطف في تقلبات الحياة لتمزقت، وقد حدث ذلك عدة مرات. بعكس حسان الذي تعلّق بها بشدة وتعلقت به، وهو أخونا غير الشقيق الذي لم تنجب سواه من زوجها الآخر. ولولا صفات أمي التي صارت تنزع إلى الطيبة المندفعة كلما كبرت لربما نفرنا منها منذ سنوات المراهقة الأولى، ولا سيما وهي تعيش مع رجلٍ آخر، بينما نعيش نحن مع رجلٍ لا يذكرها بخير مطلقاً.

أمي لم تعش معنا بما يكفي لتكتمل أمومتها لنا. إنها القندس الوحيد الذي شذّ عن العائلة فملأنا فراغها بالأخشاب والأحزان الميتة. ولم يطلّقها أبي مرتين إلا لأنها أخطأت في ترتيب السدّ الذي يريد، وافترض فيها فساد النيّة، وأنا افترضتُ فيها جموح امرأة جنوبية نادرة وصعبة المراس، وافترضَت فيها شقيقتي هند سلسلة من الأخطاء التي ظلت تعلّقها على ظهرها عقب كل حادثة، ولكنها لا تذكر ذلك أمامها أبداً لأن صداقتها المتأخرة مع أمي تتصادم مع تبجيلها لأبي

في منطقة تغلفها هند بالصمت حتى لا ترهق ذهنها باختراع المواقف. السنوات الست عشرة التي تفصل بينهما جعلتهما صديقتين. تمرِّض إحداهما الأخرى إذا مرضت، وتتسوّقان معاً، وتسلطان لسانيهما على ذات النساء، وتنتقدان كل الرجال.بمن فيهم أنا. أما الرجل الوحيد الذي لا يمكن أن تتفق أمي وهند عليه فكان أبي. فبقدر ما كانت أمي لا تكاد تذكره بخير أبداً، وتسخر دائماً من أمّيّته وجهله، كانت هند تجلّ أبي كثيراً، ولا تكاد تذكره بسوء أبداً.

كانت أمي مدينة لي بكبريائي الناقصة دائماً. استأثرت بها لنفسها ولم تورثني منها ما أعيش به بهدوء وسلام. عندما تركت البيت أول مرةٍ لم يشعر بها إلا بطني الجائع وفمي الذي ظل يفتش عن حلمةٍ لم تعد موجودة بالجوار، ثم عادت بعدها بأشهر محاطة برسولات السلام من نساء الناصرية وأزواجهنّ الذين امتلأ بهم مجلس أبي كما تقصّ علينا أمي القصة، مصرةً على أن عودتها تطلبت كل هؤلاء الوسطاء.

لم أتصالح مع أمي إلا بعد العشرين. ليس لأنها أمي التي كبرت ولكن لكونها زوجة ذلك الرجل الودود، العم إبراهيم، الذي وجدتُ في مجلسه ما لا يقدر عليه أبي من ثقافةٍ وسعة أفق وتبسُّطٍ في الأخذ من الحياة، الأمر الذي لا يمكن أن تحويه جبلة أبي التي قُدّت من صخر ورمال. أما هند فظلت على وفاق مع أمي، ويبدو أنها تنازلت عن كل ما فعلته بها أو أنها لم تجد من يتلو عليها حقوقها المسلوبة.

انتصرت جينات أمي في جسد هند، فأنستها أنها كانت طفلة مهجورة. تصالحتا على حالة اجتماعية لا تجعلهما تبدوان غريبتي الأطوار، كأم وابنتها الوحيدة، ولكنهما لم تقتسما نفس السلوك

والخصال باستثناء فضيلة التذمّر من كل شيء. غير أن هند كانت متذمّرة مقموعة، بينما أمي كانت متذمّرة ثائرة.

لا أستطيع أن أجزم أن أمي كانت تكره هند أثناء طفولتها ولكنها ربما لم تستطع أن تدلق عليها دلو الحب كما ينبغي، ربما كانت هند دائماً ما تعيد لأمي صورةً قديمةً لحمل بائسٍ أصلاً، وليلة بردٍ، وزوج ممتعض من أنوثة بكره. هند جاءت في موسم كراهية وفي مدينة تستطيع خلق مثل هذه المواسم بسهولة. وللأسف، لم تستطع بطبيعتها البليدة أن تغيّر شيئاً من ذلك. فظلّت عديمة الملامح، عشوائية السلوك دائماً.

وأنا نشأتُ وليس أمامي إلا هند. أتأملها بذهول وهي قابعة تحت شمس الظهيرة دون أن تشعر بحرارتها. تلحس الحيطان بسبب نقص الحديد والزنك في جسمها، وأحياناً تسفّ التراب وتلعق بقايا الرماد البارد في الموقد. أنفها يسيل ولا يزعجها، عيناها شاردتان دائماً في اللامكان ومعلقتان في الفراغ الذي يحيط بالأشياء. فخذها مليئة بآثار قرصات الخادمة سعدية الزرقاء الدائرية، بينما ذراعاها موشومان بخطوط حمراء طولية لفرط ما تهرشهما باستمرار وهي نائمة.

الرياض آنذاك كانت تشربُ النفط وتتضخم بشكل سريع وهائل، وأبي يلهث مع اللاهثين. لم يكن يملك وقتاً كافياً لمعالجة الصداع الذي تزرعه أمي في رأسه كل مساء، ولم تكن هي تقبل أن تعيش على هامشه قبل اندلاع الطفرة[1] عندما كان خالياً فكيف به بعدها. كان انفصالهما إذاً أشبه بوثيقة سلام وليس شرخاً في العائلة. ذهبت أمي إلى بيت خالها الذي لم تلبث فيه طويلاً حتى خطبها

---

١. الطفرة: ما يُطلق محلياً على فترة الانتعاش الاقتصادي الهائل في السعودية، التي بدأت في السبعينيات الميلادية وحوّلتها إلى بلد غني.

العم إبراهيم، وجلب أبي الخادمة الحبشية سعدية لتقوم بكل أدوار
أمي في البيت، وبلا ندم.

كنا نعيش في بيتٍ شعبي في حي الناصرية. وهو أول بيت عشتُ
فيه في الرياض أنا وهند، وثاني بيتٍ عاش فيه أبي. بعد ذلك انتقلنا
إلى حي "المربع" ثم حي "الفاخرية" الذي ما زالت العائلة تقيم
فيه. وقبل أن أولد كان أبي وأمي يقيمان في بيتٍ من طينٍ في حي
"دخنة" عقب وصولهما إلى الرياض على ظهر حافلة صدئة قطعت
بهما المسافة من أبها إلى الرياض في أربعة أيام مليئة بالغبار والقيظ
والخوف والقلق.

عشتُ في الرياض على أطراف مثلث يجمع الناصرية بالمربع
بالفاخرية قبل أن يحملني النزق إلى تخريب هذا الشكل الهندسي
بنقطة بعيدة جداً في "أوسيقو" جنوب بورتلاند. كلما تأملتُ هذه
الخريطة تساءلتُ عن الأشكال الهندسية المحتملة التي يمكن أن أخلقها
في السنوات المقبلة. أين يمكن أن أرحل؟ ومع من يمكن أن أعيش؟

تأملُ الخرائط طالما شطّ بي بعيداً عما أنشده منها. لم تساعدني
خريطةٌ من قبل على فهم الاتجاهات بقدر ما زادتني ضلالاً وغربة. نفتحُ
الخرائط لنعرف أين نحن؟ وإلى أين نتجه؟ وبما أني لم أنجح في إجابة السؤال
الأول يوماً، ظل السؤال الثاني دائماً صعب المنال، عسير الإجابة.

وخريطة الرياض التي تبدو دائماً مثل خدشٍ هائل في ظهر
الصحراء يجتمع حوله الصديد والكره كانت تحرّضني دائماً ضد
المدينة. كلما طالعتها طرحت عليّ أسئلة الانتماء والحب والذاكرة
الشقية، وبقية الأسئلة التي لا يمكن أن تكون إجاباتها مريحة أبداً.

٨٤

وعندما تركت أمي البيت للمرة الثانية ظنوا أنها ستعود عودةً شبيهة ولكنها لم تفعل ... ولم نحزن كثيراً. كان غيابها فسحة لنا من أعصابها المتوترة دائماً وضربها الموجع، وسبيلاً لنكتشف امرأة جديدة جاء بها أبي إلى البيت وأخبرنا أنها أمنا الجديدة. وفرحنا بها ككل جديد، وكانت على حيادها أسلم على أرواحنا وأجسادنا من نقيق أمي وضربها المفاجئ.

سافرت أمي مع زوجها الجديد إلى بيروت، وبقينا نحن في ربقة الناصرية نحاول أن نخترع لنا بنوة جديدة لأم لم تخطر لنا ببال. سرعان ما راحت هند تناديها "يمه"، وبقيت أنا أناديها "شيخة" كما يناديها أبي. وبرغم تقدم هند في سباقنا نحو هذه الأم الجديدة بالنداء كنتُ أنا الذي ينال منها بعض الحب والحكايات والأثرة. لا أعرف لها سبباً مقنعاً سوى أن شيخة، وهي في التاسعة عشرة من عمرها آنذاك، كانت تعتقد أن الطريق الموحش إلى قلب أبي يمرّ عبر ابنه الذكر الوحيد، ولن يمر عبر ابنته الأنثى البكر أبداً.

أما أبي، قندسنا الأكبر الذي وضع الجذع الأول نصب الثاني وقرر أن يبني سداً في وجه الرياض، فلم ينج من التيار. ابتلعه مثلما ابتلع عشرات النازحين من قبله. منذ أن كان تاجر سجاد سابق في سوق "الزلّ"، حتى انتهى تاجر عقار سيئ السمعة بعدما انفتح شمال المدينة على أهلها رغداً وعقاراً لا نهاية له، فنال أبي في بداية الثمانينيات مع الذين نالوا، وسقط وحده.

الآن هو خامدٌ مثل بركانٍ ما زال يحمل في قرارته نيّات قلق أصيلة، وتفوح من قمته أبخرة بركانية عابسة تراكمت على وجهه

كآثار الثورات القديمة. لا يتكلم أبي عن ماضيه مطلقاً، الأمر الذي يجعلني أستيقن حيناً بعد حين أنه كان ملطخاً بسوادٍ ما لا ينبغي أن تتناقله الحكايات. القليل يمكنني أن أُلمِم تفاصيله مما تبثه ألسنة أخرى، كأمي وعمتي وأقارب آخرين.

بدأ "صبياً" حتى تعلم السياقة، وأصبح سائقاً ...

قالها الرجل الأشيب الذي لا أدري كيف ساقته الأقدار من أبها إلى الرياض ليخبرني ما لم أعرفه عن أبي من قبل. جاء للعلاج واستضافه أبي في بيتنا كما يفعل عادة مع الأقارب. كنتُ آخذه إلى المستشفى وأعود به في مواعيد متفرقة إلى واحدة من غرف الضيافة في البيت. لم يكن أبي يلتقيه إلا في مواعيد الطعام الرسمية، بينما أقضي معه أغلب وقته. فعندما أيقن أبي أني لن أكون مساعد رجل أعمال، كما يريدني، قرر أن يجعلني مسؤول ضيافة على الأقل، يسند إليّ مثل هذه الأعمال الاجتماعية التافهة والشؤون المنزلية اليومية، أو أي عمل آخر يقنعه جزئياً بأن إنجابه لي لم يكن استثماراً فاشلاً.

بدأ ثابت يحكي لي عن أبي الكثير. شعرتُ بأني وقعتُ على كنزٍ صغير من حيث لم أحتسب، وفي وقتٍ حرجٍ من بحث التخرج الذي لم يكتمل قط بعد أن تركتُ الجامعة عام ١٩٩٣م ولم أعد إليها أبداً.

كنتُ طالباً في قسم علم الاجتماع بجامعة الملك سعود، واقترح عليّ البروفيسور أن أكتب بحثاً عن الآثار الاجتماعية على العائلات النازحة إلى المدن الكبرى، وكان ذلك الموضوع هو آخر ما وافقتُ البروفيسور عليه قبل أن أدخل معه في سلسلة من الخلافات والشجارات أدّت أخيراً إلى فصلي من الجامعة كلها.

كان بحثاً صغيراً في مادة جامعية، ولكنه سرعان ما التهم عقلي وتركني في حالة من الهوس لم تُقنع أحداً ممن حولي. تعملق حُلمي بمآل البحث ليتحول إلى مشروع كتاب، ثم مشروع رواية، ثم موسوعة. وفي غمرة من غمرات الهوس وجدتُ فيه بذرةً صالحةً لمشروع معارضة سياسية جيد، ثم نظرية كبرى في علم الاجتماع توقظه من سباته، ثم إلى وثائق إنسانية كبرى قد تتحول إلى دِين له أتباع بعد قرنين من الزمان. كل هذا وأنا في أوائل العشرينات، أحاول أن أخترع لنفسي مجداً يجعل هيفاء تندم تدريجياً على تفريطها بي واعتناق رجلٍ آخر.

لا أدري أين تركتُ صندوق البحث. لا بد أنه في مكان ما في قبو فيلتي في الرياض حيث كدّس الخدم بقية أشيائي بعد رحيلي. مجموعة الأوراق المليئة بالمراجعات والملاحظات، أشرطة التسجيل المليئة بأصوات أناس عديمي التأثير، وثائق مسروقة من خزينة أبي لصفقات عقارية قديمة، قصاصات صحف صفراء فتشت عنها طويلاً في أرشيفات الصحف المحلية، خرائط مرسومة باليد لقريتنا قرب أبها التي لم أزرها قط، وشريط الفيديو الصغير الذي لم يعد هناك كاميرا تصلح لعرض ما فيه من جلسات للعم ثابت وهو يتحدث بلا انقطاع عن ذكرياته مع أبي في الرياض.

اشتغالي سنتين على بحثٍ وهمي كهذا في عرض مدينة كالرياض، كان يشبه ما فعلته ماري كوري التي اكتشفت الراديوم وماتت من أثر إشعاعاته التي تعرّضت لها طيلة سنوات العمل. الفرق أني لم أكتشف شيئاً في النهاية بينما تورطتُ في جمع القبيح والشاذّ والكريه من

نقائص مدينتي وذكريات عائلتي، ولم أخرج من ذلك كله بكتاب ولا شهادة ولا امرأة!

ذلك البحث كان أسوأ قرارات حياتي. ليس بسبب فشلي في إكماله كما أردته، ولكن لأني اخترعته وأنا في حالة من الكآبة لم يسبق لي أن مررتُ بمثلها من قبل. أزمة ربع العمر كانت تفتك بي وأنا في حاجة ماسة إلى أي إنجاز أحقن به حياتي المرتبكة. كنتُ أعيش مع إخوة غير أشقاء لم يعاملني أي منهم كأخ أكبر، وأبوين لا ينتظران مني أكثر من الأدوار المعتادة، وللتو تركتني امرأةٌ أحبتني وأحببتها لأنها لا تثق بقدرتي على افتتاح حياة آمنة لنا. كل هذا يحدث في غمار فراغ قاتل، ومدينة يابسة، لتوّها نفضت عنها إثارة حرب الخليج، ودخلتْ مرة أخرى في غيبوبة الإسمنت والرمال.

ثقوب الوهم التي تركها ذلك البحث في صدري ما زالت واسعة لم تنغلق بعد، ولم أتمكن من علاجها فتركتها كما هي. حالة من حالات الفشل التي لم تتحول إلى حكاية طريفة من حكايات الماضي ولا لعنة سابقة نحمد الله على تجاوزها. ظلت قائمة كمرارتها أول يوم، أتذوّقها حتى وأنا أحاول تخليص سمكةٍ صغيرة من صنارتي على ضفة ويلامت!

محمد صلاح العزب

موت مؤقَّت

فصل من رواية

حين مات جدي للمرة الأولى، لم يكن يملك سوى عصا من خشبٍ رديء، وجلباب طويل.

حفروا له على عجل حفرة غيرَ عميقة، بجوار جثمانه تماماً، فتعفر وجهُه، واختفت ملامِحُه.

خيّطوا الجلباب على جسده من أسفل، وتحيّروا في رأسه، فوضعوه في الكيس القماشي الذي اعتاد أن يضع فيه طعامَه.

دفعوه حتى سقط في الحفرة، وأهالوا التراب على جسده، وانصرفوا دون أن ينظر أحدُهم وراءه.

طفل صغير فقط رجع بعد قليل بحثاً عن ضفدعة كان يسمع نقيقها ولا يراها، وجد الجلباب والكيس القماشي مفرودَين على سطح الحفرة الذي ظل ممهداً كما تركوه.

ناداهم الطفل فرجعوا، وحين رأوا الملابسَ طفت وحدها على وجه الأرض، دون الجسد الذي كان بداخلها، قالوا: هذه معجزة.

بنوا فوق القبر ضريحاً، يزوره المريض والمحتاج والمربوط والتي لا
تلد، دون أن يفكروا في نبش التربة حتى يتأكدوا من وجوده داخلها.

٢

لا أحد يعلم لجدي أباً ولا أماً، وجدوه متمدّداً على ظهره على شاطئ
النهر، يمد يده يغترف من الماء ويشرب وهو يبتسم، كان عمره أربعة
أعوام، وله شارب ولحية مكتملان كأنه شاب في العشرين.

هذه اللحظة تحتفظ بها ذاكرته جيداً، أقبلوا عليه وحملوه إلى بيت
كبير القرية، فأتى له بخادمة عجوز، وأمرها أن تطعمه فرفض، واكتفى
بشرب كثير من الماء، حاولت الخادمة أن توقفه على قدميه حتى يسير
فلم يستطع الوقوف، ولم يتكلم، فقط كان يبتسم ابتسامة واسعة.

اجتمع عدد كبير من رجال القرية، وجلسوا حوله وهو متمدّد
بينهم، يظنون أنه لا يفهم ما يقولون.

قال بعضهم: إنه ليس إنسياً، فرد عليهم آخرون بأنه طفل مسحور،
واعترض البعض بأنه ليس مسحوراً ولكنه ابن خطيئة ألقته أمّه بعد
وضعه، وقال عرّاف القرية إنه سيكون سبباً لهلاكهم، فاقترح بعضهم
قتله، وقالوا: حتى لا يفتن الناس، فاعترضت جماعة وقالوا: لا تقتلوه،
وأعيدوه إلى شاطئ النهر حيث كان، ولا علاقة لكم به.

رجل الدين قال: إن حالته لم يرد ذكرها في الكتب المقدسة، ولهذا
فهو شيطاني وليس إلهياً، وقال الطبيب: هذه حالة غير علمية، وربما
يكون هذا الطفل بداية تحوّل لا تحمد عقباه في السلالة البشرية.

كانوا يتحدثون، ويطيلون النظر إليه، ويفردونه أمامهم، ويعبثون
بجسده، ويحملونه ويقذفونه في الهواء، ويتحسّسون أنفه وعينيه،

كلهم جذبوه من لحيته وشاربه، ليتأكدوا من أنهما حقيقيان، وفتح أحدُهم فمه وضغط على أسنانه ليختبر قوتها. لكنهم لم ينجحوا في جعله يتخلى عن ابتسامته.

كان قد مر بنفس هذه الجلسة أكثر من مرة، في أكثر من قرية، وما زال يذكر تفاصيل كل مرة، فظل يتأمل ملامحهم التي يجدها متطابقة، ويسمع أصواتهم كصرير في أذنيه.

لم يتوصلوا إلى قرار في اليوم الأول، وأنهكتهم المناقشة، فأعطوه للخادمة العجوز ليبيت معها الليلة، وانصرف كل منهم إلى بيته، واتفقوا أن يجتمعوا في الصباح التالي ليقرروا مصير الطفل الغريب.

حملته الخادمة، كان ثقيلاً، لكنها أمسكته بيديها فقط، حريصة على ألا يقترب جسده من جسدها، وقطعت المسافة الطويلة من بيت كبير القرية حتى غرفتها المواجهة للنهر وهي خائفة ومتعبة، تنقل قدميها بصعوبة، وتجلس لتستريح كل قليل.

كانت تريده أن يكف عن الابتسام، أو أن يبكي كالأطفال في سنه حتى تطمئن، لكنه لم يفعل، فقرصته بأصابعها النحيلة في جنبه، وضغطت على جسمه بقوة، فدفع يدها في رفق، وهو يحدّق في عينيها مبتسماً، فكفت.

فكرت أن تتركه في وسط الطريق، وفكرت أن تغرقه في النهر حتى تتخلص منه، وقالت في نفسها إنها لو أضاعته فلن يهتم أحد به، وسيصدقونها لو اخترعت لهم أي حكاية بشأنه، ستقول لهم إنه تركها وجرى، أو إنه تحول إلى جني وقفز في النهر، أو إنه اختفى فجأة،

٩١

لكنها خافت من عينيه اللتين تحدقان في عينيها مباشرة، وفكرت أنها لا تستطيع قتل طفل يبتسم بهذه الصورة.

دخلت غرفتها، وأضاءت المصباح بسرعة، وضعته على فراشها، وظلت واقفة بجواره، كانت جائعة، لكنها خافت أن تنشغل عنه بصنع الطعام، خلعت شالها، ووضعته على وجهه حتى تخفي عينيه، لكنه دفعه بيده، حاولت أن تضحك له، وأن تُلَعِّب ملامحها، حملته وقذفته في الهواء أكثر من مرة حتى يضحك، ودغدغته في قدميه، وتحت إبطيه، فلم يضحك، اتسعت ابتسامته قليلاً فقط، خجلت أن تبدل ملابسها أمامه، فجلست بجواره على حافة السرير، حتى غلبها النعاس.

استيقظت بعد قليل على بلل أسفل مؤخرتها، قامت مفزوعة، فوجدت أنه قد بال على الفراش، ابتسمت برغم بلل ملابسها، ونزعت عنه ثوبه، فظهر شعر كثيف في صدره وعانته، ورأت أمامها عضواً مكتملاً لرجل، تراجعت وهي خائفة، لكنها لم ترفع عينيها عنه، وشعرت بالرغبة، أحضرت إناءً به ماء، وغسلته من أسفل، فانتصب عضوه في يدها، تحاشت أن تنظر إلى عينيه، وأطالت عملية الغسل، ثم نظرت إلى وجهه فوجدته مبتسماً وعينيه نصف مغمضتين، خلعت ملابسها، ثم صعدت فوقه، حتى شعرت به داخلها، كان مستمتعاً يتحرك بمهارة من اعتاد المضاجعة.

وهي تستيقظ صباحاً انتبهت لعريهما، فألبسته ملابسه التي جفت، ووقفت تغتسل أمامه وهي تغني، وتصفف شعرها، كان يتأملها مبتسماً، فشعرت بالرضى، فوجئت بجسدها مفروداً أكثر من

الليلة السابقة، وبشعرات سوداء جديدة وسط شعرها الثلجي، ارتدت جلباباً نظيفاً، وحملته وخرجت، فوجدت أهل القرية مجتمعين أمام بابها، حتى يشاهدوا الطفل ذا اللحية الذي لا يأكل ولا يضحك ولا يبكي ويكتفي بالماء فقط.

حين تجمهروا حولها، خاف منهم، غطت وجهه بشالها، حتى لا يحدقوا فيه، وضمّته إليها بقوة، وأعطتهم ظهرها، حتى تحميه من عيونهم، فشعر بالطمأنينة، والنساء يقتربن منها، فلا يرون إلا وجهها، فيسألنها:

ـ كيف صغرتِ هكذا؟

هرولت وهم يسيرون بجوارها، حتى وصلت بيت كبير القرية، والرجال مجتمعون لديه، دخلت فطلبوا منها الطفل، فقالت:

ـ ماذا ستفعلون به؟

نهروها، لأنها خادمة، ولا يجب أن تتكلم في مجلس الرجال، تشبثت بالطفل، ورفضت أن تتركه لهم، وأمسك هو بأنامله الصغيرة ثيابها، وجذبها إليه بقوة حتى لا تتركه، فأخبروها أنهم اتفقوا على أن يحملوه إلى خارج القرية، ويتركوه في القرية المجاورة أمام الشاطئ، لأنهم علموا أن أهل القرى السابقة كلهم فعلوا هذا، وُجد عارياً في القرية الأولى على شاطئ النهر، فألبسوه، وظلت كل قرية تلقيه للتي تليها، حتى وصل إلى هنا.

بكت العجوز، وجرت بالطفل من أمامهم، فلم يهتموا بها، وقالوا: العجوز أراحتنا.

في الخارج جرى كل أهل القرية خلفها، فجرت من أمامهم، ولم

يستطيعوا اللحاق بها، حتى دخلت غرفتها، وأغلقتها أمامهم، وضعت الطفل برفق على الفراش، ثم خرجت لهم وهي تمسك في كل يد سكيناً، وهددت بقتل من يقترب منهما.

تفرّق أهل القرية وقالوا إن الطفل مسحور وإنه أصاب العجوز بالجنون.

٣

لم تصدق العجوز في البداية فكرة أن يكون طفلاً، برغم ملامحه الطفولية، وتبوله في الفراش، كانت موقنة من أنه قزم بالغ، لكنه عاجز عن الكلام والسير، وأن أحداً غيرها لم يكشف هذا، أخفته في حجرتها، ولم تخرج به مطلقاً، كانت تحلق له شاربه ولحيته، فيبدو بريئاً كرضيع، في البداية علمته اسمها فكان يناديها به دون أن يجيد نطقه، وعلمته بعض الكلمات، وعوّدته بعض أنواع الطعام، وأتقن السير ممسكاً بيدها، وفي أيامها الأخيرة معه، صار يتكلم، ويأكل، ويسير بشكل أفضل.

كانت تضاجعه عدة مرات في اليوم، وحين يقذف داخلها لا تفكر لحظة أنه طفل، حاولت أكثر من مرة أن تسأله عن اسمه أو عن حياته قبل أن يأتي إلى القرية، فلم يبد أنه يفهمها، كانت تستغرب من نمّو جسده، ومن أنه لا ينام إلا قليلاً، لكنها أحبّت هذا حين أيقظها ذات ليلة قبل أن يلدغها ثعبان تسلل من أسفل باب الحجرة.

كانت تجلس أمامه عارية، تتأمل التغيرات التي حدثت في جسدها، نبتت لها أسنان كاملة قوية، وعاد شعرها كله إلى لونه الأسود القديم، وطالت قامتها مرة أخرى، واختفت التجاعيد من بشرتها، وأصبح

جلدها نضراً، واستعاد نهداها تماسكهما، وصار باستطاعتها أن تمشي طويلاً، وأن تجري، وأن تحمل أي شيء ثقيل، بعد أن كانت تحمل إناء الطعام بصعوبة، لكنها لم تصدّق نفسها حين نزل منها الدم أول مرة، ظنته نزفاً، لكن حين عاد إليها في الشهر التالي كانت مفاجأتها قوية، ولم تدر ماذا تفعل.

أهل القرية صاروا يخافون المرور أمام حجرتها، يقفون بعيداً يراقبون الطفل وهو يخرج ليلعب وقد صار أطول، لكن شاربه ولحيته كما هما إذا لم تحلقهما له الخادمة.

النسوة أصررن على معرفة سر عودتها إلى شبابها، فتسللن ليلاً ونظرن من فرجات الباب، ورأينها وهي تضاجع الطفل.

لم يعد أحد يجعلها تخدم في بيته، الرجال قالوا إنها مجنونة أو مسحورة، والنساء خفن على رجالهن من جمالها الذي عاد، فصارت تنزل من حجرتها إلى السوق مرة كل أسبوع، تتسوّل طعامهما، وتتحايل على مراودة الباعة لها عن نفسها، لكنها في المرة الأخيرة، تركت بائع الأقمشة يقبلها، وأخذت منه قطعة قماش وإبرة وخيطاً، وعادت إلى الحجرة تحوك ثوباً جديداً للصغير، بدلاً من ثوبه الذي قصر إلى ركبتيه.

مرة أخرى انقطع عنها الدم، أيقنت أنها ستعود عجوزاً مرة أخرى، نظرت إلى ملامحها وشعرها، فلم تجد تغيراً، انتظرت الشهر التالي فلم يأت الدم أيضاً، بعدها بشهرين أكد لها حجم بطنها أنها حامل.

انتقل خبر الحمل بسرعة البرق داخل القرية، تناقلته النسوة، ثم نقلنه إلى الرجال في لحظات المضاجعة، حتى الأطفال ظلوا يتهامسون

به في حلقات الدروس، واجتمع الرجال في بيت كبير القرية، وقرروا أن الخادمة ينبغي أن تقتل، ولكن بعد أن يعرفوا الفاعل.

أحضروها موثقة إلى الساحة، واجتمع كل أهل القرية، رفضت الخادمة في البداية أن تعترف باسم الفاعل، لكن قانون القرية كان تعذيب الزانية حتى تعترف، فأحرقوا شعرها وأذنيها، ففقدت الوعي أكثر من مرة، وفي النهاية أشارت بسبابتها إلى بائع الأقمشة، فاقتادوه معها، إلا أنه ظل يصرخ بأنه قبّلها فقط، فألصق التهمة بنفسه أكثر، طبقوا عليهما قانون السفاح: جردوهما من ملابسهما، وقطعوا أطرافهما الأربعة، وعلقوهما في نخلتين متجاورتين، بعد أن دهنوا أماكن البتر باللبن والعسل حتى تعفنت، وتجمعت عليهما الحشرات والديدان، ونهشتهما الطيور الجارحة.

في البداية مات بائع الأقمشة، ثم ماتت الخادمة وهي شابة. كانت ملامحها هادئة كأنها نائمة فقط، لم يبدُ عليها أيّ ألم، وكانت على شفتيها ابتسامة تشبه تماماً ابتسامة ذكر أقام لديها عاماً كاملاً، عشقته وضاجعته كثيراً حتى حملت منه، دون أن تفكر لحظة أن أبا جنينها لم يتجاوز الخامسة من عمره.

٤

ما إن صدر الحكم بموت الخادمة وبائع الأقمشة، حتى جرت النسوة من الساحة إلى غرفة الخادمة، كل منهن تمنّي نفسها بكفالة الطفل، العجائز كن في المؤخّرة، لكنهن جرين بسرعة كبيرة، والشابات واللواتي في منتصف العمر، كن يتدافعن بالقبضات والمناكب، وحين وصل الجمع إلى باب الغرفة الموصد، تشاجرن حتى تمزقت ملابسهن

وشعورهن، وصرن أنصاف عرايا، يسيل الدم من أنوفهن وأفواههن وأجسادهن، ولم يتوقفن إلا بعد أن ماتت معمرة القرية، لأنها تسللت من وسط المعركة على يديها وقدميها، حتى لامست باب الحجرة وهمّت بدفعه، فوقفت على جسدها عشرون امرأة وحطمن عظامها ورأسها بأقدامهن.

حضر الرجال، وحين رأى كبير القرية النسوة عرايا، أمر كل الرجال بأن يديروا وجوههم إلى الجهة الأخرى، وأمر النسوة أن تحاول كل منهن ستر جسدها، وقضى بأن تكفل كل منهن الطفل شهراً، فتعالت أصواتهن بالشجار على من تبدأ ومن تليها، حصر الرجل بيوت القرية فوجدها ١٥٠ بيتاً، وقال تقترع النسوة على ترتيب الكفالة، لكن العجائز هدّدن في السر بين النساء بفضح غرض رعاية الطفل، فطلبت النسوة من كبير القرية أن يكون الترتيب تنازلياً حسب السن، الكبرى فالأصغر فالأصغر، فتقدمت أكبر عجوز في القرية، ودفعت الباب، ثم خرجت ممسكة بيد الطفل، تضمّه إلى جسدها، وهي تضحك، ثم هرولت إلى بيتها.

لم يدرك جدي أنه كان يحب الخادمة العجوز، إلا وهو يضاجع آخر امرأة في القرية، ظل يبحث مع كل واحدة عما كان يشعر به مع الخادمة، وحين لا يجده يقول لنفسه: ربما مع التالية، وبعد نهاية الـ ١٥٠ بيتاً، كان الطفل قد تجاوز السابعة عشرة من عمره، وبلغ طوله وحجمه ضعف الرجل العادي، ووصلت لحيته إلى ركبتيه.

قرر أن يعود إلى حجرة الخادمة التي كانوا قد دفنوها فيها، فلم يجد إلا قبراً متهدماً، بنى فوق أنقاضه بيتاً صغيراً، وحفر قناة صغيرة بين

البيت والنهر، فتعجب الناس، لكنهم لم يتكلموا، لم يعرف الرجال علاقته بنسائهن، وقالوا إن بركته هي التي كانت تعيد الشباب لنسوة البيوت التي سكن فيها، وكانوا يقبلون يديه إذا لقوه في الطرقات، وحين استقل ببيته البعيد، لم يسمح لأي امرأة بأن تزوره، وكانت المياه تمر من القناة إلى داخل البيت، فيشرب منها ولا يأكل.

صادق الطيور والحيوانات، وكان يفهم لغتها، وتسير معه في موكب مهيب في القرية، وكان يخلع ملابسه في الليل ويستحم في النهر، فتتلصص عليه النسوة، وحين يراهن يقذفهن بالأسماك الكبيرة، حتى قرر أن يقيم في النهر، فقضى فيه عدة سنوات لا يخرج من مياهه، يصادق الأسماك، وأصحاب القوارب، والصيادين، حتى قرر الخروج، فخرج، ثم اختفى من القرية، ظلت النسوة يحمن طويلاً حول بيته، وحول مكانه في النهر، حتى تأكد لهن اختفاؤه.

قالوا إن النهر قد استردّه مرة أخرى كما ألقاه على شاطئهم ذات يوم، وقالوا إنه ذكرُ عروس البحر، وقال بعضهم إنه إنسي عادي، لكنه غرق في النهر، وذهب جثمانه بعيداً.

بعد عدة سنوات عاد إليهم من جديد، من النهر مرة أخرى ولكن في قارب كبير، محمل بالعطور والحلي والأغنام الصغيرة، كان قد حلق لحيته، وارتدى ملابس ليست مألوفة لهم، وحفر على صدره وشماً ظاهراً جداً للخادمة، اقتربت القرية كلها من القارب، فرأوا أشياء لم يروها من قبل، وقف بينهم وقال إن من يريد شيئاً سيأخذه، لكن في مقابل أن يدفع كل ما يملكه ثمناً له، المال والأرض والعقار، ضحك منه الرجال، وقالوا: من يدفع كل ما يملك في أشياء كهذه يرونها للمرة الأولى.

لم يرد عليهم، وانتظر، في اليوم التالي كانت كل امرأة تأتي وهي تجر رجلها فتجبره على أن يدفع كل ما يملكونه في غطاء سرير من الحرير، أو نرجيلة من الزجاج، أو حذاء بكعب عال، أو ساعة رملية.

وحين أصبح وحده يملك القرية بكل ما فيها طردهم منها، وصار يمضي وقته في بناء سور عال حولها، وحين أتم بناء السور، صار يمشي بالداخل عارياً، ويرسم على السور من الداخل صوره وهو يضاجع الخادمة، في كل مراحلها العمرية، كان يكتب اسمها تحت صورتها، ولا يكتب شيئاً تحت صورته، حتى اكتشف أنه لا اسم له، ظل يتذكر كل من قابلهم في القرية وفي سفراته الكثيرة، كان لكل منهم اسم، لا بد أن يكون للإنسان اسم، حاول أن يجد لنفسه اسماً فلم يستطع، انشغل كثيراً، وحين فشل مسح اسمها.

كان أهل القرية قد تفرقوا في القرى المجاورة، وأقام بعضهم على جوانب السور، كان يسمع أصواتهم من الداخل، وكانوا هم يتلصصون عليه، وهو يمضي عمره في هدم بيوت القرية، يهدمها حجراً حجراً، ثم يلقي بالهدم في النهر، حتى كاد يردمه، وشيئاً فشيئاً بدأت شعيرات بيضاء كثيرة تتسلل إلى شعره ولحيته الطويلة، وبدأ جسمه بالذبول، حتى انتهى من هدم بيوت القرية جميعاً عدا بيتها الواقع على الطرف، ثم حفر بطول القرية حفرة عميقة، لم يفهم أهل القرية لماذا يحفرها، كان يحفر بالفأس، وكان هو أول من اخترعها في العالم ثم قلدوه في ما بعد، يحفر ويصعد فوق النخلة العالية ليرى ما حفره من أعلى، ويسوّي حواف الحفر بدقة شديدة، وحين صعد في المرة الأخيرة، ورأى أن الحفرة تشكلت جسداً هائلاً لامرأة فتية لها نفس

ملامح الخادمة. في اللحظة الأخيرة، هدم السور، وأغلق مجرى النهر، ثم حوّله بحيث يمر بالحفرة التي حفرها، تغيّر مجرى النهر، بحيث أصبح الماء يجري مسرعاً، فيدخل من فخذيها، ليملأ جسدها، ويخرج من فمها ليواصل طريقه نحو مصبّه.

نبتت زهور كثيرة حول جسدها، وأصبحت هذه البقعة المكان المفضل للعشاق من كل القرى، ارتدى جلبابه، وحمل عصاه وكيس طعامه، حتى يخرج من القرية، لكنه حين وصل إلى قدمها، سقط على الأرض، ومات.

كان أهل القرية قد تفرقوا منذ زمن، فلم يعرفه أحد، تعجبوا من طول لحيته، كفنوه في جلبابه وكيس طعامه، ودفنوه ووضعوا العصا شاهداً على قبره، حتى عادوا ووجدوا ملابسه فوق القبر، بنوا فوقه ضريحاً، ولأنه مات عند قدم المرأة، ولأنهم لا يعرفون اسمه، سمّوا ضريحه: "ضريح قتيل السيدة".

نادية الكوكباني

صنعائي
رواية

صبحية

يحكى أن حُجرة خاصة تدعى المفرج في أعلى أدوار المباني القديمة في صنعاء تجعلك قريباً من "إلمقَّه" قمرك المعبود. وأن حجر رخام النافذة فيها، باستدارة شكله وبالضوء الخافت النافذ منه، يمنحك الجرأة لمسامرته حتى الفجر مثرثراً بعمرٍ مضى أو بعمرٍ سيأتي ...

إنه صباح السابع من يوليو ٢٠٠٩

زحام شديد للسيارات في شارع القصر الجمهوري والطرق المؤدية لميدان السبعين. جنود مدجّجون بالسلاح يفتشون السيارات والمارة ببطء شديد دون اكتراث إذا ما تأخر الموظفون وطلاب المدارس عن مواعيد حضورهم.

لم يثر الأمر فضولي فقط وأنا متجهة لمقر عملي لمعرفة السبب، بل وأيضاً فضول أحد المارة الذي سأل الجندي وهو يفتشه عن سبب هذه الإجراءات المفاجئة؟ رد عليه الجندي بصوتٍ تشوبه مسحة غضب: إجراءات أمنية لاحتفالات سبعة/ سبعة! يوم النصر! سيمر

موكب كبار الشخصيات والضيوف من هنا باتجاه ميدان السبعين،
مسرح الاحتفال ...

بدا على السائل أنه لم يستوعب الكثير، سبعة/ سبعة؟ يوم النصر؟
لكنه مر بعد أن تم تفتيشه.

التقطت اليوم: سبعة/ سبعة! والمناسبة: يوم النصر! و بدأت أفتش
كغيري في ذاكرتي عنه! نصرٌ لمن؟ وعلى من؟ مرّ عابرٌ آخر وردّد
الكلمات ذاتها وكأنما يقرأ أفكاري بسخرية لاذعة وغضب دفين،
زجره الجندي طالباً منه المرور بهدوء وإلا فسيتخذ إجراءاته! ...

حرب الانفصال، هكذا أطلقت الصحف على حرب مايو
١٩٩٤، وسمّت نتيجتها في يوم سبعة يوليو من العام ذاته نصراً
على من كانوا يطالبون فيها بالعودة للتشطير بعد أن كان مضى على
الوحدة أربع سنوات.

كان عدم الاحتفال بيوم سبعة/ سبعة لعدة أعوام مضت ومحاولة
جعله يوماً عادياً، فيه الكثير من الصواب. إذ كيف يمكن للعائلة
الواحدة عندما تحل مشكلة سبّبت لها الكثير من المآسي أن تعود
لانتزاعها من أغوارها كل عام ناسية ما يسبّبه تذكرها من ألم للمتضررين
منها من أبناء الوطن الواحد! ألمٌ، لن ينتهي إلا بوفاة آخر حفيد لكل
أولئك الذين ماتوا من الطرفين.

علا صوت أحد الجنود طالباً من السيارات التزام جهة اليمين
بسرعة، مرّ موكب مهيب من سيارات المرسيدس السوداء، انعكس
على زجاجها الفاره بوّس شعب يعاني ثلثه من فقر مدقع. حُلت الأزمة

.بمرور الموكب، لكن هذا لا ينفي أن كل من مر الموكب من طريق عمله أو مدرسته قد تأخر.

واصلت سيري باتجاه الطريق المؤدي للسائلة، دخلتُ مدينة صنعاء القديمة مخترقة أزقة ضيقة لا تسمح إلا .بمرور سيارة واحدة فقط، وضعت سيارتي في أقرب موقف لها جوار بستان شارب، وترجلت باتجاه مقر عملي. تأخري لا يمنع صالح من القيام .بمهماته في فتحه وتنظيفه واستقبال الزائرين والبيع لهم لحين وصولي.

دقائق وجاء العم محمد قلقاً ليسألني عن سبب تأخري لأني لم أُمرّ لأخذ سندويش البطاطا اليومي منه، طمأنته قائلة: اليوم سبعة/ سبعة يا عم محمد. أبدى دهشته هو الآخر من هذا التاريخ، غادر وهو يضرب كفاً بكفٍ بعد أن شرحت له السبب، عائداً إلى العربة التي يبيع فيها سندويشات البيض والبطاطا والجبنة لطلاب مدرسة نشوان، وللمارين من طريقه.

مرسمي، هو منزل قديم في قلب مدينة صنعاء القديمة، هكذا باتوا يطلقون عليها بعد قيام ثورة سبتمبر ١٩٦٢، وعندما انضمّت إلى قائمة التراث العالمي عام ١٩٧١ أصبح اسمها مدينة السور القديمة. هناك خارج السور صنعاء أخرى جديدة، جديدة بكل شيء، .بمبانيها الاسمنتية التي ترفض الحجر وبسكانها المتحضرين الذين يعتبرونها مدينة قديمة تذكرهم بعهدٍ مضى عانوا فيه الكثير من الظلم والقهر والحرمان. ماضٍ يجب أن ينسوه ولو بالابتعاد عنه. لذلك راحوا يتسربون منها كلما وجدوا فرصة مناسبة في الحصول على منزل في المدينة الجديدة.

وحدهم كبار السن باقون فيها، يمنحونها دفء ما مضى من ذكريات حياتهم ليستمروا فيها على أن يغادروها. يقومون بأعمال وطقوس مشتركة في ذات الوقت وفي أماكن متفرقة، كأنهم رجل واحد، يخرج للصلاة فجراً مهما كان البرد، ويبتهج بالجلوس عصراً مع أصدقائه في صرحة الحارة، المكان الواسع الذي تطل عليه منازلهم وذكرياتهم في آن واحد ...

اشتريت المنزل قبل تسعة أعوام، كان سعره معقولاً مقارنة بجنون أسعار هذه الأيام. مكوّن من ثلاث طبقات ومفرج علوي نوافذه حرة من ثلاث جهات، يطل على جبل نقم من الشرق، وجبل عيبان من الغرب. جعلتُ من الدور الأرضي معرضاً لبيع أعمالي الفنية إضافة إلى بيع بعض المشغولات اليدوية التقليدية التي تُحضرها لي بعض ربات البيوت من النساء وتستهوي السُياح. وبرغم حالات اختطاف البعض منهم من قبل بعض شيوخ القبائل للضغط على الدولة لتنفيذ مطالب ومصالح لهم، إلا أنهم يتوافدون إلى المدينة القديمة بكثرة طيلة أيام العام. الدور الأول جعلته مشغلاً للرسم وأحتفظ فيه بكامل أدواتي من ألوان وأقمشة وبراويز وقوائم خشبية ... والدور الثاني معرضاً دائماً خاصاً بالزوار على اختلافهم سواء كانوا أجانب من السياح أو من معارفي وصديقاتي.

في المفرج العلوي أختلي بذاتي كثيراً، يأخذني حنين إلى قليل أيامي في صنعاء وأنا طفلة قبل مغادرتها مدة طويلة والاكتفاء بزيارتها في الإجازات. أتأمل من نوافذه الواسعة المدينة المتفردة في العالم بعمارتها ومبانيها العالية. انعكاس الضوء من الخارج على القمريات الملوّنة، يجعل

من المفرج نابضاً بالرومنسية والهدوء. فأشعر بخدرٍ لذيذ باسترجاع تلك الأساطير التي لفت المدينة ومبانيها وساكنيها بعالم باهر.

أفتح مرسمي من الثامنة صباحاً حتى الثانية عشرة، أغلقه وقت صلاة الظهر. بعد ارتفاع صوت الأذان بتتابع مدهش من خلال المئة مئذنة الموجودة فقط في المدينة القديمة. لا يحب سكان المدينة استفزازهم، بالذات في أوقات العبادة. لا ألتزم بوقت محدّد للرسم فيه وأترك حالتي المزاجية هي المسيطرة. أغادر في الخامسة عصراً إلى منزلي في صنعاء الجديدة فيما يظل هناك عامل لبيع المنتجات حتى التاسعة مساءً.

نادراً ما أرسم لوحة سريالية مبهمة، أو تجريدية خيالية. أحب الواقعية. أتقن رسم بورتريهات الوجوه لكبار السن. أتحدّى نفسي في إتقانها وكأني أمدها بالحياة التي كادت تذوي فيها. ما أعشقه فعلاً هو رسم هذه المباني القديمة، والتغلغل في تفاصيلها، أتخيّل عوالم لم أعشها، وتغشاني بين الحين والآخر حالة شجن وأنا أمر بريشتي للتفنّن في إبراز ضوء خافت منبعث من نوافذ منزل صغير، أو رسم تجوابٍ عالٍ لنهاية منزلٍ مطلٍ على المدينة القديمة، تاركةً المدينة الجديدة خلفية باهتة مترامية الأطراف.

ليس لي طقوس معيّنة في الرسم مثل باقي الرسامين، لا أنكش شعري، أو أرتدي ملابس غير نظيفة. لا أدخن بكثرة لكني أستمتع بنفخ تعبي في نهاية كل لوحة بسيجارة نعناع خاصة. أستعد للرسم كاستعدادي لملاقاة حبيب. أسرّح شعري، أُكحل عينيّ، أضع مسحة ماكياج خفيف على وجهي، أرتدي غالباً قميصاً عاري الكتفين وبنطلوناً قصيراً.

بعض الأيام أشعر فيها برغبة جامحة للاستمرار في العمل حتى وقت متأخر من الليل، أضطر فيها للمبيت في المرسم الأمر الذي يزعج أمي كثيراً، لكنها تتقبّله على مضض. هي التي أصرت على أن لا نسكن في المدينة القديمة دون أن تظهر لي الأسباب. رجوتها شراء بيت أوسع من المرسم ليكون سكناً لنا ومرسماً في ذات الوقت، لكنها رفضت بشدة. شيء ما لا تريد أن تتذكره! شيء ما سبّب لها جراحاً لم تندمل بعد. لذلك بقينا في منزلنا الذي غادرناه قبل اثنين وعشرين عاماً، قضيناها في القاهرة وسمحت لي بشراء هذا المنزل الصغير.

عدت مع أمي عام ٢٠٠٠ من القاهرة بعد أن قضينا فيها تلك المدة الطويلة، تحديداً بعد وفاة والدي بعام واحد. والدي الذي برغم حبّه العظيم لليمن وبالذات صنعاء، لم يفكر مطلقاً بالعودة إليها ولو من باب الزيارة من منفاه الذي اختاره بكامل إرادته، ليكون القاهرة منذ أواخر السبعينيات.

لم يتوقف أبي يوماً عن الحديث مناجياً صنعاء، بشوقٍ كمعشوقة أبدية يحتويها كل ليلة بين جوانحه، يطبق عليها جفنيه وينام قرير العين، محتفظاً بالصورة التي يريدها وربما الصورة التي غادرها قبل انقضاء كل تلك السنين. يتناول البُن كل صباح! وكل صباح يرتشف الرشفة الأولى متعمداً إصدار صوتٍ عالٍ منتشياً. مذاقها الخاص لديه. كان يحمصها بيديه على النار، يُقسم أي كمية متوفرة إلى ثلثين يحمّصها غامقاً، وثلثها الباقي فاتحاً، ثم يضيف لها بعض الهيل ويطحنها بكميات قليلة حتى لا تفقد نكهتها التي يحب. لم أسأله يوماً ماذا يتذكر عن صنعاء، أو بماذا يشعر لكني كنت أشعر

١٠٦

بالنشوة ذاتها وأعيش معه اللحظة بمزيدٍ من الأمل في العودة لها وبناء ذكريات لي فيها، كما فعل هو حتى لو حتى جرحته بل أدمته وتركته ينزف حتى الموت! ...

كان بكل حبه لها والحديث عنها يجذّر في داخلي حبها وحب العودة إليها بل وأمل الحياة فيها. صنعاء تلك الساحرة بتاريخها، النائمة تحت سفح جبل عارٍ من الأشجار الوارفة أو الصخور الحامية، لذلك "تشعر دائماً بالبرد وعدم الأمان فيها" كما يحب أن يقول عنها أبي دائماً. صنعاء التي لا يسأل إلا عنها وعن أحوالها وأحوال ناسها بعد كل عودة لي ولأمي ولشقيقي الوحيد من إجازتنا السنوية التي كنا نقضيها بدونه.

لم تتحمّل أمي البقاء بعد وفاته وخصوصاً بعد أن اطمأنت على شقيقي الذي تزوّج بفتاة مصرية. الزواج من جنسية أخرى لم يكن يمثّل لشقيقي أو لأمي أو حتى لوالدي مشكلة. لكنه بالنسبة إليّ كان كارثة حقيقية، كيف أتزوّج برجلٍ غريب عني، رجلٍ لا يعرف عن بلدي غير ما سمعه عنه، رجل لم يشاركني يوماً السير في شوارعه واللعب في حاراته والاختباء في أركان أزقته، رجل لا يتذوّق نكهة ذكرياتي عندما أحكيها له في أماكنها ومع ناسها لأنه لم يعشها يوماً؟

كنتُ أرفض الفكرة تماماً، لكني لم أصرّح بها يوماً لأبي أو أمي حتى لا يشعرا بخيبة الأمل في تربيتي كما أرادا، تربية متحضرة جداً تقبل الآخر دون النظر إلى جنسه أو لونه أو دينه. لا يريدني أبي بالذات أن أفكر كأولئك الذين قالوا له يوماً إنه "مُولد" وليس صنعانياً خالصاً بسبب أمه الحبشية. كنت كذلك تماماً متمدّنة حتى العظم فيما عدا

هذا الجانب فقط! لذلك كنت أتقن فن خلق الأعذار لرفض كل من تقدم لخطبتي أثناء دراستي الجامعية في القاهرة. أحلم دائماً بالزواج لكن برجل صنعاني، نعم صنعاني خالص مئة بالمئة، نشأ وتربى في المدينة القديمة. يعرف أزقتها. لعب في حاراتها. وعجنته عاداتها وتقاليدها الإنسانية حتى غدا إنساناً آخر. رجل صنعاني مثل أبي ... بحميمية دقائق خباياه مع أمي، بحبه العظيم لها، بتفاصيل رجولته الصنعانية اليومية التي لا اعرف من أين جاءته، هل من صنعاء أم من أمه، جدّتي مسرّة المرأة الإثيوبية الجميلة، التي منحته لونها الأسمر وكل حنانها.

جدتي مسرة التي حكت لي يوماً عن جدي ما لا يمكنني نسيانه أبداً، جدي الذي كان ينتظرها حال عودتها من الحمّام التركي العام بكوب من ماء الورد البارد. يكون قد نقعه لها من مساء الليلة الماضية واعداً إياها بليلة ساحرة. هو الذي علمها اللهجة الصنعانية المتميّزة برنة حروفها في المخارج حتى أتقنتها، وعلمها الرقص الصنعاني بحركات الغنج والدلال التي يعشقها حتى أتقنتها أيضاً. يقضيان ليلهما بين الأحاديث الجميلة والرقص حتى يداهمهما الصباح دون أن يشعرا ... تقول جدتي مسرة "إنها لم تنم يوماً إلا بعد أن ينام و لم تستيقظ بعده يوماً إلا في ما ندر، لتكون آخر وجه يراه قبل نومه وأول وجه يستقبله حال استيقاظه".

أحببت جدتي وأردت أن أحب رجلاً كأبي الذي كان مطابقاً له تماماً ...

قابلت "حميد" أول مرة عندما جاء إلى المعرض كزبون عادي يريد شراء

لوحة لمنازل صنعانية متجاورة، داهمتني مشاعر متناقضة جديدة عليَّ أبهجتني. حجمه الذي بدا لي ضخماً نسبياً جعلني أشعر بأني سأكون كحمامة يغمرها الدفء والسكون بين أحضانه. بصعوبة تخلصت من هذه الفكرة وأنا أتفاهم معه على اللوحة وقيمتها، وبصعوبة أكثر حاولت ألا أفكر فيه بقية اليوم. لكني بسهولة نمت ليلتها في المرسم منتشية برسم سيناريو لقضاء ليلة صنعانية ساحرة! ...

لم يعد بعدها حميد لأخذ اللوحة كما وعد ولم أعد أنا لفعل ما فعلته البارحة، حتى إنني تجنّبت النوم في المرسم بعدها لشهور لأتخلص من تلك القامة الطويلة والمنكب العريض والوجه الأبيض بعينيه العسليتين! ...

وقيل إن الاغتسال بمياه الحمّامات التركية العامة في مدينة صنعاء القديمة يقي من الأمراض، وإن البخار المنبعث من حوائطها الحجرية يمدّ الجسد بقدراته الليلية الخارقة للنساء والرجال، شريطة التناوب عليها من شمال المدينة إلى جنوبها، ومن شرقها إلى غربها مرة كل شهر ... سخونة جسدك وأعضائك الحميمة ينبت منها الكثير من الصبية الأقوياء والصبايا الفاتنات بعد طول انتظار ...

حميد

تتوسّط الجنبية جسد الرجل اليمني دليل عنفوانه ورجولته. لمس مقبضها في الشجار دليل للنوايا العدوانية، وإخراج الخنجر حتى منتصف غمده إنذار بالهجوم، أما سحب الخنجر بكامله فهو المعركة والدماء التي يجب أن تسيل قبل أن يعود إلى غمده معزّزاً مكرّماً ...

١٠٩

المرة الأولى التي وافقت صبحية فيها على السير معي في الأزقة والذهاب لتناول القهوة الصنعانية في سوق الملح، لم أصدقها! ... ليس من السهل على أي فتاة يمنية قبول ذلك بسهولة! كان ذلك بعد مضي شهرين من زيارتي لها في معرضها وشراء اللوحة التي كنت قد اخترتها. قلتُ بيني وبيني إنها تكذب عليّ ولن تأتي. خيط رفيع من الأمل تمسّكت به على رغم ذلك. تأخرها عن موعدها خمس دقائق أشعرني باليأس، نهشتني فيها الوساوس وتركتني حائراً متسائلاً بين مجيئها أو عدمه! ...

لكنها جاءت، وها أنا أسير إلى جوارها، متعمداً الاتكاء على أركان الأزقة، وملامسة حجارة المنازل لأشعر بأنني لا أحلم وأنها إلى جواري بالفعل. خمسون عاماً مضت من عمري وأنا أحلم أن أسير في أزقة صنعاء القديمة متأبطاً ذراع امرأة، أهمس في أذنها بأحلامي، وأدغدغ مشاعرها بأمنياتي! ... عندما جاءت اللحظة لم أصدّقها، برغم أنها إلى جواري! ... هل أربكتني بمجيئها؟! لا أعرف! هل كانت فوق قدرة استيعابي لها كواقع بعد أن ظلت حلماً لفترة طويلة؟! لا أعرف أيضاً! ...

أخذتها في المرة الأولى إلى الصرحة التي شهدت طفولتي، حكيت لها ذكرياتي، هنا كنت ألعب الكرة وهنا مع أصدقائي نتصيّد بنات الجيران. هنا الجامع الذي تعلمت فيه الصلاة وهذه المدرسة التي تعلمت فيها القراءة والكتابة ... وها أنا أجلس إلى جوارها على ذلك الحجر المستطيل في ركن الصرحة كأني لم أحب قط، وكأن قلبي يخفق للمرة الأولى.

صنعائي

"خمسين عاماً أبحث عن امرأة تحبّني". بقدر ما أدهشتها
هذه العبارة فقد أراحتني، لأني أردت أن أحكي لها عما مضى من
حياتي، عن علاقاتي المرتبكة بالنساء دون أن أعرف هل العيب فيهن
أم فيَّ! عن صدفة مرور امرأة كل عشرة أعوام في حياتي. كان إنصاتها
مدهشاً لي، لم تخذلني يوماً عن الإنصات لي بكل حواسّها، كما لم
تخذلني يوماً في استيعاب الأزمات النفسية التي كنت أمر بها، هكذا
هي معي راقية حتى أبعد حد، وأنا كنت معها سافلاً وحقيراً حتى
أبعد حد أيضاً.

حكيت لها عن تقية، التجربة الأولى التي مررت بها وأنا لم أتجاوز
السابعة من العمر. لم أكن أدرك سر انجذابي إليها، هل حنانها الذي
كانت تتعامل به معي ومع أولاد وبنات حارة طلحة، أم جمالها الباهر
الذي كانت تهبنا إياه ولا تضع اللثام لتغطي به وجهها وهي تلعب
معنا في الحارة، وكأننا مميزون لديها، أم هو شعوري بأني وحدي مميّز
لديها لدفاعها عني وضربها وتهديدها كل من يتعرض لي. تقول إني
"حالي" ولا يجب أن يتعرّض لي أحد.

تقية تكبرني لا أعرف بكم لكنها أطول من كل الذين كنت ألعب
معهم من الأولاد والبنات، لم أكن أعرف ما الذي كان يعنيه لها الاختلاء
بي في دهليز منزلهم المظلم بعد المغرب واحتضاني وتقبيلي لتشكرني
على شراء الحلويات التي كانت تطلبها من الدكان في آخر الشارع. كان
لعبث أصابعها على تفاصيل جسدي الحميمة لذة خاصة، تقول: "يا
رب احفظ حميد الصغير". وبعد مرات عديدة أصبح حميد الصغير
يستمتع بملامسة جسدها. وبصوتها الذي كانت تصدره بعد كل

١١١

ملامسة، صوتها الذي يحتل أذني حتى هذه اللحظة. وفي نهاية كل مرّة
تحذرني من أن لا أخبر أحداً بملامستنا حتى لا تموت تقية. كلمة موت
كانت كابوساً جاثماً على صدري لأنها تعني أن أفقد تقية وهذا ما لم
أكن أريده لكنه حدث سريعاً! ... فبعد عام تزوّجت تقية، رأيتها مع
أولاد وبنات الحارة وهي مرتدية الفستان الأبيض في انتظار شقيقها
ليصطحبها إلى منزل الزوجية. لمحتني من بعيد مختبئاً بين باقي الأطفال
ودحرجت لي ابتسامة خفية وهي تعضّ على شفتها السفلى.

ليلتها لم أتوقف عن البكاء حتى غلبني النوم، وفي الصباح كان كل
شيء في حارتنا بلا طعم، لم تعد تقية إلى الحارة أبداً ولو لزيارة أهلها،
ذهبت مع زوجها المغترب إلى السعودية ولم أرها بعد ذلك. لكنها تعود
إلى مخيلتي بين حين وآخر مرتدية ستارتها الملوّنة وواضعة اللثمة على
وجهها الأبيض، تسبقني بين الحارات وأنا أتبع الضوء الصادر منها
دون أن أعرف أين ينتهي بنا المطاف.

في أول بلل شعرت به وأنا في الرابعة عشرة من عمري، داهمتني تقية
بقوة، استعذبت لسانها وأصابعها من جديد قبل أن تختفي من ذاكرتي
للأبد. عندما حلت مكانها حضية بنت الجيران، تناسيت كل ما حدث
في دهليز تقية، واكتفيت بتبادلنا للنظرات بذلك الوجد من نوافذ منزلينا
المتقابلين، لم نتحدث يوماً أو نلتقِ، أنهت حضية كل ذلك بموافقتها على
الزواج. لتتسرّب هي الأخرى من حياتي كأنها لم تكن.

في الرابعة والعشرين مرّت المرأة الثالثة في حياتي، وجدتني بقرار
مسبق لا أجيب عن أسئلة الامتحان في الجامعة حتى لا أكون العام
المقبل مع أمينة، زميلتي التي أحببتها بصمت طيلة ثلاثة أعوام

وعندما صارحتها بذلك رفضتني، لأنها أحبّت صديقي صديقي دون أن يخبرني هو ذاته عنها، ربما كان خفف عليّ وطأة ما حدث لي من جُرحِ رفض امرأة لحب رجل.

المرأة الرابعة هي زوجتي وأم أبنائي الأربعة. زواجنا كان تقليدياً، اختارتها والدتي من أقاربنا، قالت لي في أول وصف لها إنها جميلة وبشرتها بيضاء وهذه مواصفات يفضّلها معظم الرجال، كانت كذلك، لكني بعد أن تزوجتها اكتشفت أنني لا أحب ذوات البشرة البيضاء كما لا أحب المرأة الصارخة الجمال! ... خشيت أن أصارح أمي بذلك حتى لا تقول إنني غبي في فهم جمال النساء. لذلك طيلة العشرين عاماً التي قضيتها معها لم أحبها الحب الذي أريد، تعوّدت عليها لتسير الحياة. كان من الصعب أن تلبّي نداءً خفياً في أعماقي وتكون تقية وحضية وأمينة في آن واحد ...

لقائي بصبحية ليس صدفة كما تظن بل هو قدر وعليّ الإيمان به. ليس صدفة أن يكون والدي ووالدها في المعركة ذاتها للدفاع عن صنعاء في حرب السبعين يوماً ويُستشهد أبي وينجو أبوها لنكمل نحن الحكاية. تلك الحرب التي جعلت منّي يتيماً في سنّ مبكرة عاشقاً للعزلة وحاقداً على كل من لديه أب، كما جعلت من صبحية يتيمة أيضاً بفقدها للوطن وبقائها طيلة كل تلك السنين بعيدة عنه.

القدر أن تتحقق أمنيتي بعد مضيّ كل تلك السنين وأجاهر بسيري إلى جوارها من دون اكتراث بتلك النظرات التي تلاحقنا كلما مررنا معاً بأزقة المدينة وحاراتها. لم تستيقظ المدينة يوماً على وقع خطوات عاشقين كما فعلنا، ولم تنم على مناجاة أمنيات ذات

العاشقين بالتوحّد مدى الحياة ... هناك من قام بفعل خبيث ليفرقنا، لينهي كل هذا الوجد بقليل من الجهد وكثير من الألم ...

يحكى أن طائراً ضخماً بجناحين أسودين اقتلع "لحجر النَّفاسة" من ركنها بعد أن أصبح البصق عليها حولها وطلب إبعاد العين المؤذية لهم هاجس أهل المدينة للحفاظ على ممتلكاتهم وصحتهم وسير نمط حياتهم، وبعد أن كاد الزحام الشديد يسبّب موت أحد الأطفال الذي نجا بأعجوبة ...

ناصر الظاهري

حجر الرغبة

"ليس في المكان ... غير الحر والبرد، الجفاف والرطوبة.
النار حارة جافة، والماء بارد رطب، الهواء حار ورطب، والتراب
بارد وجاف.
ومن هذه الخواص يمكن للإكسير أو الزئبق الأحمر، ذلك السائل
من حجر الفلاسفة أن يعطي شيئاً من الخلود، والكثير من الرغبة".

في محاولة لفهم جابر بين حيّان، ولما كانت العبادة للحجر!

في منزل المثّالة، التي غاب اسمها في مهنتها عند الجيران البعيدين، لا
يرد إلا على لسان صحافيين ممن يفرحون بأيام الافتتاح لمهرجانات أو
معارض فنية مقترحة، وكأنه واجب مهني أو نقّاد قادرين على النفاذ
للعبة الأصابع على الحجر.
الصومعة كما تحب أن تسمّيه في لحظات مرحها القليلة، ذلك
البناء الحجري الذي يستقر في طرف المدينة، كدليل كد سنوات طويلة
في العمل الدبلوماسي الخارجي، لرجل ضاع بين الخدمة الملكية،

والقراءات، والمتع الناقصة، والأسرة غير المكتملة، وأوجاع زوجة من بنات العم، لم تعش طويلاً.

في ذلك المنزل الذي تحيطه حديقة برية متوحشة، عملت عن قصد، لكي تتواءم مع نزق الحجر، وجفاء المكان شبه البعيد، فيما تتوزع منحوتاتها الزوايا، والأركان الصغيرة، ومرات تجدها مبثوثة هنا ... وهناك، عند خاصرة البيت مثلاً، تحت شباك مضاء، ومزيّن بزجاج معشق، في الحديقة التي تشبه مقبرة كاثوليكية في قرية صغيرة.

"حجر ... حجر، ما أروع الحجر، من قال إنه لا يطوّع؟ من قال إنه صخر صوان، كتلة حجر؟! حجري ناطق تجري فيه دمائي وعرقي، وتلك الأحاسيس التي أبثها له وحده، تلك الوشوشة، والحديث الصامت بيني وبينه، شوقي له، بحثي عنه، لا يدخل بيتي إلا حجر منتقى، لأن كلام الإزميل والمطرقة ورقص الأصابع والفرشاة، حديث همس له كل المعنى، يكاد يسبر الروح في متاهتها البعيدة.

الآن ... حين يستوي التمثال، ويصبح كائناً مكتملاً بكل عافية الحجر، وحلمي المتخيّل، وحين تنطق تفاصيل الجسد، ويتهيّأ لي مثل بطل أسطوري تهمّه الانتصارات، وأتهيّأ له مثل نساء المعبد، الشرقات باللذة الصامتة، ينطق الحجر، وأغيب في دفئه: حجري غير الحجر"!

هكذا شهقت المثّالة بحديثها ساعة التجلي واكتمال المولود، غصّت بالفرح وهي خارجة من بحر نشوتها، وهي تغطي التمثال، الرجل الجديد، بغطاء سريري أبيض، مضمخ بسر عطرها.

تمضي المثّالة جل يومها تحاول أن تستنطق انفعالات الحجر، وتفصّل

شجر الحديقة، فليس يعكر زهو الصباح، مثل وظيفة دبقة على روح
فنان، هكذا كان قرارها، برغم إلحاح معارف الأب الكثيرين الذين
بودهم تقديم خدمات مجانية للـ"بيك يوسف" ووظيفته المحترمة.

كانت تعشق ظل الصباح، وروائح زهر الليمون، لقط أوراق
الشجر اليابس المتساقط على مهل، كانت تعطي الأمور شيئاً من
نكهتها، وتفصّلها وفق فلسفتها الجمالية الخاصة.

فناجين القهوة في فترة راحتها، واستراحتها، تنتقل معها من ركن
إلى ركن، مرة تحت شجرة التين، ومرة أخرى تحت شجر اللوز، وهي
تستمتع ببرودة الجدار الحجري المسندة إليه ظهرها، لا يشاركها
وحدتها، ووحدة فنجان القهوة، غير أصابع السيجارة التي تستلها
من العلب العديدة من ذلك الصندوق المعزز على الطاولة.

في يومها الذي يبدأ إن لم يكن ليله قلقاً في الفجر الذي يضحك
مع أول ضوء الشمس، تظل تعمل حتى منتصف النهار، بعدها
تذهب في رحلة الماء، وتتناول إفطارها الخفيف، تغط بعدها ساعة
زمن، لتخرج من جديد هذه المرة متزيّنة، متعطرة، لتنسج عملاً جديداً
أو نحتاً استعصى عليها في ساعات الصباح الأولى.

تبقى متأخرة حتى العصر، بعد أن تأخذ إغفاءة داهمتها فجأة،
وطرأت على جفنيها المتخفيين خلف نظارة سميكة، بإطارها المذهب،
وخشبها العاجي، الذي كان يوماً ما قيمة غالية.

تنزل حديقتها بعد أن تصبغ الشمس كل الأجواء بلونها البرتقالي
الغائب، ليخلق مع حجر الدار تلك السكينة المشتعلة.

تضحك بصوت عال، إذا كان يومها على درجة من الرضى،

بينما تكتفي بابتسامة خاصة، إذا ما سارت أمور اليوم بطبيعة كسلى، تبتسم وهي تهم بدخول باب البيت المنحوت بطريقتها، مطبقة على ما بقي في العينين من منظر تعشقه، ولا تعوّضه المدن الكثيرة الأخرى.

الليل ... عندها له طقس آخر، وتدبير مختلف، فبعد أن تحضّر وجبتها النباتية، وتستقر زجاجة النبيذ الذي تحرص على انتقائه من أركان دافئة في مطارات مختلفة، بجنب الحواضر، وكأسها الخاصة، تذهب من جديد إلى رحلة الماء الثانية، وترتدي خفاف الملابس، بألوانها المدعاة للمشاغبة الليلية.

الليل عادة ما يمضي بين القراءة، والتلذذ بالأوراق النباتية المغسولة بالحامض والخل، وتلك الكأس المشربة بحمرة دم الأتقياء، وحين يبدأ الجسد يرتجف بأول هزات النشوة، ترفع من صوت الموسيقى ليؤنسها، ويؤنس وحشة البيت، والليل الذي بدأ يغوص في ظلمته، تبقى في متعتها تلك، حتى تشعر بالخدر يسري في كل الجسد، ويستدعي أحزاناً مستقرة في الرأس، ولحظات فرح كانت غامرة يوماً ما، حين كانت صغيرة، مستبشرة بتمدّد الجسد، وبداية تفاصيل النحت الأنثوي فيه، وتلك المغامرات الصغيرة صوب براءة التكون، التي تعنّ اليوم، وكأنها لم تغب طيلة هذه السنين، وحده وهج النور يطفئها، لا تأتي بها إلا هبوب الليل الباردة، والتماعة الكأس التي نادراً ما تفرغ، وإن فرغت، كان الجسد يتفصد عرقاً، منهكاً من التعب، ومن تلك النشوة حين تذهب إلى مداها، دافعة ضريبة العمر، والجمال غير المكتمل، والآيل بسرعة نحو العطب.

تتكوّم كقطعة حجر بدائية تضمها الكنبة العتيقة، لا توقظها إلا الأحلام التي تهاجمها بشراستها أو تلك الكحة التي توقظها أحياناً في منتصف الليالي الشتوية، وحين تئن العظام من برودة الحجر، والصمت الذي يضفي عليه الليل شيئاً من سواد الشر، تسحب قدميها، لتلقي بجثتها على السرير الكبير، وتنغمس في فراشها الدافئ، والوثير، باحثة يدها عن شبح رجل ليته كان هنا ... الساعة.

ضوء الصبح يكشف عن ملامح امرأة خمسينية، ينتعها الطول، وتصقلها النحافة، لولا سمنة العمر، وترهل الوقت اللذان يحيطان الخصر والأرداف، ويثقلان الصدر للأسفل.

ينحسر الشعر المحنّى عن الجبهة، ليضاعف من سنواتها الخمسين، والنمش المتناثر على الوجه والصدر، وقليل منه على اليدين، بتلك الأصابع الطويلة التي تشبه أصابع عازف تدرب كثيراً، تزيّنها خواتم الفضة والأحجار الكريمة ذات الفصوص المهيبة.

شيئان لا تجد فيهما اللمعة الحقيقية: الأظافر الدائمة التكسر والتقصّف، والأسنان التي اعتادت القهوة اليومية والنيكوتين، وحده الجلد ظل محافظاً على نظارة ما.

كانت دائماً تفتش عن حجرها الخام، تبحث عن الأشياء المركبة من الناس أو تخلق تلك العلاقة بين المرأة وبين الموجودات، كان جسد الرجل هو فرحها الحقيقي، كانت تتعامل مع كل عضلة فيه، تطرقه بقوة جسد أنثى مسكونة بحرقة العطش، كان رقص الأصابع يوحي وكأنها تحمّمه بالغار أو تغسله بعطر الورد، في لحظات النحت كانت كل الحواس تتجاذبها مع لغة التواصل، وإلى أن يمنحها الفم الإحساس

بتلك القبلة الغائبة، تظل درجة رضاها محل اختبار، أما حين يكتمل التمثال، فليلتها ليلة عرس وثني، يظهر هيامها بالمعبود الجديد، تجلّ حضوره بطقوس الصلوات القديمة، تظل مثل كاهنة المعبد تتلوّى على نشيد رب الخصب والنماء، تتحدى مطره، وتنتظر عشبه الذي يخضرّ حولها، ليلتها تشعل ناراً من بقايا نار المجوس، وطلاسم من أناشيد الهداية الأولى، وتظل تطوف بالنار، وتهب للجسد انطلاقته وعفويته حتى يسقط في بحر الرجس!

تصحو بعد تلك الصلاة الوثنية، خفيفة متطهرة من جروح النفس، وكأنها عروس الخصب الجديدة، تفرح بلحظة التملك التي تتمنى لو كانت تدوم بصيغة أخرى، أي صيغة في الحياة ... حتى ولو كان ذلك الحدّاد الكافر الذي حضر مرة وهي صغيرة يركّب بوابة البيت الكبير، كانت معجبة باليد المعروقة، المتعرقة، وبتلك البدلة الزرقاء التي تخفي تفاصيل جسد فارع، كانت تراقب ثني الحديد ونار الأوكسجين التي تذيب كل شيء، كانت لحظة مراقبة طفولية، لأشياء ستحبها في أيامها المقبلة، غير أن نظرة الحدّاد جرحت عمرها، وشغفها بمراقبة اليد وهي تعمل.

اليوم ... ليته يأتي بكل رغبته الشيطانية تلك!

أما ذلك الذي هرب بزهر العمر الغض، وبتلك الرسائل المدرسية الوردية، فليعش مع زوجته تطحنه لقمة العيال، ولعنة السكّري الذي حوّله إلى شبح مخضرّ مطارد، مثلما هرب ذلك اليوم متخلصاً منها، ومن كل عطاياها، متذرّعاً بأنه عاطل من العمل، وغير قادر على الارتباط الزوجي، وكل همّه أن يجد فرصة السفر إلى الخليج بأي

ثمن، ساعتها أخرجت من صندوقها الذي ورثته عن أمها ربطة نقود،
ورمتها في صدره، أخذها ولم يعد من الكويت إلا وهو يجرجر زوجة
سبقته إلى هناك، تعمل بوظيفة مدرّسة مطلقة، وتعيل بنتاً وولداً في
الخامسة، أجبره عليها طمع مستقر في النفس، والأيام الرجولية في
مدن السواحل التي لا ترحم!

يومها نحتت وجهاً نصفياً لرجل متأنّث متخنّث، ونصفه الآخر
متفتت، محفور، وكأن دواب الأرض جلست تنغل فيه، وتقتات به
لأيام متواصلة.

استقر ذلك التمثال خارج البيت، ترمقه بنظرة كلما سنحت
لها فرصة التذكر أو السهو. مضت حياتها بعد مغامرة ذلك الرجل
الهارب بنصف رجولته تسير نحو نجاح في الحياة والشهرة التي تحظى
بها من خلال الصحف والمجلات والمعارض، وكلمات النقّاد اللعابية،
والسفرات الكثيرة، والمشاركات العديدة، وجلسات زوّار طارئين من
مثقفين عابري المؤتمرات الوهمية، وعشاق فنها، والتي عادة ما تنتهي
بقبلات من تعتعة السُّكر وقلة الحيلة، والتعلل بضرورة المبيت عند
الزوجة المثقلة بنداءات الانتظار.

كانت ليالي ... تبتدئ بالفرح الأولي، سرعان ما يخلو البيت،
وتبقى طاولات العشاء بصحونها الرابضة، التي تتمنى لو لم تكن
تخصها ساعتها، كلبوة ملت من الشبع والتسافد، ليال ... سرعان ما
تخبو، سارقة إتمام الفرح الأنثوي الذي كانت تمنيّ النفس به دوماً، لا
يبقى عادة بعد تلك الجلسات الحميمة إلا ما يوجع الرأس من ذكرى أم
لم تستطع أن تكبر معها، وأب ستتآكله العواصم السياسية، والزوجة

الثانية، وسنوات طويلة من الغياب كفيلة بأن تجعله يشبع من ابنته الوحيدة بلقاءات فاترة، سرعان ما تنتهي بكثير من العتب، والنصائح المتأخرة والمسرّبة بلسان الزوجة الثانية!

هكذا سار بها العمر الذي كان يفرض عليها مقاييس جديدة لطريقة الحب، ولنوع المغامرة، كانت شروطه تزداد يوماً بعد يوم، وهي لم تعد قادرة على إعطاء سر الجسد المتحوّل لكل شخص، حتى قرع بابها ذات يوم شحاذ أعمى يقوده طفل في الحادية عشرة من عمره، فقدّمت له من فطورها الباقي، وأرادت أن تعطيه أشياء كثيرة بكرم.

أحست لأول وهلة أنه مشروعها الفني الجديد، وأنه يمكن أن يعالج البكارة الذاوية بطريقة جلفة، كانت تتأمله وهو يأكل، وهو يشرب، وهو يمسح شاربيه، وكيف يتحسّس الأشياء، تفاصيل الجسد، يقظة الإذنين، الأنف المتوثب، اللحية النافرة كعشب ليل بري من قلة الحلاقة.

كانت تسترق النظر إليه حيناً وهو يعبث بالفراغات، مشكّلاً حواره معها، وحيناً آخر تشاركه في حديث كله أسئلة.

صبي الشحاذ تنبّه لنظراتها، وكادت ترتبك، رمت في حضنه حبّة برتقال، كنوع من طلب الرضى، وتشتيت الرأس الصغير، وشراء الصمت!

بعد تجشوْ الشبع، دعا لها الشحاذ الأعمى كعادته حين يرضى عما يقدم له بطول العمر، والصحة، ومباركة الرزق، والولد، وعمار البيت.

شعرت بأنه يقولها بصدق أو هكذا أوهمت نفسها، طلبت منه أن يزورها كلما مرّ من هنا، وحاولت أن تفهمه أنه مشروعها الفني المقبل، وأنها تريد أن تصنع منه تمثالاً.

لم يفهم كثيراً، ولم يقتنع كشحاذ محترف خبر الطرقات، قائلاً:
"يا ستي ... حنا دراويش على باب الله ... قولي: يا رزّاق ... يا
كريم"!

قالت له بطريقة مومس مبتدئة: "سأعطيك عن شهر من العمل
مئة دينار، وستأكل وجبتين كل يوم، وربع بطحة عرق ...".

قال: "موافق ... بس انطيني فوقها علبة سيجارة كاملة كل يوم".

ضحكت، وقالت: "كنت لن أوافق ... لو طلبت ربع لفة
حشيش".

برقت عينا الأعمى في الغبش، وبان نابه ضاحكاً: "والله يا ستنا ...
أنت كريمة ... ومن ناس أجاويد، وأنا استاهل عطفك".

لحظتها كانت تريد أن تسبر ما تحت ثيابه، تظاهر الشحاذ بسواد
عماه، وأتى بحركة تنمّ عن خبث علّمه إياه العمى من وقت مبكر، لم
تعرف ساعتها، هل كان يقصدها ذلك الأعمى النجس، ليبصر طريق
ظلمته نحوها، أم جاءت هكذا كعفو خاطر، لم تقتنع بالثانية، ولكنها
اقتنعت بعملها الفني القادم، رضي هو بعرضها السخي، ضامناً
شهراً من المتعة: الأكل، الأجر، قلة المشي، وكيف قادر على أن يسد
أذنيه عن مشاجرات لا تنتهي عادة كما يشتهي مع أم العيال بإراقة
ماء ظهرها.

فقط ... بقي سؤال يؤرّقه، هل يساوي كل هذا العرض الذي
قدّمته؟ وماذا فيه من أشياء لا يراها في نفسه؟

كان حديثاً مقتضباً، وطارئاً بين الشحاذ وابنه، لكنه استهلك كل

الطريق، كانت أسئلة كبيرة لصبي اعتاد أن يجيب عن أسئلة أبيه غير المبصرة، كان هو عينيه، لكنه هذه المرة، تمنى لو كان هو هالة العينين!

ثمة أمر يبدو أنه يخص الفحولة، تمنّى الأعمى أن لا يدركه الصبي أو يسرّ به إلى أمه الغاضبة دوماً، الحاصية عليه كل شيء في مسائها الضجر عادة.

قال الأعمى لصبيّه المرافق: "يا ابني ... دعنا نوكل وجبتين في اليوم، ونقبض الميّة دينار، ونقول لأمك، أنّا كسبنا نصف المبلغ، وعلبة سيجارة بحالها، بتدخن منها لوحدك خرطوشة بعد كل وجبة، شو رأيك؟ خلنا نقضي هالشهر دون أن تدري أمك الساحرة، هذا إذا بدك توكل زي الناس، وتطعم البرتقان عن حقّ، وتجرب السيجارة، وتخف المشاوير السابقة الطويلة".

همهم الصبي، وتمنى لو كان يعرف كل شيء بسرعة، وبوضوح.

تتالت الأيام من حضورهما قبل الموعد، كعادة الناس المغبشين قبل أن يخطف الطير رزقهم، والذي كان يضايق المثّالة، ويسبّب ضغطاً لا يتناسب مع إيقاع يومها الذي تشتهيه أن يسير كمجرى الماء.

الابن ظل يتذكر تلك البرتقالة الناضجة التي رميت في حضنه ذاك النهار، وذلك الفطور الذي حافظ على موعده في الحادية عشرة والنصف تقريباً، وذلك الظل الذي يجلب نعاس الظهيرة الذي ترسله شجرة التين الكبيرة، ونظرات تلك المرأة التي حاول أن يفهمها بعمر لذة الاستمناء، ويفهم كلامها العذب، مثلما حاول أن يتصيّد لها تشكيلاً أنثوياً يسحبه إلى تلك الفرشة المتهالكة الرطبة، وصور آخر الليل العارية، التي يستدعيها العمر في المخيّم البائس.

الأب جلس بعد تلك الأيام المقلقة مع ابنه بعد عودة المساء، كان يريد أن يعرف منه شيئاً نسيه أو شيئاً يريد أن يفيض به، ولما اطمأن دونما جواب من الابن ... ذهب متسللاً يتعكز على أصابع يديه، ويتلمّس خطواته في الظلمات، ورضي بالسكون، ومشاغبة امرأة عرفها باللمس، ونشدان النشوة معها من تلك التضاريس التي تلتقي بالأصابع، وتستدل عليها دونما عناء، منتزعين الرغبة الساكنة من وجع التعب اليومي، الذاهب في المشاحنات واللغو وتفاصيل الأولاد، ومضايقات الحارة المكتظة، وسكانها الذين يجبرهم الفقر على خلق يومهم وعوالمهم، وتلك الأمور الصغيرة التي تعطي للحياة حيويتها الناقصة أحياناً.

لم يكن ليستطيع في ذلك المساء، وهو يلامس زوجته، عدم إدخال صوت المثّالة طرفاً بينهما أو محاولة خلق تمثال لها في ظلام العيون، كانت الصورة الجديدة فاعلة، مثلما هي الليلة، حيث كانت ضحكة زوجته، ورضاها قد تحوّلا إلى يدين ناعمتين، مسّدتا ظهره، وأطرافه المتيبسة، وجعلتاه يخرّ في سبات لم يستدعه طويلاً.

كان حضوره اليومي إلى دار المثّالة يتبع ابنه، لا شك في أنه أربك برنامجها، ووتيرته الكسلى بلذة، لكنها حاولت أن تكيّفه بقدر ما استطاعت، وبقدر فهمها، وفهم ابنه، حتى وضعتهما على خط سيرها، وضمن تفاصيل يومها المجبرة عليه بفعل مهنتها.

الابن كان في بدايته ملازماً لأبيه، إلى أن اخترعت له ألعاباً تتناسب وسنه الراكضة نحو الرجولة المبكرة، فقد ضمنت سكونه، وركونه بذاك الجهاز المدهش الذي قلما تفتحه إلا إذا كانت هناك برامج تسجيلية

أو أخبار لا تسرّ خاطرها أو تلك التي تذكّرها بوجع الوطن القديم،
والقرى المتناثرة على الضفة الأخرى المنسية، كان التلفزيون مسكّن
الصبي، والأفلام التي تبث بالأبيض والأسود مصدر سروره، وضحكه،
واحتلاماته. الأعمى في بداية الأمر، ظن أن الاهتمام الموجه للصبي، أنه
هو المعني بالأمر، وأن وجوده هو مثل كوز الماء، فحاول أن يفهّمها أن
لديه وجهة نظر، وأنه رجل، ويريد أن يعرف: "الاتفاق ما هيك يا ستنا
... وإذا بدك إياني، أنا مستعد"!

كان الشك يسيّره مثل أي أعمى، فهمت المثّالة بعض نيّاته، وحاولت
جاهدة أن تثبت له، أنه مجرد مشروع فني وحسب، وعليه أن يلتزم بهذا،
ولا يزعجها بأموره الخاصة في عملها، أما الأساسية منها فإنها ملبّاة.

صرخ من شكه:

— ولكن يا ستي ... الصبي بعده صغير، ولسه ما طرّ شاربه، شو
طلباتك ... عندي أنا ... الله يرحم والديك.

— افهم يا رجل ... خلي الصبي يلتهي ... بدنا نشتغل.

— أنا يا ستنا والله حاضر ... بس تشري بصباعك ... كرمك
مغرقنا من تحت لفوق.

— أسمع ... أفهم عليّ ... بدّي أصب لك قوالب لكل شيء فيك.

— أنا يا ستنا حاضر ... شو ما بدك ... أنا حاضر، ولو إني ما
فهمت ... بس خليك بعيدة عن هالصبي.

— أسمع عاد ... هلكت ربنا بالصبي ... شو بدي بالصبي، أنت
موضوعي ... بتفهم، وإلا ... لا.

— ستنا مثل ما بدك ... أنا من إيدك هاي، إلى إيدك هاي.

"بلاش ستنا ... هلكت ربنا فيها ...

– مثل ما بدك ...

– تعا معي ... بدي أعمل قوالب ... بس ما بدي ولا نفس ها ...

– حاضر يا ستنا ... الله يوفقك، وينجّح مقاصدك.

– الله يطولك يا روح ... تعا معي ... عالساكت، بلا غلبة.

– والصبي ... يا ستنا.

– خليه يشوف التلفزيون ... وإلا بدك إياه يكون أعمى
زيك ...

– يا ستنا خذينا بحلمك ... نحن ناس غلابه، دراويش ... على
باب الله.

– بلا كثرة حكي ورغي ... خلينا نشوف شغلنا ...

امتثل لها مثل صبي نُهر على غلطته، لكن داخله كان يستصرخ
خشونة الرجل، وقسوة الحياة، حين تصنع رجالها، كان يشعر بأنه
مقبل على ضوء جديد سيسعد أيامه، شعر لحظتها، وكأن مسالكه
البولية تريد أن تتسرب في اتجاهات جديدة، وبطرق سيراميكية لامعة
لم تعتدها حياته في المخيّم، ولم تسمح الظروف بتجربتها على مهل.

كانت تتعامل مع جسد الشحاذ كخامة مختلفة عن الحجر، كان أشبه
بلحم ميت، وهي النباتية، ليس فيه صلابة الرخام، ولا مطواعية
الحجر، كان شكلاً لا يخصها، ولم تشهد التكوين، انتظرت لحظة
النضج، واكتفت بالوداع قبل الباب، وكأنها كانت مرغمة على شيء

لا تحبه، ولكن تأتيه، ففي ليلها الضجر ذاك، عليها أن تهزم الرجل الهارب، والعمر الهارب، وتكتفي بما تصنعه يداها!

فرّغت من طقوس يومها الشحاذ وابنه، وطعامهما الذي لا ينتهي، فقد اشتاقت أن تبقى متوحدة مع طقوس اعتادت أن تعطي أشياءها ظلاً من حنين.

كلمة شكراً كان يمكن أن تكفي، لكن في منطق شحاذ أعمى، وابن على طريق التسوّل، فالأفضل منها فتح الثلاجة على مصراعيها، وتفريغها من حاجاتها التي قد تفقد صلاحيتها بعد وقت قليل.

لا تعرف لما طرأت عليها فكرة الاعتقاد بفساد الأشياء، وهي ماكثة في مكانها، حرّك ذلك التفكير في وجهها عضلة نائمة، بدأت تنتفض، وتتراقص بلا إرادة منها، لكنها استسلمت لفرحة الوحدة من جديد، وأن هذا الحيّز من القلب والمكان لا يمكن أن يتسع للكثير، وفي كل الأوقات.

وحده الابن ظل متعلقاً بالباب، وبكل المسرّة التي دخلت يومه، منذ أن ولج تلك الدار، وبها كتمثال أنثوي سكن رأسه، ولا يشبه أمه، ولا يعرف أن يقبض عليه، كما ينبغي للحالات، وبمنحوتاتها الكثيرة، وبتفاصيل عرفها خارج عطن المخيم، بات ليلتها ضائعاً، كيف يمكنه أن يمسك كل تلك الأشياء مرة واحدة، ومن جديد؟ وتذكر ... أكثر ما تذكر تلك البرتقالة التي استقرت في حضنه قبل شهر تقريباً!

بعد واحد وعشرين عاماً، وسبعة أشهر، وسبعة عشر يوماً، عند ناصية الشارع الذي أخذ اسماً جديداً "شارع أحلام المجيدي" وفي دوار حديقته الصغيرة التي استقر فيها تمثالاً أزاح عنه الستار محافظ

العاصمة اليوم، وقبل أن أتجه إلى طريق منزل عرفته قدماي الحافيتان لأول مرة، تركت شيئاً من زهر الليمون يؤنس وحشة المكان الجديد، ويذكّرها بعطر كانت تحبه في حياتها، أشعلت الغليون، ورميت بشالي الكشميري حول رقبتي، ولم أنتظر المطر حتى يتوقف، فقد كنت، وكانت روحها، وكانت المدينة بحاجة إليه، في يوم استثنائي على الأقل بالنسبة إليّ، كرجل تغيّر منذ دخل بيت المثّالة مشدوهاً، ومعنيٌّ بالأسئلة، يقود شحاذاً أعمى.

مرّرت يدي المبتلة على وجه التمثال المبقع بالنمش، وتحسّست النظارة السميكة، شاعراً لحظتها بقيمة العاج، وطال تأمّلي لتلك الجبهة الحاسرة قليلاً، ثم طبعت قبلة الرضى على شفتي المثّالة، لا تعني غير تمجيد ذكراها، وغير الحب لشخص عاشر كل تفاصيلها، وانغمس في يومياتها، وعلمته الكثير في آخر عمرها، والرضى عمّا أنجزت يداه على هذا الحجر!

المساهمون

أليس غوثري: بريطانية. درست اللغة العربية في جامعة إكستر، وفي المعهد العالي للغات الأجنبية في دمشق. تعمل مترجمة أدبية وإعلامية، وقامت أخيراً بترجمة بعض أعمال الكاتبين الفلسطينيين عاطف أبو سيف وعلاء حليحل.

إنعام كجه جي: عراقية. مراسلة صحيفة "الشرق الأوسط" في باريس. تُرجمت روايتها "الحفيدة الأميركية" إلى الإنكليزية، ووصلت إلى القائمة القصيرة للجائزة العالمية للرواية العربية عام ٢٠٠٩.

بول ستاركي: بريطاني. أستاذ الأدب العربي في جامعة دورهام. كتب عن توفيق الحكيم، وألّف كتاب "الأدب العربي الحديث"، وترجم العديد من الكتب عن الأدب العربي الحديث.

بيتر كلارك: بريطاني. يترجم الروايات والشعر والمسرح والتاريخ عن العربية منذ عام ١٩٨٠. عمل وأقام في سبع دول عربية، وهو أمين الجائزة العالمية للرواية العربية، ومحرّر مساهم في مجلة "بانيبال".

جبور الدويهي: لبناني. يعمل أستاذاً للأدب الفرنسي في الجامعة اللبنانية. روايته "مطر حزيران" وصلت إلى القائمة القصيرة لجائزة الرواية العربية لعام ٢٠٠٨.

ريم غنايم: فلسطينية، تحمل شهادة دكتوراه من جامعة تل أبيب، في الأدب المقارن. ترجمت الشعر الفلسطيني، وتكتب المقالات عن الأدب.

علي عازريه: مغربي. يحمل شهادة من جامعة باث وسوني في بينغهامتون، الولايات المتحدة. عمل بالتدريس في كلية الترجمة في جامعة الملك فهد في طنجة، ويعمل حالياً مدرّساً في جامعة الأخوين، أفرين، المغرب.

كمال الرياحي: تونسي. يرأس قسم الترجمة في المعهد العالي للترجمة في الجزائر. نشر رواية واحدة، ومجموعتين قصصيتين، وثلاثة أعمال نقدية.

لانا عبد الرحمن: لبنانية مقيمة في مصر. تحمل شهادات من الجامعة اللبنانية والجامعة الأميركية في القاهرة. صدرت لها روايتان ومجموعتان قصصيتان، وتعمل في الصحافة الثقافية.

محمد حسن علوان: ولد في الرياض في المملكة العربية السعودية. يحمل إجازة في إدارة الأعمال من جامعة بورتلاند في ولاية أوريغون الأميركية. صدرت له ثلاث روايات، وبعض القصص القصيرة. يكتب زاوية أسبوعية لإحدى الصحف السعودية.

محمد صلاح العزب: ولد في القاهرة، وصدرت له روايات ومجموعات قصصية. من بين الجوائز التي فاز بها جائزة سعاد الصباح للرواية.

منصورة عز الدين: ولدت في قرية في دلتا مصر، وتعمل في الصحافة والتلفزيون. روايتها "ما وراء الفردوس" وصلت إلى القائمة القصيرة للجائزة العالمية للرواية العربية عام ٢٠٠٩.

منصور الصويّم: سوداني. ولد في الرياض، في المملكة العربية السعودية. يعمل صحافياً في الخرطوم، وقد نشر روايتين ومجموعتين قصصيتين. تُرجمت بعض أعماله إلى الإنكليزية والفرنسية.

ناديا الكوكباني: ولدت في مدينة تعز في اليمن، وتحمل شهادات من اليمن ومصر. تعمل أستاذة في هندسة العمارة في جامعة صنعاء. صدرت لها ثلاث مجموعات قصصية.

ناصر السعيد النور: سوداني، ولد في إقليم دارفور. يعمل صحافياً ومترجماً وباحثاً في القضايا الأدبية والسياسية، ويعمل حالياً مترجماً في المملكة العربية السعودية.

ناصر الظاهري: إماراتي، ولد في مدينة العين في الإمارات العربية المتحدة. أكمل دراسته في الإمارات وفرنسا. يعمل رئيساً لتحرير جريدة "الاتحاد". صدرت له تسع مجموعات قصصية وعدد من المقالات.